Journey's End

Book III

By George Lendon

Nobody knows what tomorrow holds

Journey's End

Published via www.pgprintandofficeservices.co.uk

Contents

The Preface

Dear Readers,

Our train is now waiting, so please come on board where you will meet up with many old friends and make new acquaintances. We have reserved your seats for the last leg of our story – 'Journey's End'.

Sir Claude Dibbs is now the chief general manager of the London and Edinburgh Bank and has to face numerous problems on all fronts, but he is widely respected in the City and by the media.

Edgar, after an army career in the Paras, seems to have lost his way. Initially, he started a small building company, Wadham Developments, but, after a bereavement, he changed direction and set up a special school, which caused him much anxiety.

Vicky and Todd continue farming on the Yorkshire moors, which is an arduous way of life, but Vicky's wedding hire business is going from strength to strength.

You will meet an interesting galaxy of people who we all come across in our daily lives, and are assured of an exciting journey but, like me, will possibly feel saddened to say farewell at our final destination. However, fear not; we will not desert you but will endeavour to chronicle their lives in future offerings.

Happy reading...

Best wishes, George Lendon

List of Players

SIR CLAUDE STOCKER DIBBS (CD), Chief General
    Manager of the London and Edinburgh Bank (LEB)
Lady Pat – wife
Rosemary – sister to Pat
Bob – husband to Rosemary and
    Godstone United's football coach
Don Rowbotham – Chairman, Godstone United
Ted Drake – Manager, Godstone United
Dolly – CD's sister, lives in New York
Steph – lively granddaughter of Dolly
Hilary Hilton – famous American icon
Roy Tibbles – CD's chief clerk
Sir Peter Lipton – Chairman of LEB
Philip Beaumont – previous Chief General Manager of LEB
General Sir Waldron Harding - Chairman of the
    Shareholders' Association
Sir Clifford Butler – senior civil servant at the Treasury
Prof. Amos Gold – Vice Principal, London School of
    Economics
Gareth Jones – head of security at LEB
George Draper – bank manager at Croydon branch of LEB
Ted Stubbs – Secretary, National Association of Building
    Societies
Christopher Barrington – acting chief general manager
    at LEB
John Baxter – surgeon
Kathleen Darnley –surgeon

CAPTAIN EDGAR COLLINS – Chairman of
    Wadham Developments
Heather – deceased wife
Simon – adopted son
Charlie – father-in-law, a fish and chip proprietor
Vicky – Heather's sister
Todd – Vicky's husband
Charlotte – Vicky & Todd's daughter
Caroline – Heather and Vicky's sister
Neil Skerritt – Caroline's husband, a solicitor
Renée Kingdom – runs wedding hire shop with Vicky
Carlos – Renée's boyfriend, who is bad news
Rod – ex. agricultural student, worked for Vicky & Todd
Gloria – Rod's wife
George and Marilyn – Rod's parents
Philip – architect for Wadham Developments
Joan – Philip's mother
Claire – Philip's lively lady friend
Barbara – Philip's latest partner
Lord Callington – owner of Callington Estates
Henry – Lord Callington's son
Bella – Lord Callington's daughter-in-law, Henry's wife
Leonard Holdsworth – Dept of Education inspector
Dr Hester Hubbard – Dept of Education inspector
Ian and Mary Hogg – Bennington Grove School
    house parents
Dick Loxton – school director of studies
Carol and Bradley –disruptive pupils
Tom Owen – retired vicar
Jennifer – Tom Owen's daughter
Lord Marchant – resides at Hannington Court
Diana – Lord Marchant's wife
Peter Irvin – Heather's ex-business partner

BOOK III
Journey's End

Chapter 1

Claude eventually got off to sleep and was dead to the world when suddenly, at 5.00 a.m., his phone rang. He jumped up and picked up the receiver.

"Dibbs here; this is rather early!"

"Sorry to disturb you, Sir. I am the duty officer at the London and Edinburgh and we have just had a red alert."

"Did you say a red alert?" Claude quickly came to life. "Look, give me a minute and I will take this in my office."

He scrambled out of bed. Pat did not move but was snoring softly. He put on his dressing gown and made for the office.

"A red alert; this must be serious. We have only had three such alerts in all my time."

"Yes, Sir. I have just had a call from our agent in Hong Kong to report that one of our principal trading partners in the Far East, Barchester Investments, is in serious trouble, and I have been made to understand they are in the process of calling in the receivers. Again, Sir, it has been difficult to ascertain all the facts but it would seem that they employed a rogue trader and, due to lack of supervisory management, he has been running wild. It would seem it's the old story: gambling on investments and trying to make up the shortfall."

"Well, however did this come to light?"

"It would seem there was a disaster in Hong Kong on their Stock Exchange relating to cashflow problems and a run on their currency and so the Trading Houses were closed for three days. Again, it cannot be confirmed, but at the same time London received a report from a firm of actuaries questioning the outstanding returns. Head office became suspicious and sent out a team of auditors. Fortunately, these losses could not be hidden in time."

"How did this trader... what was he called?"

"Ben Larson. It would seem that he carried out the dual roles of floor manager and security officer so had ample opportunity to hide some very substantial losses. The company losses appear to be in the region of $45 million, so it is rumoured. They approached the Bank of England for a loan but their requests were refused. Of course, I do appreciate they are our principal trading partners in the Far East and they are holding large sums of our clients' money."

Claude's mind raced back ten years to when the company was floated by a Brian Perkins and Sir Edmund du Cann. He knew Perkins from way back; he was a rising star in the Northern Insurance Company, which was taken over by the Commercial Union where he became a very dynamic chairman. He had rubbed shoulders with Sir Edmund in the House of Lords and was a very popular figure in the City.

"Good god. I must quickly get moving and try to contain this disaster."

"Sir, I will complete my reports and get them dispatched to you immediately."

"Now, I must prepare before the story hits the national press, and then we will be besieged with the usual sensational coverage, but thank you for being so prompt."

Claude rang the car hire company and then quickly washed and changed. He popped into the bedroom with a cup of tea for Pat. She put on the light and sat up. "You're early this morning. What's the hurry?"

He tried to explain to Pat why he was leaving early.

"What has this trader done wrong?"

"Well, it's a bit difficult to explain in a sentence, but he was arbitrating derivatives and,"

"Hang on, what does that mean?"

"Well," said Claude, moving towards the door, "simply, he was buying and selling shares in the Futures market and got greedy; he waited for a higher price and simply got caught up in heavy losses. Matters then started to spiral out of control."

Pat put down her cup. "Well surely, it's not as bad as all that?"

"Sadly, this has been going on for some time, and we are talking about millions."

"My word, I can now see why you're in a rush but, darling, do give me a ring later in the day. I should be home late afternoon." He leaned over and kissed her as she lay back in bed.

"Now I must rush. The first thing is to ring the chairman, then no doubt he will convene a full board meeting, so I don't know what time I'll get home; it's going to be a very hectic day."

Claude arrived at the office at the same time as his chief clerk, Roy Tibbles, a tall red-headed Scotsman.

"Sorry to drag you in so early, but I want an up-to-date report on our financial holdings in Barchester Investments. This could not have come at a more inconvenient time. We are being stretched financially on all fronts and I am fully aware that we will have to write off possibly... well, it could be as high as $45 million plus. Now I want to see Dan Parker, head of foreign banking, immediately and then I better speak to the assistant governor of the Bank of England."

Parker seemed to be in the picture. He was a short fat morose man with a fine head of black hair. Most of his colleagues thought it was a toupee. He was obviously very worried and Claude was sympathetic, although he had not been impressed with his general performance and was due for the chop in the next round of reorganisation.

Claude looked over his desk and took off his glasses. "I appreciate that all our dealings with Barchester have been conducted at arm's length but, as you are fully aware, they have been our principal partners in the Far East. Are you able to furnish me with an accurate figure of all our holdings in this bank? From what I can glean it would seem that they are going to the wall. I am due to speak to the Bank of England, but I am not very optimistic. So, to put it bluntly, I must have in my possession a clear picture of our financial standing before I report to the Board later today."

Parker looked embarrassed and coloured up. "Yes Sir, I do appreciate the gravity of this disaster, which we were not prepared for. Please find enclosed in these folders all the relevant transactions which have been placed with Barchester over the past three years. I have a team at this moment collating all the figures and will report back to you at midday with a clear picture."

Claude got back to his chief clerk. "Well Roy, what's on the agenda? I must make two urgent phone calls: one to the deputy governor of the Bank of England, who I find to be at times very difficult, and, more importantly, to Sir Peter Lipton, our chairman. I'm sure he will have heard of our problems."

"Sir, I have just received back from the Chancellor a revised copy of your speeches on the forthcoming trade mission to New York."

"Yes, I must check them through. I'm certainly not going to adhere to any views which I disagree with. I was surprised to be invited to speak on the same platform as the PM, certainly quite an honour."

"Sir, I also had a call from General Harding, seeking an appointment; since being elected Chairman of the shareholders, he has been very vociferous."

"Not again! Well, what did he want this time, although I think I know? I really must make arrangements for him to see the chairman; his demands are well over the top."

"Well, his demands have not changed, Sir. Briefly, he wanted the appointment of three shareholder directors, reports on our progress with the banking unions and early warning of wage rises."

"Look, make an appointment for him to see... better still, I'll have a word with Sir Peter, but really I haven't got the time or the authority to handle these demands. I know he means well but he will continue to be a thorn in our side if not seen to."

"I also had a phone call from Hilary Hilton asking if you could ring her back." Her name quickly aroused Claude's libido and her beautiful face and plump legs flashed through his mind. He could feel the beginning of some sensual excitement. He took in a deep breath. "Yes, yes; I'll ring."

"Also, don't forget, Sir, I had the call from that equerry at Kensington Palace asking for you to communicate with them regarding some fiscal matters appertaining to a member of the Royal family."

"Yes, I was very intrigued. There had been reports of various members experiencing financial difficulties, but it would seem that in most cases it was just sensational titbits. What else did he say?"

"It was all to be very hush-hush, strictly confidential, and they wanted direct access to you. Again Sir, I'm guessing, but there has been a whisper of late that Princess Margaret has fallen out with her bank. I don't know the details and it all sounds very strange. It's also been rumoured that the Queen Mother is sitting on a sizeable overdraft, but I would have thought the Queen would act as a guarantor."

Claude took off his glasses. Of course, the Princess had not married into money and it had been reported that she had given her two children a helping hand in securing substantial properties. "Still, we must keep an open mind. I think there is a danger we are getting in front of ourselves. This is all conjecture. It could possibly be a minor Royal, and there are quite a few."

"Finally, Sir, I have a long list of investment portfolios sent over from the strategy department asking for your comments."

"Well, with the present state of play, I must study these applications, but in most cases I shall be using my red pen. Right, I better get on and start making some phone calls. I will start with Sir Peter – always a difficult chap to corner."

"I'm glad I caught you, Sir. You probably heard."

"You mean the problems at Barchester Investments?"

"Yes."

"The City is all talking about it; I think it was such a big surprise. Still, I fully understand why you're ringing, but is there anything we can do?"

They had a chat about the implications and agreed to arrange a board meeting, when an up-to-date picture of the bank's involvement could be discussed and any possible action to be taken. Claude then turned his attention to General Harding.

Sir Peter laughed. "Yes, I realise the general is becoming more than just a nuisance, but also an embarrassment. His cohorts have been lobbying all and sundry. I even had the Prime Minister moaning about him. I gather his father had served under him on Monty's staff and couldn't stand the chap, but agreed he was a brilliant tactician. But look, I know what his demands are, and they are well over the top. I've been thinking a lot about this. It might be an effective solution to invite him to join the board."

Claude leaned back. "What an excellent idea, as long as he takes the bait."

"You leave it to me; this is the only answer. My concern is trying to win over the directors who have all suffered at his hands, and they are an obstinate bunch. Still, leave it to me. Now, I must get on and call that board meeting; I would suggest for 6.00 p.m. I am sure it will be a lively gathering. Just to remind you, I am off to Jamaica next week to watch the cricket, so I would like to speak to the General this week. I'll see you at 6."

Claude was about to ring the Bank of England when he had a call from Kensington Palace.

"Good afternoon, Sir. I am Colonel Geoffrey Gunstone, Equerry to Her Royal Highness the Princess Margaret. She has asked me to arrange a meeting to discuss her long-term investments. As you will appreciate, this is a very sensitive subject and she has insisted that she wants to deal with you direct. The Princess has been very disappointed with her bank and feels she wants a fresh approach regarding her estate. I am sure you understand she is very busy but feels a face-to-face meeting might help to resolve some of these problems."

"It will be an honour and a privilege to assist the Princess in any way I or my bank can."

They finally agreed on a date and time to take place at Kensington Palace. Claude was asked to come to the rear entrance by taxi.

He was trying to finish the final draft of his three speeches which he was to give in New York during the forthcoming trade mission. He was checking the alterations made by the Chancellor when Roy came through.

"Sorry to bother you, Sir, but we've had a problem just blown up in Edinburgh. It would seem that a cashier is complaining, in fact threatening, to sue the bank because she has alleged she was raped by the manager. I gather this took place in the branch in Queen Street. The manager is very bright and highly thought of by the regional director. He has a law degree and only got married three months ago."

"Well, how far as this gone? Are there any more details?"

"I'm waiting for a fuller report but, as you would expect, he denies all the charges and states the lady's brother came in for a loan for his business, which is a holiday letting agency and is in dire straits, but the loan was refused. I think the legal boys are a bit concerned because she is demanding an immediate payment of damages or she will take the story to the Edinburgh Chronicle and then of course in no time it will be national news."

"How much are they asking? What, £75,000! And how can they arrive at that figure?"

"I gather they came up with permanent loss of employment and psychological stress. I gather she is receiving psychiatric support. They also hinted that they will be selling the story nationwide."

"That's one big bluff. Look, get me the legal department. I know from past experience they always see the worst side of these scenarios and think a large cheque is the only solution."

Claude finally spoke to the assistant manager of the legal department. "Yes Sir, I do appreciate your concerns and we are trying to get this misunderstanding dealt with to avoid any unnecessary publicity."

"I will send Gareth Jones up to look into these allegations; he will soon get to the bottom of it. I'll come back to you as soon as possible. In the meantime try to slow them down and tell them compensation will have to be sanctioned from the top. Now tell me about this manager. You say Ken Sturtridge. From what I've read, he is quite young. Send me a full report. I hope to get back to you in the next three days."

Roy put his head round the door. "Don't forget, Sir, you are due to attend a meeting with the trade mission delegates and the Chancellor tomorrow, followed by a session with the world's press."

"Yes, I have not forgotten. Please get me a list of all the delegates, the government officials and their American counterparts, and send Gareth Jones in immediately."

"Yes Sir. I had the General back on the 'phone hoping to have a word with you, Sir."

"I have spoken to Sir Peter and he will arrange a meeting with the General, but in the meantime he'll have a word with the directors, where there's likely to be a big explosion."

Gareth Jones was a retired Metropolitan Police Inspector and head of security. He slipped in and Claude spelt out his difficulties. "Gareth, I want you to go up to Edinburgh," he said, handing him the file concerning the rape accusation. "Look into these allegations. I think the whole thing smells and I want a man up there on the ground. If you have any queries, liaise with the legal department."

"Right, Sir. I'll book a flight for tonight and hope to be back later tomorrow."

"Thank you, Gareth. Now I must prepare for this meeting with the Chancellor tomorrow and my forthcoming trip to New York."

He was about to ring Hilary Hilton when he had a call from the assistant governor of the Bank of England. It was short and sharp and very much to the point.

"We are aware of your bank's involvement with Barchester Investments but can only assist in an advisory capacity. Now, off the record, we have numerous requests from small financial institutions who have been seeking loans due to the inclement state of the economy, but it is the policy of the Bank of England to refuse these requests, and their only alternative source of income is to seek financial support on the open market." It was as Claude expected; he now felt it was imperative to have a clear picture of the state of the bank's involvement when he reported to the directors that evening.

Finally, Claude decided to ring Hilary Hilton, the celebrated American icon he had met at the bank's luncheon club with the American Ambassador. He became excited; he could see that beautiful face, her large blue eyes and curly blonde hair and short plump figure. He felt aroused; suddenly his libido took off and his body started to pine for her. He had taken her out for the day to Eastbourne and they had arranged to meet up in New York after the trade mission. Unfortunately, the outing had been noted by the paparazzi and was reported in a tabloid. He was expecting to be quizzed by the world's press when the trade mission faced the media and he was not looking forward to having to explain to Pat about their day out.

"Claude, thank you for ringing." She had a rich American accent." I so enjoyed the day in Sussex with you; such beautiful countryside and your quaint little churches. Hope to see more on my next visit but I had enough of cocktail parties; it's all so artificial. Well, I am off tomorrow. I came really after an invitation from the ambassador's wife; she is an old girlfriend of my brother's, but the poor darling is not well and I had to stand in for her last night. It was quite a big evening. We had Prince Edward and the Duke of Kent; they were great guys and invited me down to their country homes but I'm off tomorrow. I am so looking forward to being with you at the end of your trade mission; can't stop thinking of you. I'm looking forward to returning your kind hospitality. I have got an apartment on East Side, so please come and stay; it's so much more discreet than a hotel."

Claude now felt fully excited at the thought of Hilary and a quiet weekend together. "I'd love that. I just can't wait. I'll give you a ring when I arrive and we can go from there."

They parted on the most amicable terms but Claude felt guilty he had not told Pat about their day in Eastbourne, and there was the question and answer meeting with the press corps. Hilary was an American legend and the world's media were always hungry for news of her social life. Her brother had been in the running to be the next Vice President. Sadly, his life was cut short due to a massive heart attack. Her godfather had been the late President Eisenhower, so she had moved in the higher echelons of American society.

Claude finally got home completely exhausted after a stormy meeting with the directors. It started very peacefully. He delivered a report on the difficulties being experienced due to the demise of Barchester Investments and the action that the bank had taken to cover the shortfall. They appreciated the trading difficulties in the present economic climate and fully supported the action of taking up an option on £5 billion, to have on call at short notice to cover any emergency crisis. The meeting then became very noisy and strident when the demands of General Harding were discussed, and his requests were all quickly rejected. Sir Peter then suggested offering him a seat on the board; this was vehemently voted down. It was obvious the board had had enough of the General. Sir Peter warned them this problem was not going to go away and he was open to any other solutions. He pointed out that matters were getting out of hand and the work of his cohorts was giving the bank a bad press. It was finally agreed to bring this matter to the attention of the board at the next meeting but in the meantime he would have consultations with the General to try and head him off.

Chapter 2

Vicky was small in stature, with black spiky hair and dark grey piercing eyes. She was Edgar's sister-in-law. Vicky finally got to bed; it was now 12:30 am. Todd was snoring and their baby was sleeping soundly in the cot at the foot of their bed. *I would love to be a fly on the wall in Rod's bedroom tonight.* She could see Gloria was flaming mad at Rod for taking Bella home after the dinner party. *No,* she thought, *I would trust Rod, although I certainly wouldn't trust Bella; the more I get to know her, the more I realise she is a man eater, and has a drink problem.* She noted Bella was giving Rod the glad eye most of the evening, but then Bella was very unhappy. Henry, her husband, had recently come into the title of Lord Callington of Torrington. In all fairness, she never tried to put on any airs and graces, but could be difficult and was most unpopular with the estate workers. She adored her baby, Paula, and was in the process of joining Henry in Sidmouth where he had moved after his father's death. Their marriage was strained and it was rumoured that he had girlfriends.

Vicky was fond of Rod. He had been their farm manager until a disastrous accident. He finally recovered but in the process lost a leg. The more she got to know Gloria, his girlfriend, the more she liked her, but could see she had a mind of her own.

As she snuggled down her thoughts turned to Edgar, her brother-in-law with the school near Manchester. He seemed beset with problems and now there was this poor girl who was found hanging in the woods. It didn't seem long ago he was suspended because he had assaulted one of the pupils. *Well, we all have our problems; the grass always looks greener but it is not always the case.* She thought about the dinner party earlier that evening. It had not been a great success; poor Renée had suddenly left early, rather tearful, and Bella's behaviour did not help. She was very fond of Renée, who had been very kind to her and now wanted her as a partner in her wedding dress business. The poor thing was lonely and, though only 67, seemed suddenly to have aged now with her only niece suffering with cancer; it was causing her much distress. *Yes, I'd take her up on her offer and become a partner, but I certainly can't take on any more work.*

Suddenly she had a fright. *Did I leave the microwave on?* She padded down the back stairs to check and in the dark kitchen found Gloria sitting by the window waiting for Rod. She was small and pretty but looking very angry. When Rod had taken Bella home after the dinner party it was 12 o'clock, and now it was 2 o'clock. She sat down at the kitchen table. "Can I make you a hot drink? I hope you're not getting cold sitting down here."

"That's very kind of you, but I'm just waiting for Rod. Where the hell is he? It doesn't take all this time to take Bella home. Oh God, I love that man. I seem to eat, sleep and dream about him. I want to have his child, just like little Heather. I do envy you with your little family living in the country, although I do appreciate running a farm has its problems. I want to leave London. I'm fed up selling perfumes to ugly old ladies trying to score, and the younger ones, some of them are on the game. I want to keep chickens and grow herbs and have a little baby girl. Suddenly, car lights shone through the window as it drove up the drive. "That must be him at long last. Where the hell has he been? Look at the time!" Vicky thought, *there's going to be fireworks. I think I'll slip up the back stairs*, but she heard the beginning of the row.

"Where the hell have you been, and what have you been doing with that woman? It was 12 o'clock when you left here."

Vicky slipped up the back stairs and quickly got into bed.

"Yes, I am sorry, but she was very depressed and I had to listen to all her problems. She said her husband's got a lady friend and does not make any secret of it. She can't stand her mother-in-law and his sisters are not friendly. He allows her very little money and she would like to stay up here. Look, I did try to get away but she became difficult and started to get nasty. I think she was tight."

"Now tell me the truth: did anything happen?"

"Look darling, I promise you I did not touch her. She was very emotional and looked a real mess."

"Well, what does that mean?"

"Darling, you know I am not interested in anybody but you. I have never been unfaithful to you since we first met."

"Now don't rub that in; it only happened once and I have regretted it ever since."

"Sorry, I didn't mean to bring that up. Let's change the subject."

Gloria still looked very fierce. "You can sleep with me tonight, but I don't want you to touch me. I'm not ready for all that." They finally slipped into bed and rolled away from each other. Rod was sleeping lightly when he felt her hand on his shoulder.

She whispered in his ear, "Sorry, darling. I'm a real bitch. It's just that I love you so much and I want all of you and I want to have your baby. Oh my God, that dear little baby makes me want to be a mother. She melts my heart. I love that baby as if it was my own. A few days down here makes me want to get out of London and change jobs. I'm fed up with selling perfumes, and the modelling business is corrupt and full of pimps; you have to sell your body to get on the cover of a magazine. I know they are all at it. I don't want to talk about it. I'd love to live in the country with a few animals and raise our little family. Now, come on big boy; make love to me. I want all your juices and I want to have your baby, and damn the consequences. You're the greatest love of my life."

Rod was now lying on his elbows. "I feel I want to get back to real farming. Crunching numbers all day and then having to put the boot in can be most disheartening. I'm not like my dad; he deals with these problems every day."

The next moment her arms were around his neck and they were soon joined together. He was very gentle, which Gloria enjoyed. *Mother of Jesus, please hear me. I so want a little baby just like little Heather, a dear little girl. I have never felt like this before but then only a woman could understand.* Gloria had reached the crossroads; she had finally made the big decision. She would marry Rod and leave London.

She had never really liked sex; it always seemed to hurt, but this time it was just heavenly, having a breath-taking organism after feeling the joy of his warm juices entering her body.

o o o

Vicky swiftly ascended the back stairs and slipped into bed. Todd was lying on his back snoring. She suddenly heard a crash downstairs but decided to roll over and go to sleep. Todd grunted and moved onto his side. She was now very tired and quickly drifted off to sleep, dreaming of her childhood and her dear old dad who had been an archdeacon, a kind but frail old man, and then mum who was very much the disciplinarian and had made her three daughters toe the line until her eldest sister Heather rebelled and left to go and live with her father, Charlie. Mum's life had not been easy; she married a fish and chip proprietor, Charlie, from Brighton, and they were just not suited. After her elder sister was born, they parted and she finally married the Reverend Nigel Jackson Stevens and they both seemed very happy; then she and her sister Caroline were born. She continued to dream of her mother, who was very strong-willed, and her elder sister Heather who had a similar disposition, and then of one of the saddest days in her life when her sister was killed in a car crash. She dreamed of Todd and her two little daughters and finally woke when she heard Todd moving about the bedroom.

She heard him in the bathroom and slipped out of bed. Little Heather was sleeping soundly; she was such a dear, never any trouble and very rarely woke during the night. The house was very quiet and she descended the back stairs into the kitchen where she put on the kettle, and in no time Todd was down, fully dressed sitting at the table drinking from a large mug of tea and chewing on a thick slice of toast. "I must get out and see the boy is feeding the pigs properly; he's so unreliable and never clears up." Vicky smiled to herself but kept silent.

o o o

Renée got home early from the dinner party feeling very depressed. She was lonely and wanted some male company. *Surely I'm not too old at 67; I've still got a slim figure.* But men seemed to avoid her. Her marriage had been an unhappy affair. Arthur, her husband, had been a jobbing painter and decorator scratching a living on building sites. She had come into a large legacy when her father died and bought a string of upmarket building plots. This soon put Arthur on his feet but he started to get home later and she quickly realised he had lady friends. She threw him out twice and they split up and he went to live with an old scrubber, but finally he became very ill and came back. She did not have the heart to turn him away and nursed him on his deathbed. He died of cancer of the oesophagus, all very painful. He could not swallow because the radium treatment had burnt his throat. He lost a lot of weight. It was all very sad. She had quickly realised he was most unreliable, particularly where money was concerned, so she took charge of the building company and it quickly took off. She built up a small land bank of very desirable building plots which increased in value in time. But then he started to wander. However, she was very perceptive and owned 70% of the company so, on his death, she sold out and was quite a wealthy woman, which she kept under wraps.

Slowly, she undressed and studied her body in the wardrobe mirror. *I would so love to have a nice gentleman to caress me*, and then she thought of Carlos. He was 20 years younger and she knew he was using her; the only person he loved was Carlos. When they first met he was very attentive and convincing. She remembered that first night when he was so gentle. She never had enjoyed sex more; Arthur was pretty useless. Carlos was half Italian, tall, slim, with large dark brooding eyes and well endowed. *Should I ring him? No, no, I must control myself. I know he's a waste of time – he's just after my money.* He had an estranged wife with two grown-up sons but never had any money and she was always expected to pick up the tab. *Should I join a dating club? Knowing my luck, I will land up with another scoundrel. God*, she thought, *will I ever find a gentle, caring partner? Sex would be a bonus.*

She switched on the answer-phone. "Darling, I just bought some tickets for a Gilbert and Sullivan show the students are putting on up at the tech. It's 'Trial by Jury'. I got the tickets then I thought we could have some supper afterwards at Don Giovanni's. I'll ring you tomorrow. Bye darling. Love you, Carlos." *I know who will pay for the supper*, she thought. *God I've got to be strong*, but she knew she could not resist that man. Suddenly she felt excited with hot flushes as her hormones started to race around her body.

She climbed into bed and drifted off to sleep. She had a wet dream thinking of Carlos making love to her.

o o o

Claude was not looking forward to the question and answer session with the media regarding the trade mission. It was going to be a very intense meeting, commencing with a briefing from the Chancellor and then the meeting with the world's press. The day arrived and over coffee he was introduced to the delegates. He knew many of them and it was a very friendly get-together. The Chancellor chaired the gathering. The PM, who was due to be with them, was tied up with an engagement at Buckingham Palace and tongues were wagging, but all his officers were very tight-lipped; there was a whisper on the street that he was about to resign.

There were 20 delegates from the world of commerce representing all facets of British industry, including banking, engineering, ladies' fashion, catering, and a list of minor innovative outlets. Claude had prepared for the meeting and was aware of all the delegates and the civil service support team. The Chancellor was an academic and had a very smooth relaxed style but took some stick from the tabloids because of his lack of experience in the day-to-day running of a commercial enterprise. They were all presented with a folder which gave details of their opposite numbers, a diary of the conventions and the list of the support team. Claude was very impressed with all the preparations; the Chancellor was very resourceful and seemed to have a phenomenal memory. He was pleased to see a sprinkling of ladies and found out later they represented travel, fashion and catering. The Chancellor, who was in his late fifties, thick set with grey short hair, gave a short address welcoming everyone and thanking them for joining the trade mission and assuring them of his support. He introduced them to the team of civil servants and stressed he was part of the back-up: if they experienced any difficulties he was always available. Claude was quite impressed; he seemed very natural and it was all put across in a very friendly manner.

"Well, ladies and gentlemen, my most precious commodity is time and I am forever chasing my tail. We have an important vote on the Immigration Bill this evening in the House and a three-line whip is out to ensure our presence. Now, if there are no more questions, please accompany me to the Great Hall where the world press are waiting to meet us."

They crossed the quad and entered the hall which had originally been built in the time of Henry VIII and had witnessed many important events in the history of the English Parliament. It was a large hall with open rafters, stone walls and a flagon tiled floor. There were approximately a hundred reporters from the world press including a large group of photographers and a number of television cameras with their crews. The noise was deafening but started to abate on their arrival. There was no seating but a large low stage with chairs.

The delegates trooped onto the stage and sat and faced the media. The Chancellor quickly introduced them and the senior civil servants. He then spoke briefly for 20 minutes highlighting the importance of the visit and his confidence in the members of the team. There was a low buzz from the TV cameras and the muffled voices of the interpreters. He mentioned the help and support he had received from the Confederation of British Industry and stressed this was very much a team effort and felt confident much would be achieved. He then invited them to question members of the delegation and apologised they were working to deadlines because of the forthcoming vote in the House. The Chancellor then sat and a young civil servant orchestrated the questions; he seemed very familiar with the world's press, and questions in a range of accents were soon flying across the hall to the various delegates. The media had news channels in Australia, Europe, the Far East, but mainly in the United States. Claude fielded a question dealing with the abortive negotiations to purchase two American banking institutions, which seemed to go down well. As the meeting was drawing to its close, he was faced with another question concerning the American diplomat, Hilary Hilton. *Here we go,* he thought, but the Chancellor put his hand up: "Really, we are not here to discuss personal matters."

Claude stood up. "I am more than willing to answer the question. Yes, I had the pleasure of meeting Hilary Hilton when she was a guest of the American Ambassador at the Bank's luncheon club. She requested a wish to visit; I think it was an English pub and a quaint old country church in that order. A smile went around the room. So on Saturday I drove her through Sussex to Eastbourne and we had lunch in a pub and visited the church at Wilmington. So please do not misconstrue the outing. Needless to say, she enjoyed the visit but had to rush back to the Embassy for a formal dinner with members of the Royal family."

The Chancellor then stood. "Thank you, Sir Claude. I'm sure the outing helped the Atlantic alliance. Now, sorry gentlemen, but I must curtail this press conference. No doubt, we will be meeting up with many of you at the various venues in New York. Thank you." There was warm applause from the media. All the cameras were flashing and the TV announcers all looked very busy. The Chancellor quickly jumped up, went around and swiftly thanked the delegates, warmly shaking them by the hand. He spoke briefly to Claude. "I thought you handled the Hilton question well. I had a feeling it would arise and of course with the media they have an irritating habit of making something out of nothing. I shall look forward to seeing you on the flight next week."

Claude sat back in his chauffeur driven car on the way home feeling quite relaxed. The meeting went very well and he was glad the question regarding Hilary Hilton was out of the way. He realised to the Americans she was their equivalent of royalty and had a big following in the States and of course was watched all the time but, unlike our Royal family, was not surrounded by a team of security specialists. *Now*, he thought, *I must have a word with Pat, and that might be difficult.* Thank goodness she was now picking up and getting back to her old self. He could see that this might be a bit tricky.

Claude knew that Pat was worried about her sister Rosemary; the baby was lying in the wrong position and it was due in the next fortnight and Pat felt she was working too hard. It seemed the catering business had taken on a lot more assignments and was building links with various churches to cover funerals and weddings, which were more lucrative. He was thinking about Bob, Rosemary's husband, who it seemed was getting bored with electrical contracting and wanted to get back to the excitement of football, possibly in some management role.

Claude was pondering his visit to Kensington Palace the next day when his car finally arrived outside a very smart block of apartments in Holland Park; he climbed out feeling very tired.

o o o

The following day, Claude arrived at the back entrance of Kensington Palace in a taxi. He was met by the Princess' Equerry, Colonel Geoffrey Gunstone, who was tall and quite young. He shook Claude's hand warmly. "I'm so pleased to meet you, Sir." He had a rich plummy accent and looked to be in his late thirties. He had fair hair, large pale blue eyes and a toothbrush moustache. They entered a large square hall and ascended a grand, wide, sweeping staircase to the first floor. It was all beautifully appointed with large canvas pictures and an enormous chandelier. He led the way to an impressive door and knocked softly and then stood aside.

Claude entered a luxurious drawing room exquisitely furnished with antique French furniture. It had dark red walls covered with masses of family photographs and paintings.

A little lady sitting in the corner of the room jumped up, removing her glasses, and came striding towards him with her hand extended. "Sir Claude, it's so kind of you to come." She was wearing a dark blue twin set, was very small with a petite figure, and had large grey eyes and a big smile. She shook his hand gently. "Please," she said, pointing to a large easy chair. "Thank you, Geoffrey. We shall be about 45 minutes." He closed the door quietly. "I shall miss Geoffrey when he leaves; he's not cut out to be an equerry and wants to get back to his regiment and be a real soldier. It's really a boring existence being a dogsbody to members of the Royal family, quite a thankless task. Still, to business."

She sat back and looked at Sir Claude. "Now, what can I get you? Would you like a coffee, tea or something stronger?"

Claude smiled. "Whatever is the easiest?"

"Well, I feel like a real drink. I know it's early, but I could kill a gin and tonic. Please join me."

"Well, thank you, a small whiskey and water." She picked up the phone and ordered drinks. She offered him a cigarette then lit up the end of an ornate cigarette holder. "I must try and curb this habit; my family are chiding me all the time.

"Well now, I have a serious problem: my income." There was a soft knock on the door and a footman entered carrying a large silver tray with drinks and some small biscuits. He finally slipped away. "Now, where was I? Yes, my income has declined to a very alarming level. Really, I am living quite simply above my means and this is becoming very alarming," she said, picking up her glass.

"Well, ma'am, this is not an uncommon problem, but for me to advise you I will need to study your portfolio, in particular all your investments and sources of income."

Princess Margaret inhaled deeply. "Yes, yes, I'm happy to furnish you with all this, but I am feeling very despondent. Still, you were strongly recommended, in particular by the Prime Minister. Now, Sir Claude, before we go any further, I'm sure you appreciate my position and I do not want our discussions circulated outside this room."

"Yes," said Claude, sitting up. "I will be the only one privy to this information, but I feel it may be a wise move for you to use a pseudonym, a fictitious name. Have you any suggestions?"

"Well, yes. She scratched her head. Let me think. What about... yes, what about Lady Pamela Black? This should pass by without attracting any attention. Yes, I'll be Lady Pamela Black. Now, I have here a folder with all the information you require: my investments and income, but I have not outlined overheads. I think that might frighten you. Look, to be honest, I have made some substantial items of expenditure. I assisted my children to secure their houses; they did not marry into money, and also I am having a house built on the island of Mustique through a friend and will lease it when I am not resident. In fact, I'm due to go there at the end of the month. But still, here's the folder containing the information. Five years ago I had £17.2 million in investments; now it has shrunk to £9.8 million, although my bank is not entirely blameless. They have introduced me to a galaxy of investment brokers who really took risks and certainly did not fulfil their earlier promises." She leaned over and stubbed out her cigarette and then picked up her glass and finished her drink. "Well, I'm not in the blaming game; I am too old for all that. Incidentally, may I ask what your fees will be?"

Sir Claude put down an empty glass. "Well, normally it is a sliding scale, but my Bank will be honoured to carry out this service at no charge."

"That is most generous of you. Now, I think we have covered the subject pretty well, but naturally if you require further information..." She stood up and looked at her watch. "Sorry to push on but my mother rings daily at this time and I can never get her off the phone. I shall look forward to hearing from you."

The next moment the door opened and he was escorted off the premises by the tall young Colonel.

Chapter 3

Captain Edgar Collins, a former paratrooper late of the SAS, had certainly had a momentous life since leaving the Army. He was now in his late forties, with blonde hair tinged grey, large blue eyes and was always popular with the ladies; they seemed to want to mother him. Initially, he had worked part-time for a highly regarded security agency involved in protecting foreign dignitaries but also set up a building company, buying up freeholds which he developed.

Edgar had a passionate affair with Pat before she had met her husband Sir Claude but they still carried a torch for each other. Claude was put into contact with Edgar when he was being blackmailed because of his relationship with a Mayfair prostitute. Edgar retrieved some very incriminating evidence; needless to say Claude was relieved and grateful to him.

Edgar had a sticky start with the business but married Heather, a bank executive. She quickly put the business on a sound footing. As they could not have a family, they had adopted little Simon, but suddenly Edgar's life came to a halt; catastrophe struck when Heather was killed in a car accident. He later found out she was pregnant. After much thought, he decided to resign from Wadham Developments and set up a school for disadvantaged children. He had been warned about the stress and commitment but had not envisaged the emotional and rigorous challenges.

What a nightmare of a month Edgar had. He was now driving back to his school for emotionally disturbed pupils where he was the Principal to face another crisis after one of the pupils, Carol, had been found hanging from a tree. It would seem that she had committed suicide. He thought about Carol, a very disturbed young lady who was nearly 16 but with all the emotions of a mature woman; she had never had a chance. There was no father. Mother was an alcoholic with psychological problems and poor Carol was in love with an Asian boy who had groomed her with drugs; then she had been controlled by a very vicious gang. Although social services and the police knew of their whereabouts, the gang restrained the girls with a reign of terror.

Edgar was driving up, to Yorkshire to visit his son, Simon, when he had the emergency call from the school,

So here he was driving back to school to face a police enquiry concerning Carol's death, which on the face of it looked like suicide, but that had to be established. The gravity of the situation worried him. If the school was found to be at fault then it would be closed and possible criminal charges could follow. He had been warned that there was a posse of reporters at the front gate with a large television van. This certainly was not the type of publicity the school needed.

o o o

At last Edgar reached his destination. The school was deserted but for a large TV van which was parked by the side of the entrance. It was past midnight when he finally entered his flat and picked up a letter in the hallway from Ian Hogg, the senior house father. "We have all missed you. The Department of Education are due to be with us tomorrow morning and Chief Inspector Roy Eggleston will be over at 2.00 p.m. to complete his enquiries. I spoke to the Department; they thought it would be sensible for all the pupils to return home. So they have been collected by their welfare officers and we have just a handful to be collected tomorrow.

Edgar was quickly in bed. As soon as his head hit the pillow he was asleep and up at 7 o'clock to the sound of his alarm. Breakfast was a quiet affair, with just five pupils, after which he carried out an inspection of the buildings and noted outbreaks of graffiti on the walls in the bedrooms and in the wash area; also, two broken windows and some damaged furniture. This was always a bad sign. He wrote a note to the caretaker to deal with these damages, and then held a brief meeting with the senior staff: Dick Loxton, head of education, and Ian and Margaret Hogg, head of care. They brought him up to date regarding the police enquiries. By 11.00 a.m. all the children had been collected. Later in the morning, the Department of Education arrived and was soon entrenched in Edgar's office.

HMI Holdsworth, a Staff Inspector in his mid-sixties, was short and stout with a large black moustache and a bald head. Dr Hubbard was tall and slim with short hair, pale grey eyes and wearing a twinset. Holdsworth put his cup down and looked at Edgar. "This is not the first fatal accident I have been involved in but we do appreciate at this juncture it all looks very grim, and of course the media do not help; they are very adept at twisting the truth. But keep your head and it will pass over. Dr Hubbard and I have been impressed with what you and your staff have achieved in your first year and we are here to give you support and guidance. Incidentally, I have met Chief Inspector Roy Eggleston before. I looked up my notes; it must have been 20 years ago – he was a sergeant and we were dealing with an unfortunate but common problem: a member of staff had been interfering with a pupil in a school in Liverpool.

"Now, down to business. I would like to reappraise myself with all the reports appertaining to Carol and in particular the psychiatrist report and the documentation from the child guidance clinic. Dr Hubbard would like to tour the buildings with Margaret Hogg. I feel she is a very perceptive lady and had a good working relationship with Carol."

Finally, after a light lunch, Chief Inspector Roy Eggleston arrived, escorted by a lady officer. Edgar noted that he spoke to the media on the way in and suddenly they all seemed to disperse; even the television van started up and moved away. The chief inspector was tall with dark hair turning grey; he had small dark guinea pig eyes and looked very solemn and had a commanding presence. He quickly took charge. "Yes, I spoke to the media on the way in and promised them a statement at the police station at 6.00 p.m. if they departed immediately. I appreciate they have a job to do but at times they can be an utter nuisance. Now, I would like to speak to Mr Holdsworth and Dr Hubbard; I appreciate they rushed up here in the middle of their assignments, and then I would like to see you, Mr Collins, and then finally have a word with your senior staff, Mr and Mrs Hogg and Dick Loxton. My sergeant would like to speak to some of your junior staff and then I would like to be away by 4.30 p.m. so I can collate all my reports at the station."

As they sat in the common room, Mr Holdsworth smiled. "We have met before." The chief inspector was looking at his files and looked up with a quizzical look. "Yes, it must have been 20 years ago. It was in a Catholic school in Liverpool where a housemaster had been accused of interfering with one of the pupils, but as I remember there was insufficient evidence. I think he was called John Dunstan."

The chief inspector put down his coffee cup. "Oh yes, I remember; it was certainly a long time ago. Unfortunately, this is becoming a common problem in residential institutions. Well," he said closing his file, I do appreciate your report is in the pipeline but tell me briefly about the school: its strengths and weaknesses. I have been inundated by enquiries from children's departments asking about the school, questions which really should be addressed to you. Mr Holdsworth, please briefly outline the recent full inspection, finishing with the conclusions you had reached."

"Yes, I have been closely involved with this special school for emotionally disturbed children for the past year and I have been impressed with the dedication of the staff and the leadership exhibited by the senior members, in particular Ian and Margaret Hogg. We are pleased with the way the school has developed and feel confident given time and under the existing management it will be granted a full licence."

"Thank you, Mr Holdsworth. I fully respect your experience in this field and now feel more confident to speak with some assurance and answer the enquiries which my department has had to deal with. Thank you for coming up. I will not need you again but, between you and me, I feel it is a straightforward case of suicide while her mind was unbalanced. Now, I must get on and see the senior staff and Mr Collins."

Edgar had a brief word with Mr Holdsworth and Dr Hubbard as they were leaving. They took him to one side and offered him some encouragement and then they drove off together. The chief inspector had a short meeting with the senior staff; he focused his attention on Margaret Hogg. "Tell me: was there anything going on between Carol and that boy Bradley?" She hesitated. "I must have the truth."

"Yes, I overheard her bragging to Gladys that they had sex and he didn't know what to do; then she said that Bradley had been boasting that he had sex with his social worker but, according to what I heard, she would not let him put it in, but the details were all rather vague. I put it down to bragging and, really, I hear so many wild tales I put it to the back of my mind."

"Thank you, Mrs Hogg. I do not feel this changes the cause of death but I must send a confidential communiqué to the director of social services stating what you have told me." After a few more questions, he closed his file and gave them a friendly look. "I understand the great stress you're under but the inspectors were very supportive and felt much has been achieved in the past year. I often wonder what would have happened to these poor youngsters if they were not in your care. So please rest assured, I am not here to find fault and the dedication of all your staff is fully appreciated. I am a family man and have a niece Carol's age, and it makes my blood boil when I think what that poor girl has experienced in her short life. Unfortunately, the powers that be are more concerned about political correctness than in bringing these people to justice and frequently our hands are tied. Thank you for all your help; it has made my job so much easier."

Edgar then joined the chief inspector and was quizzed about the staffing levels, pastoral care and the financial structure of the school. "Were you aware that Carol had a sexual relationship with Bradley? She was heard bragging about it."

"No, I was not aware. She had an abortion when she was 14, but again that has not been confirmed."

"Well, Mr Collins, I must get on, but this does not change my judgement that this is a case of suicide. Now, I must get back to the station and make up my reports and then send them on to the coroner's office and he will in due course issue a death certificate. This has been a most unpleasant case but I have been very impressed with all your staff, and the inspectors respected your leadership. Mr Collins, one final piece of advice: be on your guard regarding the physical relationships between staff and pupils. Of course, it can affect all genders but frequently I have found it to be single men and boys. Make sure you have ladies, possibly older women, who are involved during out-of-school hours, putting them to bed, et cetera; sadly, there are sick people who are attracted to residential institutions and it is becoming an increasingly common problem. We have teams of police officers bringing the culprits to justice years after the serious misdemeanours were committed. Well, I really must be off. I will speak to the media and hope that will keep them out of your hair. My reports will be sent to the coroner's office and, as there is no evidence of foul play, they will issue a death certificate, then this unfortunate incident can put be put behind us. Now, I must be off, but thank you, Mr Collins. I must get back to complete all the reports and I hope it's the end of this unhappy affair."

o o o

Claude felt very much under pressure. He had been putting off speaking to Pat concerning Hilary Hilton and their day out in Eastbourne. He knew she could be very fiery, and this was just before his trip to New York. She was not unintelligent and would quickly guess he was possibly going to meet up with Hilary in New York.

He was very concerned that the bank was standing still and needed changes in the top echelons; in particular, three general managers were really past it and major changes had to be made because of the ever-increasing demands.

He had a report from Gareth Jones who'd flown up to Scotland regarding the grievance from the cashier complaining she had been assaulted by her manager. He quickly read his account. It was not as simple as he first thought, but they never were; it was open to various interpretations. This was the type of story the tabloids thrived on and it could become rather messy. According to the report, they had lived together and then fallen out and he had refused a loan to the cashier's brother who ran a holiday booking company which was in dire straits; the manager was claiming he was the innocent party. Claude pushed it to one side, after writing a pungent note for the attention of the legal department.

He then turned his attention to reorganising the top structure and offering early retirements to the three general managers, and bringing Lawrence Davies down as an assistant general manager for special projects to use him as a trouble-shooter. He wrote a short confidential report for the attention of Sir Peter Lipton, the Chairman, outlining his plans.

His eye caught a long list of speaking engagements which he wanted to peruse. He also noted the final paper on sponsorships which he would like to read before it was implemented. He noticed the list of dining room guests over the next month. General Sir Waldron Harding was due to attend. He felt guilty but had arranged for him to meet up with the Chairman, Sir Peter. He could clearly see the General would be a long-term problem, with his aggressive demands. He smiled to himself and decided to avoid lunch, when he had a call from Hilary. "Sir Claude, how are you, and how is Pat? I do hope she is on the mend and feeling better. I'm so looking forward to seeing you; it's only next week."

Claude took off his glasses. "Where are you? You seem to be a long way away."

"I'm visiting my daughter in LA but flying back to New York on Friday, preparing for our get-together. Darling, I can't wait to be with you. I own the lease on an apartment in the centre of town; you must come and stay – it is so much quieter and certainly more discreet than a hotel."

"Yes, I am so looking forward to seeing you. We've all been briefed and had a session with the world's press and I've prepared my speeches but, darling, I'm awfully sorry but I must rush. I've got your number and I will ring you as soon as I arrive." They parted very amicably and Claude felt a pang of guilt. *Really*, he thought, *I should not be seeing her.* But it was the same old story: his heart said yes but his head said no.

He finally got home to find Rosemary with Pat and little Freddie running around the flat laughing. They kissed him then Rosemary had a fruit juice and Claude and Pat had a sherry. Rosemary was now expecting any day and looked very well. Pat picked up a toy. "I keep telling her to take it easy and let the staff do more."

"They are all very good, but we were a bit stretched last week; we did two functions on the same day. It was too much; we just did not have enough staff. Still, you live and learn."

"Well," said Pat, lifting up her glass, "when are you going to stop?"

"I will finish this Friday for a month but will continue to keep on top of the office work. I'm hoping Bob will carry on helping in a part-time capacity. He's fed up with electrical contracting and wants to get back to his first love, football."

"What about his wages?"

"There might be a drop, but really if it makes him happy... he's been in the dumps, but then he's always serious at the best of times. Mind you, the big problem is the unsociable hours. I'll have to make sure he is not out every night. He can help with the children. I've now got a part-time nanny, a young girl; she never minds what she does and Freddie adores her. Oh, did I tell you I had a call from Joy? You remember Joy Bulley. She always spoke so highly of you. Well, she got married last month and is coming back for a delayed honeymoon."

"Of course, I remember her very well," said Pat smiling. "She had that rather dishy cricketer; what was he called?"

"Shane," said Rosemary, standing and grabbing Freddie as he ran past. "No, she married a retired farmer called Angus." She looked down. "And you, my little man, better go and pick up your toys. We've got to get back to feed your dad."

Claude had arrived home with a bulging briefcase and spent the early part of the evening in his office reviewing the major applications for commercial loans. As they sat in the lounge after supper, Claude put down his newspaper. "This may amuse you: remember I told you about the Shareholders' Association and the Chairman, General Sir Waldron Harding? Most argumentative and difficult man to appease, but he means well. He has a daughter up in Wrexham who is pally with the wife of the regional director and they walk their dogs twice a week. Well, the General has a girlfriend; he must be in his mid-eighties and she's younger than his daughter, who finds it very embarrassing. He is a widower. I think he's 84 and is planning to marry her. I gather she's been married three times and is in her mid-fifties. I like him, but he has organised his committee to campaign for seats on the board and they want advance notice of all-important decisions. He behaves as if he was back in the desert with Monty where, I gather, he was responsible for the deployment of all the mechanised units. He seemed to have set up regional committees all over the place and his office is full of maps and the names of some very influential shareholders. Still, darling, I must not bore you."

"No, I find it very interesting. He sounds a bit like old Archie MacDonald, Lady Ann's old boyfriend."

"Well, not really; Harding is very resourceful and very bright, but they both can be rude."

Pat put down the paper and leaned back and smiled. "I remember when I first met Lady Ann Patterson. At the time, I was David's housekeeper and of course she was his sister. I knew within two minutes I would like her. I can see her now, all dressed up to the nines when she looked in to see her brother David, but he was away in Paris. Mind you, I think she looked in to see me. At the time she was Princess Margaret's lady-in-waiting, or something like that, and was about to go on a tour of the West Midlands, but she was so natural and had a marvellous sense of humour. I remember she stayed for lunch and invited me to visit her in Wales. Dear David, her brother, was really a lovely gentleman and a pleasure to work for. I had some serious problems at the time with Jim, my ex, and the riffraff he was mixing with. But David kindly gave us the use of his flat over the garage and made no charge, and when Emily, my mother, joined us and she was seriously ill he welcomed her as if she was a member of his family. Did I tell you David proposed to me? He was very ill and I was at the time fed up with men, but I was seriously thinking of taking up his offer."

"Well, thank you very much," said Claude smiling, "and where does that leave me?"

"Don't be a chump: it was before you came on the scene. If you remember, we first met at David's funeral when we shared the same hymn sheet."

"Yes, of course I remember," said Claude smiling. "It was one the greatest days of my life and I shall never forget it." Suddenly he felt a pang of guilt as a picture of Hilary appeared in his mind.

Pat suddenly got up and padded across with nothing on her feet. She sat on his lap, put her arms around his neck and kissed him passionately. "I can feel you're pleased to see me; you've been playing hard to get of late, so look out tonight," she whispered in his ear. "I love having sex in a single bed: you can't get away from me when you're done."

Claude arrived at the office early to try and clear his desk before his trip to the States. He had promoted Christopher Barrington to be the senior Deputy Chief General Manager, but he would continue to be responsible for Domestic Banking

"Sir, I've got the General on line three."

"Good morning, Sir."

"You must call me Waldron. I just rang to wish you a successful visit to the States. I am due to see Sir Peter next week and then my Association will expect to have a meeting with the board of directors. We need to negotiate the role of the shareholders so that we can play an active part in the company's affairs. I have been in touch with a director of the Bank of England who was very understanding and felt there should be more transparency. Now look, I realise you're preparing for your trip but I hope my committee can see you when you get back."

"Sir Waldron, I have taken into account all you have said but I can only repeat that I am not free to enter into any discussion concerning the long-term plans of the bank."

"Yes, yes, I thought that would be your response, but events are moving swiftly and soon shareholders will be granted access to all of the bank's affairs." They finally parted on amicable terms.

o o o

The big day arrived. Claude was up early and after breakfast and an affectionate cuddle and kiss from Pat, he arrived at Heathrow. They were due to leave at 11:00 a.m. via a chartered flight comprising the government's team, including the Prime Minister and the Chancellor. There was a large posse of correspondents from the media and they were due to meet up with the World Bank the following evening. Claude was pencilled in with the Chancellor to speak at a fringe meeting. As he sauntered onto the plane and sat and studied some papers, without warning the seat next to him was occupied by the Prime Minister.

"Sir Claude, thank you for joining the delegation. I am hoping to move around and speak to members of my team." The PM was quite young, in his late forties, ex-Eton and Oxford with good looks and a very relaxed style but always seemed to be in a rush. "You possibly heard that Professor Gold can't make the trip; his wife has been admitted to hospital, but I gather she is now much better. Now, I have been hearing encouraging news that the London and Edinburgh are shortly introducing a new structure into their operations." The plane was soon airborne, and Claude explained the reorganisation of the bank into the three divisions, ring-fencing domestic investments away from the commercial lending. The PM seemed very impressed and then turned to the question of quantum easing. They seemed to be very much in agreement that it was a short-term measure and only to be used in an emergency. The PM finally came up with a question regarding General Sir Waldron Harding. "My father was with him in the desert and, between us, could not stand the man, but he did say he was very resourceful and courageous and had the greatest respect for his tactical abilities. Needless to say, his shareholders have been bombarding my MPs. Although we are quite sympathetic to his demands, he is using this issue as a national crusade and he is a difficult man to shake off. Still, it's been useful having this chat. Just one very last thing – I'm trying to strengthen the Exchequer's team in the House of Lords and, if we were to invite you, naturally you would receive a life peerage. Would you be interested? Look, just think about it and I will be in touch. Now I must run along and have a word with the Chancellor."

Chapter 4

Rod's dad George flew back from Italy to attend a partner's farewell dinner and left his wife in Italy. Rod finally was able to have a chat with him. "I miss home and my old ladies at the Citizens Advice bureau. I get so bored with nothing to do. Mind you, mum would like to live out there permanently. Since taking up Bridge we have met some very interesting people, but I seem to have more arguments with your mother regarding her erratic calling. She wants to join a local club and I hope I've put her off. Now, tell me how you're getting on, and how is Gloria keeping?"

"Well, dad, I decided I'd like to go back to farming. No offence but, really, crushing numbers all day is so impersonal."

George looked very cross. "That's a silly idea; you are with a well-established company and your long-term prospects are very promising."

"Dad, you and mum have given me a wonderful education, but my heart is not in it. Yes, I can see that in time I will be able to attain a senior position in the surveying department."

"Well, this is out of the blue; just sorry we did not buy Uncle Albert's farm when we had the opportunity."

"No, dad, I'll start off as a tenant farmer and then try buying small parcels of land, but for the time being I will continue to work as a surveyor. You have been wonderful parents and now it's up to me."

"What about Gloria? How does she feel about all this? Is she willing to be a farmer's wife?"

"Yes, she is fed up selling perfume and has also lost interest in modelling and would love to live in the countryside and start a family, and she'd like to keep chickens, and grow herbs."

"Well, that's one for the book; I always thought she was a city girl, but what are you going to do for money?"

"Yes, we have thought it through and to start I will continue working as a surveyor and Gloria will have to find a job."

"Did I hear you mention marriage? I do like Gloria and thank goodness your mother has now come to accept her, but I certainly will expect you to get married if there's going to be a family. Incidentally, what does her father do? I remember he was very argumentative and a very keen socialist."

"Well, yes, he is a bus driver and the shop steward; her mum works in Tesco's. They have been very kind to me. But, really, her old man is great company as long as you avoid politics, and then he can become a real pain."

"Well, Rob, whatever you decide, your mum and I will give you all the support we can. If we can help you in your farming aspirations, we will help you to get started."

"No, dad, I am going to do this off my own bat, and if it is a failure then I have only myself to blame, but thanks anyway. Now, I have got to try and convince mum, and that's not going to be easy. Then there is the question of the wedding, and that's going to be a real nightmare. I will have to face that when it happens. To tell you the truth, I would like to slip away with Gloria and quietly get married in a registry office, but I know mum will do her nut."

George smiled. "I fully understand how you feel and if that is what you want I should go and get on with it and face the consequences when you get back, but whatever you decide you will have my blessing."

"Well, tell me, dad," said Rod, picking up his glass of wine; they had just devoured a pizza and seemed very relaxed. "How did you start? You have in the past told me in dribs and drabs but not the complete story."

George got up and, carrying his glass of malt whiskey, went and sat in an old armchair in the corner of the kitchen. "Well, it's a long story. As you know, I was one of five and dad was very friendly but could not handle money; plus he had a drink problem and rather liked the ladies, so as you can imagine my poor mum had a hell of a life. She worked as a waitress, or barmaid, and we always seemed to be in debt. I was the youngest of five: two girls and three boys, but sadly I have just one brother left and I have lost contact with him. Poor mum was barely 50 when she died of cancer and my eldest brother Ted really brought me up. Dad seemed to disappear. I think he went to prison, something to do with changing the mileage on the cars he was selling. Yes, he was a salesman but was always changing jobs. Of course, he died years ago. I was very fortunate to pass the 11+ and went to the local grammar school. I was one of the poorer pupils. There were not many of us who lived on the estate, so we did get ragged, but that's life. I left school at 16 and went to work for the local council in the accounts department where I was articled. God, that was a boring place, so depressing, a great junk of a building, ten stories high and nick-named the Kremlin. I finally qualified during my national service in the Royal Army Pay Corps and then came out and decided to get a job in accountancy. I certainly did not want to go back working for the council.

"This was one of the most important decisions of my life: should I go for a large upmarket firm of accountants where I would be well paid or go for a small firm where the opportunities would be greater but the money poorer? I decided to go and work for Stevens and Willie, just two partners, both in their mid-fifties, and not very ambitious. They never looked for work but were the cheapest firm in town. It amused me because some of their clients were poached but always came back; they knew we were the cheapest. The long and short of it was more business was coming in than they could cope with. As they were not very ambitious and I was very much the new boy and left to myself, somehow I seemed to make all the decisions because I could never seem to find them. They were always out of the office seeing to their customers; I became the unofficial office manager. But they were two lovely blokes. John Willie was short and fat with a big Jewish nose and a strong Somerset accent; he was quite a comedian and used to attend parties in care homes as an entertainer. I can see his wife; she was the complete opposite: tall, always impeccably dressed with a large hat and spoke with a lardy-da accent. They had no children. I remember the offices were above a pet shop and we were always being plagued with mice, not that we ever had any food in the place. They shared one part-time secretary and she was rushed off her feet, but they both seemed to live in a different world and they were just working quietly towards their retirement.

"Look, do stop me if I am boring you."

"No, dad, I'm all ears and, really, I am just about to make that important decision which you made many years ago."

"Well, of course, I met your mother when the bank invited us to a Christmas lunch and she, as you know, was the manager's only daughter. He was always very friendly but her mother, quite naturally with her being the only daughter, was protective. Mum at the time was studying art at Goldsmiths College, which was full of the arty types: scruffy, bearded, and with earrings and dirty nails. Her mum didn't take to me initially. I had to make myself a nuisance to get her daughter's attention. She thought I was rude, self-opinionated and was not going anywhere, but she changed her views when a friend gave me a glowing character reference. Plus the fact I don't think she was very enamoured with some of those arty types. We finally got married and lived happily ever after, but your birth was the greatest moment in her life; her dad had died but her mum was over the moon.

"Well, there you have it. When I retired we were the sixth largest accountancy firm in the United Kingdom with 80 offices and a labour force of 1,200. I left most of my shares in the company but, between you and me, I am thinking of selling up. I am not happy with the new managing director and the direction the company is taking."

"But surely, dad, you appointed this guy. Did you make the wrong decision?"

"No, no. We have always been a very democratic outfit and he was elected by the board. Really, since retiring I've lost interest and there seem to be tensions amongst the directors. Still, keep that to yourself, but if I do decide to sell our shares then I will have to decide where to invest it. Of course, your mother was left very comfortably off, but she's got no idea about money. I invested some of her inheritance in the company.

"Still, tell me Rod, any news of Claude Dibbs? I don't know him well, but he used to put business our way for some of his wealthy clients. Every time I look at the business news his name is mentioned."

"Well, yes, I did hear from a reliable source that the London and Edinburgh are closing down their surveying department because it's too costly and want to go out of house for valuations, which means in the long run I will be in the right position to pick up some of this business."

Rod stood up and stretched. "Well, I think it's time we went to bed. I'll just put these plates in the dishwasher."

o o o

After a wonderful holiday, Edgar and his son Simon spent Christmas with his sister Rita and husband Doug in the New Forest. Their son Freddie was older than Simon but he enjoyed his company. Rita had not changed; she was always worrying about something and was busy being a part-time teacher and, of course, the vicar's wife.

They spent a few days in Surrey where they were received with a warm welcome from all sides. The building business, Wadham Developments, was now very much on its feet with healthy reserves, principally in building sites. The three directors, Philip, Maggie and Sally, had decided to concentrate on small developments and resisted the opportunity of purchasing large locations. They were only too conscious of the additional finance this would entail and also the extra pressures. Philip, behind his boyish charm, had not changed and could never sit still for long, but he was very astute in buying and selling sites and much of the profits had been accrued in this way. Sally, the marketing director, always seemed to find a buyer, but she was now part-time. Philip missed his mother, Joan, who had taken a great interest in his work and was coming to accept his new wife, Claire.

Edgar spoke to a director of Irvin Financial Services, the company which his late wife had set up. He had sold out all her shares to the directors and they seemed to be holding their own but reported competition was fierce and the fluctuations on the stock market made it difficult advising customers. Although they invited him over for lunch, he sensed they were being polite, and he now had no interest in the business. He was very saddened to see that his father-in-law, Charlie, had aged and was now confined to the house. June, his ex-barmaid, looked in most days and she was now happily married and settled with three children. Charlie was pleased to see Simon, gave the boy a big hug and pushed some notes into his hand. Simon looked upon him as a stranger but was friendly and polite. June took Simon home to meet her three children, which gave Edgar and Charlie time to have a natter.

"Well, I'm pleased I've sold all the chippy shops and finally sold that pub which was a real pain. In fact, that Sally Bridgeman who you use was most helpful; she certainly knows the market. Mind you, I had to drop the price. Still, I'm out of it and at last in the black; must be the first time ever. Needless to say, my bank manager is delighted." Suddenly Charlie seemed to be like his old self. "Tell me, Edgar, what are you up to? You still got that school? I did hear that you'd had some difficulties. I know that's a job I could never do; they would probably lock me up for being too strict." Edgar spoke about his work as they sat in Charlie's comfortable little lounge sipping whiskey. Charlie put down his glass. "I shouldn't really be drinking this stuff. My doctor – actually, she is a lady – if she knew she would do her nut."

Edgar could see that Charlie was now getting tired. "Look, I must pick up Simon. I'll be in contact."

Charlie looked sad. "Please, please come and see me again. When I see you I think of my daughter, darling Heather, such a clever girl. I do miss her. She was one of the best things that ever happened to me and the older I get the more I think of her." Suddenly tears appeared in his eyes and he took out a coloured handkerchief and wiped his face.

o o o

Edgar started to feel under the weather, and it seemed to be getting worse. He found it difficult to sleep at night. He seemed to be haunted with pictures of Carol, and the thought of returning to Bennington House filled him with dread. He enjoyed Simon's company; he was a determined boy and never stopped asking questions.

They finally made their way back to Harrogate. He had spoken to the head of St Michael's preparatory school where Simon had been offered a scholarship, which in simple terms meant the school fees were reduced by 25%. "Simon performed quite well; he was very much borderline with the written papers but came through very strongly when interviewed; we all felt confident he would do well here. Now, Mr Collins, don't take offence, but what are your plans in the long term, bearing in mind he will be leaving us when he is 14? I am sure you appreciate we do not like to see all this grounding wasted."

"Well, thank you. I'm very impressed with your long-term commitments and I can assure you I will endeavour to send him on to an established public school."

Simon was very excited to be starting at a new school. "Look," said Vicky, "I'll see to his uniform and all the items he will need."

"Oh, thank you; that will be a great help. Just send me the account. He has quite a lot of money in his trust fund. Also, I will continue to pay the monthly cheque for his board and incidental expenses. Now, that is settled, and I don't want any argument." Finally, after a short stay he reluctantly bid farewell to Simon, Vicky and family and was soon in his car making his way back unwillingly to his school.

After the long journey, Margaret Hogg was there to meet him. She could see he was not himself and appeared to lack any enthusiasm. Everything seemed to be an effort. Finally, the children arrived in dribs and drabs. They were all very excited and needed firm leadership, but Edgar passed over his evening duties to Ian Hogg. The following day he did not arrive on duty but sent a note to Ian. Suddenly it became common knowledge that he was sick and needed help. Ian went to see Edgar. "What is the trouble?"

"I'm sorry, but since the death of Carol I have not had a good night's sleep; her death is haunting me, and I feel responsible that I should have done more."

Ian gave Edgar a hard look. "I think you need some help and I am sure this is not the right environment with the anxieties you are experiencing."

"It's just I'm fine until I have to face the children and then I get stomach cramps and my nerves seem to go to pieces."

"I think you should see a doctor and find out what he has to say, but I do remember years ago a colleague having similar problems; he eventually resigned."

Edgar loosened his tie. "I'll have a chat with Mr Holdsworth, the HMI, and come back to you; I found him to be most supportive."

"Well," said Ian, pulling off his glasses, "now we have the two extra house mothers we are well staffed in the childcare department, but with your absence I feel we will need a senior management officer. But if this should occur, I insist that Dick Loxton and I attend the final interview with the school trustees."

"Yes, Ian; much of the success of the school is due to you and Margaret, and you will be fully involved in any senior appointments."

He decided to ring Leonard Holdsworth immediately. "You just caught me; I am just about to go out of the door. I'm on the road for four days. Still, how can I help you?" Edgar spoke frankly about the problems he was experiencing and Holdsworth listened without a word.

"I have witnessed breakdowns in health more times than I would like to admit; in fact, I had to close down a school recently because the head tried to carry on. Now, some advice: you must get away. You will not recover staying there – your health will only deteriorate. You will possibly need psychiatric help, and recovery can take time, but it is essential that you appoint an experienced principal to carry on the good work and maintain the high standards you have achieved. It is essential that all the recommendations made at the last general inspection are implemented. Finally, you must not feel ashamed to get medical help. It may mean you will be absent or possibly you may have to change direction in your career. Look, do come back to me. I will consider this call unofficial and private. The Department will start to flap if they learn of your condition. I suggest you appoint a new head immediately and then put the Department in the picture. But, Edgar, I do wish you success. Come back to me in a month's time again in an unofficial capacity; until then, I do hope everything goes well for you."

Edgar decided to get out. He had a brief word with Ian Hogg and Margaret and explained his phone call to Leonard Holdsworth. "I am very sorry to be running away like this, but if I stay I will be just one big liability. Look, I will speak to the bursar and also my brother-in-law, Neil Skerritt, who as you know is a solicitor and a Trustee, so everything will be in place. Finally, I will ask Neil to advertise for my replacement; he will be in contact with you and Dick."

Both Ian and Margaret became watery eyed; she produced a handkerchief and blew her nose and he wiped his eyes with the back of his and spoke. Edgar looked up. "The school won't be the same without you; we shall all miss you and it's all so very sad. I felt we were at last turning the corner and great things were ahead. You will be in our thoughts and, naturally, you leave with our very best wishes. When are you planning to go?"

"Early tomorrow morning. I don't want a lot of fuss. I'll just slip away and I promise to give you a ring in a week's time and hope by then to have a clearer picture of what my plans are. Never thought it would come to this and it is with a very heavy heart that I am leaving but since coming back my anxieties have got worse; if I stay, I will have a complete breakdown."

Margaret got up and went over and kissed Edgar on the cheek and left the room. Ian shook his hand warmly. "We shall look forward to hearing from you and pray that you are on the mend." He left with his head bowed, walking with a slight stoop.

At the break of dawn, Edgar was in his car heading south. The further down the road he got the more relaxed he felt. By lunchtime he was in Salisbury where he rang Rita. "We're all looking forward to seeing you tomorrow, and the boys are so excited." Edgar bit his tongue. "Now, stay as long as you can. I can't tell you how much we are looking forward to seeing you."

Edgar thought about the boys and how they loved a good old rough-and-tumble. He smiled, hoping they were getting past that sort of thing. "Well, yes, I'm looking forward to seeing you all, and don't go to too much trouble. I shall probably move on at the end of the week. Till tomorrow. Bye."

He decided to stay in Salisbury and spent the afternoon in the cathedral. As he knelt down in prayer he was suddenly overtaken with a glow of peace and serenity. He felt as if his problems were lifted and in a strange way he was looking in at himself. He felt he was at peace with the world. He was leaving when he heard a voice address him. He looked up to see a tall frail old man looking at him and was very much surprised to see it was the Reverend Tom Owen who had been his vicar near Guildford. "Tom, it's lovely to see you after all this time."

"Yes, I retired to a little village called Chilmark. My darling wife Mary died last year after 52 years of marriage. My son Michael is now the medical officer of health for Hampshire and my daughter married a farmer and is living in Cornwall. They both want me to come and live with them, but I don't want to be a burden. I will shortly be 84 and I am moving back to Surrey into a small flat with 24/7 cover." By then they were in a small teashop. "And you, Edgar: last I heard, you had changed direction and set up a small school for less fortunate youngsters – a very commendable vocation. Still, what brings you to Salisbury?"

Edgar took in a deep breath and quickly thought, *yes, I will tell him everything.* He suddenly felt he wanted to share his problems. "I don't know where to start."

Tom looked up. He had a long haggard face with piercing dark eyes. He smiled. "I've got all the time in the world and clerics are good listeners." Edgar told Tom the whole story and did not hold back: the death of Carol and his difficulties in facing up to her suicide; the responsibilities and pressures of managing a small school and the sadness of being separated from Simon; and still feeling an agonising hurt and anger at the death of his dear wife Heather. By now it was getting late. "Where are you staying tonight? You can come to my place, near the village of Chilmark, about seven miles down the road."

"Well, thanks very much, but actually I have booked into a small hotel and then tomorrow I'm off to the New Forest to see my sister and her family."

Tom looked very serious. "From what you have said, it is obvious that you have got to find yourself again; all the psychiatric help in the world is no substitute for a real faith and believing in yourself. I think that brief visit to the Cathedral is a small step in the right direction. I'm sorry Edgar, we clergy do tend to pontificate but please give our dear Lord the chance to help you. I know in this materialistic world people scoff at our beliefs and often their only religion is money, but I think you can see that there's more to life than worldly possessions. At the end of the month, as I mentioned, I am due to move into some sheltered accommodation just outside Guildford. If I may, when I settle in I will give you a ring and we must get together and have a real drink." Edgar shook his hand warmly and suddenly seemed to feel better. They agreed to meet up in the very near future.

Chapter 5

Finally Bob, Rosemary's husband, was invited to join Godstone United as the assistant manager and trainer. The manager, Ted Drake, was on his way out. The team had dropped down two divisions over the past four years and the supporters' club were up in arms. They owned 38% of the shares, but the largest shareholder was Don Rowbotham; he wanted to sell up but the shares had dropped like a stone and he felt the only way out was to get results but he could not afford to sign up experienced players. Bob felt sorry for Ted, whose wife had died of breast cancer, and he seemed to be having problems with his son-in-law. He frequently arrived late for the training sessions, often smelling of alcohol. The club had a pool of 28 players and ran two teams; Bob was appointed as the second team trainer but was now very much in charge of all the training sessions. It was hard work but he was in his element and they started to string some away victories. The club had now climbed to the middle of the table and suddenly they started to feel confident, and the supporters were delighted with the change in fortunes.

Bob had never met Don Rowbotham but he heard he was living in Marbella and was recovering from open heart surgery. He could quickly see the team's limitations; they were missing three quality players and the club was running a large overdraft. The bank was concerned and had issued a closure on any further credit. Bob was in his element; all the players were part-time professionals, including Bob who had a part-time day job as an electrician.

The players were watching the TV in the clubhouse; the FA draw for the minor clubs was being made. They had a difficult draw away against East Lee, a team on the outskirts of Birmingham who were in a higher league, and who had only lost two home games that season. Bob decided to travel up to Birmingham to watch them play. He had a chat with Ted, who was always very supportive. "Bob, this will be my last season so if you want my job it will all depend on results. Naturally, you'll have my support but a run in the cup would certainly help." So on the following Saturday Bob left early and travelled up to East Lee. He finally came away realising it was going to be a tall order to outclass the opposition. They were slow and robust; half the team had Division I experience and they built up their attack in a solid but slow formation. He studied their strengths and weaknesses but felt they could be beaten; it would have to be with quick breakaway attacks. He had watched the game incognito and as he drove back home he thought about the composition of his team and decided to bring in two younger players and put them on the bench to play on the flanks in the second half.

He got home and put Freddie to bed; he had wanted to come but had left him at home. Rosemary mentioned that Godstone United had lost playing at home.

Bob took the training session on Monday afternoon. He was full of ideas and couldn't wait to put them into practice. He was quietly spoken and very rarely shouted but was respected by all the players. "Now, they are older and a more experienced team, but they can be beaten. I noticed in the second half they tired and that is the time when we will have to hit them hard on a quick break. In the first half we will play a defensive game and try to absorb their attacks. But in the latter part of the second half I will then start to switch players, bringing some off the bench, and then it will be all systems go." They were sitting around the changing room with a large blackboard. He picked up the chalk. "Let's be honest: we do not have a ball carrier in the team so we will have to attack down the wings, and it is in these breaks that we will beat them. They have two very talented forwards, one in particular, Wilf Mannion, who really is their match winner and I shall have him shadowed, if possible starved of the ball. He is small, very nimble and will take some catching and I gather has been watched by some of the big league clubs." Bob turned to the blackboard and started chalking up the names of the players with their positions. "Yes, yes, I know you are surprised, but I will be altering the composition of the team in the second half so it will be very much a game of two halves. Now, please remember this game against East Lee is the most important of the season up to now. We have stopped the rot but really we are not going anywhere, but if we can get past East Lee and then have a lucky draw and win the next game we'll be in the big money. It's not going to be easy and we've got to believe in ourselves. Now, I appreciate it's been a long hard season with some very tough games so the coaching now will involve planning set pieces in pinpointing the long ball. I believe in keeping it simple; we have got to find our wingers and get the ball across, but it is all about speed, so we will be concentrating on this. You are all fit, and I am cutting out all the stress training programmes. Now, let's get onto the pitch and start to practise some of these set moves."

They then trotted onto the pitch and started to practise the planned moves, at first walking through them, and at the end of an hour they were completing the moves at a neck-breaking pace. He then turned to defence, in particular free kicks and corners.

Ted Drake, the manager, was sitting in the small stand with another man. He waved Bob over. "Bob, this is Don Rowbotham. As you are aware, he is the principal shareholder."

They all shook hands. "Nice meeting you, sir. I think we are slowly turning the corner, but I have been practising a plan of attack against East Lee in a fortnight's time."

Don smiled. He was in his late fifties, wearing a light brown overcoat and a hat. He looked very pale. Bob thought he looked like Del Boy. "Sorry, Bob, we have not met before, but I haven't been well. I had open heart surgery, but felt I must come over for the big match and see my family. Wish I could offer a bonus to the players but really we are carrying a large overdraft and the bank have us against the wall. Of course, if a miracle does happen and we get through the next two games then it will be a different story."

Bob slipped on his track suit top. "Yes, just think of it, a game against Liverpool and then we would be in with the big boys. Still, must keep our feet on the ground."

Don suddenly seemed to shiver. "Sorry Bob, I must go. I can't stand the cold but, look, big decisions will have to be made at the end of the season and much will depend on the next two games. I will be in contact."

o o o

All of a sudden Edgar felt depressed and didn't want to see anybody. The death of his wife Heather had been the start. He had decided to change direction and leave his successful building company to start the school for emotionally disturbed pupils. Initially, it had been a great success but tiring and then the death of the pupil Carol pushed him over the edge. He finally decided to rent a small cottage on the Marchant estate near Salisbury; it was very isolated and peacefully situated close to the woods. He had appointed Ian Hogg as principal of his school, although the children were away on holiday. The thought of returning, with all the pressures associated with the death of Carol, filled him with anguish.

The cottage was very primitive, with a grubby interior, worn out furniture and inadequate heating. He had a mobile phone which he had turned off and he spent much time reading and drinking. He lost all account of time and the days and nights seemed to drift by. He slept in the kitchen in an old armchair fully dressed and neglected his personal hygiene, which was so unlike him. As he was dozing, he heard a banging on the kitchen door. He finally opened it to find nobody there. When he was shutting up he heard a shout and opened it again to find a distinguished man in his mid-sixties, tall and thin with a large ginger moustache, wearing hunting tweeds and carrying a rifle with a brace of grouse. He gave Edgar a broad toothy smile. "I'm Lord Marchant." He looked closely at Edgar. "Are you alright? We have not seen you and I'm just checking to see that you are coping." He came into the kitchen and looked around. "When did you last have a meal?" He looked at the waste container overflowing with empty bottles. "Look, old boy, you better come over to the Manor and have a meal, but do have a shower." He had large grey eyes and a friendly face. He squinted. "We can have a chat this evening." Lord Marchant then picked up his rifle and birds and departed, shouting over his shoulder, "Make it 6:30." He had a plummy accent and walked with a limp.

Edgar stood and stretched. He looked in the mirror and received a shock. He had thick stubble, needed a haircut and had dark bags under his eyes. He looked at his mobile. *No, I will not turn it on*, he thought. After a shave and a cold shower, he turned his attention to the cottage. He put out all the dead bottles and generally tidied up the place and made up the bed. At 6.20 p.m. he made his way up to Hannington Manor after finally getting his car started.

He was met at the main door by a small hunchback servant; she nodded to him, and he followed her through the majestic hall with a grand staircase. The walls were adorned with past members of the Marchant family. It was very dim and quiet, and he followed her down a side corridor, arriving at the kitchen. There was a large bulky woman bending over a huge Raeburn typical of that period, and in the room was a big solid pine table covered with utensils and dishes. She stood wiping her brow; she had a friendly face. "I am Edith and that's Emily. She's as deaf as a post so she won't hear you, and you?"

"Oh, sorry, I am Edgar and was invited to come up for a meal."

"Yes, his Lordship did mention you were staying in the gamekeeper's cottage. It's a bit lonely down there."

"But it's just what I want." Edgar had to think quickly. "I'm writing a book, and the peace and solitude is all I need."

"Oh, that's interesting; what's the book about?"

"The Army. I was a soldier for 22 years, but it probably won't go far."

"Is that so?" said Edith, lifting a large baking tray with a sizzling side of beef. "Funny, but my husband was in the army before he ran off with the housemaid, and he was old enough to be her dad!"

Edgar was soon sitting in the corner of the kitchen tucking into roast beef with all the trimmings when two small Jack Russells came bouncing into the kitchen. As soon as they spied Edgar they started barking. Edith looked up. "Don't worry about them: they're quite harmless, but I think her Ladyship is on her way." The next moment, a tall slim lady in her mid-fifties came sweeping in. She was wearing a heavy tweed skirt and a dark woollen jumper. She had dark hair and looked very stern.

Edgar jumped to his feet. "Hello. Henry did mention you were coming up. I am Elizabeth. He was hoping to see you but got called away. I hope Edith has looked after you." She looked at the table. "Edith, haven't you got some beer or wine for our guest?"

Edgar smiled. "No, please: I am fine. I think it would do me good to go without."

"No, milady; the last shooting party seem to have cleaned us out, but we do have the big order coming in tomorrow."

"It's Edgar, isn't it? Well, I better let you finish your meal. My husband would like a word before you leave – he should be home very shortly."

Edgar sat back and was finishing a cup of tea when the phone rang. "Yes sir. I'll get Emily to bring him up."

Edgar was ushered into Lord Marchant's study. He followed Emily as she scuttled along the corridor. "Glad to see you again," he said, holding out his hand. He was tall, with a large moustache and a toothy smile, and was dressed in a light grey suit. "You looked a bit peaky this morning. Hope you're feeling better. Come in and have a drink. I must join the family for dinner in a moment."

"Thank you, Sir, but I am now going to try to get on the wagon. I've been drinking too much of late." His Lordship smiled.

They were soon sitting in easy chairs in his large office, with an enormous desk and a large log fire burning in the grate. Lord Marchant picked up his cut glass tumbler; the liquid inside was the colour of bark. "You sure you won't join me? Incidentally, were you military? You have the posture of the parade ground."

"That was a good guess. I was in khaki for 22 years and came out as a captain in the SAS, but was originally in the Paras."

"Well, that's a coincidence," said his Lordship, taking a long pull from his glass. "I was Coldstream Guards and miss every moment of it; they were wonderful years." They chatted on about various personalities.

"The only chap I knew in the Coldstream Guards was Colonel Thomas Taylor."

Marchant's eyes suddenly lit up. "Good lord, I knew him well; he was a brilliant soldier – clever but difficult to work with, had no sense of humour. I think he got a degree in Arabic, but tell me how you knew him?"

"Well, he was attached to the SAS and was my company commander. Then when he left the army he ran a security company protecting VIPs. He was closely involved with the

Crown Prince of Saudi Arabia and I used to carry out part-time assignments for him, in the main protecting VIPs."

Suddenly the door flew open and Lady Marchant appeared wearing a full-length evening dress. She ignored Edgar. "Henry, we are all waiting to start supper, do come."

"Just coming, dear." He stood and picked up his glass and started to go. "Sorry, Edgar, but we must have a natter tomorrow." He winked and moved towards the door. "I'm sure you understand."

Edgar got back to his cold deserted cottage feeling so much better. *I must start to get myself into shape. I'll go for a long walk tomorrow; it will do me the power of good.* He was dozing in front of the TV when he heard a noise outside the back door. He put out the lights and looked through the window and saw a shadow moving around outside. He decided to go out and investigate and opened the door when he was suddenly blinded with a strong light shining in his face.

o o o

Philip missed his mother and now had been joined by Claire, his new wife. She was a very noisy boisterous young lady and was out to have a good time. His mother Joan had not fully approved of her and Philip was slowly getting to see why. Sadly, his mother Joan died suddenly but had made the effort to be present at the wedding, although she frequently had to bite her tongue. "She's noisy, outspoken, and those short dresses! I think she wears too much make-up." Claire resented moving down south from Newcastle but she quickly made friends and joined the ladies' darts team in a rough local pub Philip disapproved of, and then, with a troop of girls, she joined a dance club. She started looking for a job but had little success and stayed in bed for half the morning and then seemed to spend hours on the phone. Philip was becoming very disenchanted with her behaviour and then suddenly, without warning, Claire became pregnant. It was a big surprise to Philip; the little bits of lovemaking that took place were never very successful. Even so, he was over the moon and hoped the responsibilities of a baby would make Claire stay at home. But, sadly, it was not the case and they seemed to have a row every day, either about money or the choice of some of her unsavoury friends. It seemed to be a short pregnancy; Philip was becoming very excited. Claire became moody and apprehensive and even suggested that she would like to have a termination, much to Philip's consternation.

The building business seemed to have settled down and the firm Wadham Developments where Philip was the architect became selective in planning its future expansion. Maggie, the secretary, was now working part-time and Sally Bridgeman, the sales director, was only working two days a week; she had married her retired bank manager and suddenly seemed to have lost interest in the partnership. Philip had taken on some outside work, in particular for Harris and Reid; they had grown and always came knocking on his door when they had particular planning problems and tried to utilise his services, but Sally had always firmly refused their requests. The business was going well; they had built up a large land bank of building sites and were developing them slowly, at the same time as buying and selling. Much of the success was due in the main to Sally's skills in finding buyers.

Maggie was worried about her husband, Ron; he had prostate cancer and was unable to walk far so was now restricted to a wheelchair. Her daughter Mary had settled down with her partner who now had his own scaffolding business. She had come to like him; he was always very sensible and obviously adored her daughter, so she finally lent him a small sum to buy more equipment. She was hoping they would start a family but only after they were married. She felt Wadham Developments seemed to be losing its way and thought it needed to attract some new blood, possibly a new dynamic chairman. Philip obviously had problems of his own; he kept the company ticking over, but his heart did not seem to be in the job. She and Sally would like to sell up and get out; the problem was how to unload their shares and get a fair market price.

o o o

Suddenly Claire was rushed into hospital. She had been behaving very peculiarly of late, but Philip was excited and hurried to the hospital. He was spoken to by the staff nurse. "Sir, I think it has been a false alarm, but we will keep her in. Please stay, but it is impossible to give you an accurate time concerning the birth." He could see that Claire was very depressed. They finally gave her a mild sedative, so he decided to go back home.

It was 4 o'clock in the morning when he had a call from the hospital to tell him things were happening if he wanted to be there at the birth. He rushed over and was met by a consultant. "There have been some problems. The midwife called me in. I don't want to be too technical, but I will have to perform a Caesarean procedure. There is nothing to worry about; I deliver healthy babies every day, so please do not worry. Your wife is under heavy sedation to combat the pain; all I need is for you to sign the consent form."

Philip had tears in his eyes. "Is the baby okay?"

"Yes, rest assured, if I do not immediately operate there is a danger you will lose your baby, who is lying in the wrong position and the umbilical cord has got tangled."

Philip sighed. "Where's the form? The sooner I sign it the better."

"Right, sir; this should take two hours. We will have to get your wife back into the operating ward and I want just a few more X-rays before I proceed."

Three hours later Philip was dozing in a waiting room when the staff nurse shook his shoulder gently. "You are, sir, the father of a big bonny boy. Both mother and baby are doing well."

As he walked down the corridor, he could hear the baby squealing. He was met by the surgeon, dressed in a pale green shirt, trousers and a loose-fitting skullcap. He was a tall man in his late fifties and gave Philip a big smile. Philip shook his hand vigorously, with tears in his eyes. "Thank you, sir, for everything."

"It's been a real pleasure," he said with a wry smile on his face. "I think you're going to be in for a big surprise."

He followed the staff nurse into a small operating ward. The walls were covered with various pieces of equipment, dials and charts. On the solitary bed, sitting up, was Claire, holding a handkerchief to her nose. A young plump West Indian nurse was skipping around the ward with a little baby wrapped in a white shawl; he could hear it crying.

Philip rushed over and kissed his wife. She started to cry and then the young nurse came up. "Now, young man, this is your dad," and she passed the small bundle over to Philip. He took the parcel and looked down, and he was in for one of the greatest shocks of his life. It was a dear little chap, but he was dark skinned and had Negroid features. Philip quickly realised this was not his son. He looked at his wife, who was crying into a large blue handkerchief.

She looked up. "It was all a mistake; it should never have happened. He took advantage of me." Philip quickly passed the baby back to the nurse. Tears were running down his cheeks. He was lost for words.

"Darling, darling, it was a mistake; it only happened the once. I was drunk and he, and he took..." She was now sobbing and choking. "He took advantage of me. I love you. Please, please, don't go."

Philip was overcome with grief and quickly turned on his heels. "I can't stay." He half ran out of the operating ward, along the hospital corridor and made his way out of the hospital to his car and drove away at a break-neck speed.

Chapter 6

Sir Claude Dibbs accompanied a small group of delegates to their hotel on 42nd Street. It had been a tiring journey. The PM had cornered him on the plane, and they had a useful chat. He mentioned that he was trying to strengthen the government's representation in the House of Lords concerning banking issues and had asked if he was interested. "Of course, you will receive a life peerage." He marvelled at the PM's energy; he spent the whole flight moving around amongst the delegates, discussing various issues, and never seemed to fumble with their names or their business activities. He was disappointed that Professor Gold could not make the trip; his wife had been admitted to hospital. He enjoyed his company. He was a red hot socialist but would have been an asset on the stage at Yale.

The party was staying at various hotels and after an early dinner he was finally taken to the City Hall where he was escorted into a large auditorium packed with members of the Small Businesses Guild. The Chancellor and the PM were staying at the Embassy. The PM finally arrived 10 minutes late to address the packed assembly. They were soon sitting on the stage facing a hall crowded with 400 delegates. The lighting was so dim he could not see the audience. The meeting started with a prayer led by the Catholic Cardinal of New York. This was followed by a list of notices which included mention of members of the PM's delegation. Finally, Claude was invited to speak. He stepped forward and stood behind the lectern on the large stage, after having been introduced by the chairman, a bulky coloured man with a broad New York twang.

Claude was now becoming very fluent at speaking at this type of gathering. "Well, my friends, I realise bankers are not the flavour of the month and, yes, on occasions they can be very difficult." There was a soft applause across the hall. "But please remember we are in this together and your success is reflected in our profits which in turn keeps the shareholders off our backs. But, ladies and gentlemen, let us start with the basics. What are the essential ingredients of a successful business?" He felt they were all listening with rapt attention, although he could barely see his audience. He spoke with no notes and moved from behind the lectern and stood on the front of the stage. "Yes, I know much of my deliberations are common sense: having the right product which is in demand, and then much can depend upon your market strategy." He then covered a wide range of advertising and marketing procedures. "Now this leads us on to overheads, which cover a range of costs from banking charges, labour, marketing, property specialists and legal advice, not forgetting accountancy and pension liabilities. I must stress relationships with your workforce; I have in the past six months been very involved in examining and designing a programme of inducements for my employees." He paused. "I am hoping this will put the bankers' union in a friendly frame of mind." He heard a faint cheer. "But ultimately, at the top of this list should be cash flow. I stress this time and time again; if this is neglected then the most successful business with all their products in demand will go under. It should be studied not monthly, not weekly, but daily and firm action should be taken on all outstanding accounts."

He then moved back to the lectern. The audience was sitting very quietly. "It has been a great privilege to address you all. These are the problems of business worldwide and I do hope I have helped to focus your attention on some aspects of your work. Thank you for having me."

After a short pause, there was enthusiastic applause from the packed room, and you could hear shouting in the background. It seemed to go on. Claude sat and the Chairman of the Guild, who was wearing an ornate chain of office, gave a vote of thanks. He turned to Claude. "You Brits seem to understand our problems: we're faced with high costs and red tape whichever way we turn, but thank you, Sir Claude. I wish I had you as my bank manager."

After a round of applause, he turned to the Prime Minister. In that broad New York accent, he introduced the PM. "We have now our most distinguished guest, the Prime Minister of Great Britain, the Right Honourable David Patterson." There was some muted applause. The PM jumped up with a bundle of notes and stood behind the lectern, put on his glasses and was quickly addressing the auditorium as if he was in the House of Commons. It was a very polished performance, stressing the importance of working together and highlighting members of the delegation with their specialist skills in the field of commerce. He spoke for 25 minutes and then fielded questions from across the hall, some very unfriendly, particularly the question of tariffs and the European agricultural policies; also, steel imports were discussed. But the PM managed to dodge the flak and spoke of his respect for their great nation and how he was so looking forward to meeting their president.

After a vote of thanks, the PM and Claude, with their entourage, slipped out of the hall to waiting cars. As they were about to leave, the PM spoke to Sir Claude. "You were outstanding. Now, would you like to come over to the embassy for a nightcap? The ambassador has lain on a small party of distinguished guests which I'm sure you would enjoy." Claude thanked the PM but refused his kind offer and pleaded he had some private work to catch up with. "Yes, I can fully understand; I have my dispatch box which my PPS keeps opening and I shall have to spend at least an hour tonight trying to sort out problems of the state."

Claude finally got back to his hotel and managed to slip past a group of delegates who were commandeering the bar; they all seemed to be in good form. He decided to have a bath and get to bed. He calculated it would be some ungodly hour in the UK so decided to ring Pat in the morning. It must have been 1 o'clock; he was in bed dozing, with papers scattered all over the floor, when the phone rang. He woke with a start.

"Claude, is that you?"

"Hilary darling, how wonderful to hear you. I'm so looking forward to seeing you. It will make this trip worthwhile. I can't stop thinking about you."

"Claude, I was so disappointed. This evening I attended a cocktail party at your embassy and had expected to see you. I know your ambassador, Sir Humphrey Morehead; he was at your embassy in Rome, so I managed to get an invite. We had a lovely evening. I met your Prime Minister; what was he called? David Patterson, a real charmer, but I was so hoping to meet up with you. Even so, I had a pleasant evening, only there were too many showbiz people there; they are so noisy and never stop showing off. Still now, tell me how long are you staying?"

"Well, the main party are leaving on Wednesday evening and I have booked a flight for Friday morning."

"Oh dearest, I wish you were staying longer; I've got so much to show you. Still, what will be, will be."

"Yes, I wish I could stay longer, but I will be free all day Thursday. I'll ring you Wednesday night, then we can discuss our plans."

"Sorry, did I wake you up? You sounded very sleepy. God, I'm missing you. I could do with you now, but you won't get much sleep when you're with me," said Hilary, laughing. "I'm so looking forward to that moment. Still, sweet dreams darling, until Wednesday night."

Claude had a busy three days. He joined the Chancellor to speak at a fringe meeting of the World Bank. The meeting was very poorly attended. On Wednesday morning he was at

Yale for a question and answer session. He joined the team of distinguished economic gurus. The hall was packed, with students standing everywhere. The meeting was televised and the students had no respect for the speakers. At times, they asked personal questions. Claude enjoyed the free-for-all. 'How much is your yearly salary? ...Do you have share options? ...Is there a gender pay gap? ...Which nation when lending would you avoid? ...Have you ever been refused a loan? ...What have you done for world peace?' Claude found the questions refreshing but he sensed some of the panel were ill at ease. They were sitting on a platform in a small packed room and the chairman found it at times difficult to keep order. He learnt later that the meeting had been infiltrated by an extreme left group. The panel comprised of two Americans from the State Department, a woman from the American Banking Union, and a representative from the World Bank. Finally, after an hour and a half they were able to leave the dais after much heckling. The chairman was a grey-haired Economics professor in his late sixties; he looked a little dazed. "I don't want to go through that again. Still, I've just heard that the TV producers are delighted and plan to show us on the national network at peak viewing times." The chairman thanked them for coming. "I found out later that we were the target for a far-left political group. Still, I'm sure some will find it entertaining. We will certainly get a splash in the national papers tomorrow."

Claude got back to his hotel and took a call from the PM. "Sir Claude, thank you for all your support. I feel the mission has been a great success. I had a meeting with the president this morning and my team have been busy negotiating some very lucrative trade deals against, I might say, stiff competition. Well, I will be in communication about what we discussed, supporting my team in the House of Lords Incidentally, I saw a clip of your meeting at Yale; it certainly was a lively get-together, but the economic correspondent was very impressed with your openness. I am just sorry

Professor Gold could not be with you; he would have been in his element dealing with the students. Look, we are moving here. I will be in touch." They parted in a most amicable fashion.

Claude was in the hotel having afternoon tea with three of the delegates who were staying on seeing to possible business contracts. They were bewailing their problems, in particular the weak pound; he was just about to discuss exchange rates when a porter leaned over to inform him that he was wanted on the phone. He took the call at the desk and quickly realised it was Hilary. "Look, I'll ring you back in 15 minutes." Eventually he got back to his room and spoke to Hilary.

In the early evening, Claude took a taxi from the hotel to an apartment on Upper East Side. It was a small block of opulent apartments. He was stopped at a small kiosk by the duty porter who announced his visit. Hilary was delighted to see him and rushed into his arms and kissed him passionately. "Now, my darling, let me see you," she said, leading him towards the window. "You look tired." He noticed her blonde hair was longer and she had put on a little weight. Her voluptuous figure excited him.

"Yes, it has been a long tiring three days. I've met so many people."

"I saw a bit on the TV; your visit to Yale had a very rude lot of students. I should think a faction of them was from a socialist movement and most of them are commies. Now, listen: I plan to take you out tonight to eat at a new French restaurant, the Charles de Gaulle; it is very good and has only just been opened and has not yet caught on, but it is in a rather rough area. I know the manager. Actually, he is Italian. Having worked in Italy, he likes talking to me. Mind you, they're having troubles and want to move into a more upmarket part of town. Still, darling, tell me all your news. I like your PM; he was easy to talk to."

Claude then outlined his engagements. "I'm so sorry I did not come to the reception at our embassy; if I had known you were there I would naturally have come."

"Dearest, you didn't miss much; there were too many actors and they can be so noisy and insincere."

Claude walked around the flat. "I must say, this is very much larger than I thought."

"Oh, yes. I had a small pad in LA which I sold and bought this. It was not cheap but, still, what's money for? Let's have a cocktail. I booked the table for eight." They finally rang the porter to order a cab, and after a drink and a brush-up they were soon on their way to the restaurant. They had a table in a quiet corner. The dining room was dim with candlelight on every table. It had luxurious fittings and an intimate charm.

As they sat, Claude heard his name and looked up to see an old familiar face. "It can't be, but yes, George Draper. I've not seen you for years." They shook hands and he introduced him to Hilary. "This is one of my colleagues; he is the area manager for Croydon, a very busy borough in London."

"You mean I was. I retired six months ago. My darling wife Ruth suddenly died. My pension was up-to-date... sorry, let me introduce you to my younger brother, William." They shook hands.

Claude was standing. "Do join us for a drink." The waiter quickly came and drew up two more chairs.

"Let me see," said Claude. "Isn't Edgar Collins a relation of yours?"

"Yes, my son Douglas who's a vicar is married to Edgar's sister, Rita."

"How is Edgar? Last I heard he was having problems with the school he was managing."

"Oh, yes; all rather sad. I don't know the details, but I gather one of the students died. I think it was all rather tragic. I spoke to Rita, and Edgar seems to have disappeared.

I gather he had a breakdown; but there was a police enquiry and the school was exonerated."

Claude turned to William. "So George is your elder brother."

"Yes, dad was married twice so I'm the last edition," he said smiling. He was slim and very short with jet black hair and light brown skin, as if he was half Indian.

"Tell me about your father."

"Well, we all lived in Brighton and he was the area manager for an insurance company."

"And where are you working now?"

"I work for a shipping company in New York. We are quite small and have some very profitable contracts, but it is very much on the cards; we will be taken over in the next six months, then I think I shall go home."

George emptied his glass and stood. They could see the waiter was standing discreetly waiting to take their order. "We must let you get on and enjoy your dinner. It was so nice meeting you again."

Claude stood up. "I do hope Edgar is found. He was a very good friend to me."

Hilary looked bored. "I thought they were never going to go." The waiter came over and took their order.

They ate by candlelight to soft background music, sipping a delicious French white wine, just slightly chilled, and exchanging stories of their families and their friends. The evening went like lightning and they were soon back in the cab making their way to the Upper East Side to Hilary's apartment. They were let in by the duty porter and were soon opening the door to the apartment. Claude suddenly bent down and lifted Hilary and carried her in and then on into the bedroom. In no time, they were undressing each other; their insatiable hunger could not be abated. They were soon in bed, kissing and fondling each other. It was all so exhilarating. Hilary could not remember the last time she had gone to bed with a man. She had resisted so many opportunities but now she could feel his weapon rubbing up against her vagina. The sensation of her pubic hairs set Claude on fire. He pulled her on to his body. She was now astride him. He was squeezing her bottom and she felt the thrill of a deep penetration and she worked slowly as they were kissing and experiencing the joys of madness and passion, but suddenly there was a noise at the door and the lights went on. She rolled off to find three masked men in the room pointing pistols at them.

o o o

Bob still worked as a part-time electrician; he was self-employed and was in constant demand, but his first love was Godstone Football Club. Rosemary was delighted. He seemed to be in his element. They now had two young sons; the baby George was into everything and needed constant supervision. He never seemed to sleep at night, so they took turns. They employed an outside young nanny; she was a Cypriot and very fond of George. The luncheon club Rosemary ran with the new directors was busy, but the margins were tight. She was studying possible changes and was considering taking on weddings and funerals and family parties, but a suitable venue would be essential. She had carried out a trial balance covering the past three months and it was not good; in fact, the directors were taking home less than the employees. Bob was taking a big drop in his income since his playing days with Chelsea, but they had put away some of his insurance money for the future of their two boys. Rosemary was worried about her elder sister, Pat, who had brought her up. She had recovered from the operation for the removal of a cyst in her brain but suddenly seemed to have aged overnight. She lost interest in her appearance and seemed to have gone into her shell. Most days she came over to help out with the boys; she adored George. Pat's husband, Claude, seemed to be away frequently. He was due to visit the States to represent the Institute of Bankers at a conference in New York; she had heard he was to speak to a distinguished gathering of American bankers at the end of the conference. Rosemary had her suspicions that he was going to join up with Hilary Hilton. She held her own counsel but was very worried about Pat.

Bob's dad had died, and his mother was living alone and was not well. Although Rosemary disliked her since she had been against their marriage, she felt sorry for her – Bob was her only child. He was now very involved with Godstone United and seemed to be everywhere, helping to cut the grass, designing the programmes, giving talks to the supporters' club, and was now a very popular member of the community. He even got involved with canvassing for sponsors for the big cup game. They had a coach company who had been supporting the club but was about to pull out. Bob managed to persuade them to carry on to the end of the season. Ted Drake had a chat with Bob. "One of our biggest problems is finance and, in particular, sponsors. I've had a chat with Don, and we are of the opinion that it is urgent for us to employ a professional fundraiser, but we have been advised they will charge a large percentage and can be very unreliable, and of course our most generous supporters are on our doorstep. The long and short of it is we feel you will be the best guy to do the job; we agree to employ you full-time, mainly as assistant manager, but you will also be responsible for fundraising."

Bob smiled. "I'd like that, although I have a feeling it will encompass a lot of evening work which my wife has been dreading; she likes me home in the evening to help with the children. I would expect the club to pay at least on par with my electrical work which brings in approximately 40 grand."

Ted frowned. "I can see where you're coming from. Yes, we will guarantee to cover your electrical salary for six months and then review the situation."

Bob stood. "I must go. I've got two players who are fighting to be fit for the game on Saturday and I must check on them. I must also check on three of our younger players who are always out on the tiles boozing and chasing the girls, and that's the last thing we want at this time of the season." Ted Drake had been a playing hero in his time but was really just marking time until the end of the season. He was fond of Bob and hoped he would get his job. "If I hear those three juniors have been misbehaving I'm going to give their parents a real earful and warn the boys they could jeopardise their careers. I've already threatened that we may not renew their contract at the end of the season." Ted blinked; he had never seen Bob quite like this before. There was obviously another side to him. "Now I must be off, but when do you want me full-time?"

Ted looked serious. "Well, as soon as convenient with you, although we do appreciate you may have to complete some jobs first."

Bob shook Ted's hands vigorously. "Thank you for your confidence in me. I won't let you down."

Friday afternoon arrived and Streets Coach Hire came to take them up to East Lee, which was seven miles from Birmingham. Three large coaches had been hired for the supporters and a larger crowd were coming up in private cars with the supporters and relations. The secretary of the supporters' club, Johnnie Mortimore, with his wife and young family, was travelling with the team. He was an ex-premier player with Portsmouth and now worked for the Godstone Journal. He worked hard for the club and was able to sign up sponsors by selling them space in the paper at a discount price. There were three estate agents heavily involved in giving the club much needed publicity. Bob realised this match was going to be the most important game of the season. Success would lead to an increase in revenue and the supporters would come flocking back. Godstone

United's ground had a capacity of 6,000 but the gates had dropped off from nearly 3,000; now it was just under 800. The players sat together. They wore smart navy blue blazers with the club emblem provided by a generous sponsor, Thanet Pharmaceuticals. So, the big day had arrived and they were all geared up. Most of them were experiencing butterfly tummies as they travelled up to East Lee.

Chapter 7

Claire decided to go home, she rang her mother in Newcastle but only told her that she was a grandmother of a little boy. Her mother was delighted with the news and looking forward to seeing her, but Claire knew her dad would be furious. She also had two brothers who had in the past worked for dad in a garden maintenance company erecting fencing.

After a most uncomfortable journey, she finally got home, having caught an early train. Mum was in the kitchen. Claire stepped inside with little Winston sleeping in a carrycot. She put him down and threw her arms around her mother and started to cry.

"What is it pet? Come and have a cuppa tea, but first I must look at my little grandson." She leaned down and took the little bundle from out of the carrycot. She pulled back the white woollen blanket to reveal little Winston, a dear little black baby who was whimpering. "Whoever is this? You've got the wrong baby. There must be an error."

"No, mum. Sorry, I had an accident. I made a mistake. I had too much to drink and he took advantage of me."

Her mother lifted up the little parcel and looked closely at Winston. "Oh my God. What have you done, pet? I can't think straight."

"Mum, mum, it was a big mistake. I know you did warn me, but it will never happen again."

"Well, I should hope not. I am worried about your father. Look, you better leave me to explain it. Yes, I can guess what's happened and I've warned you countless times. Well it's happened; now you have a dear little boy."

He now had a big smile on his face and kept dribbling. "Have you got some baby food or are you still breastfeeding him?"

"No, I can't seem to make any milk. I know it's not his fault, but I just can't. I've got a bottle here."

"We better sort out where he's going to sleep and then feed the dear little mite. Dad will soon be home so you better leave him to me. He is always best after he's had supper so I will feed him first."

Claire's father could be difficult. He had been to prison on two occasions, the first after stealing lead off the church roof and then on another occasion for assaulting one of his girlfriends. In fact, he was a nasty piece of work. His two sons could not wait to leave home and Claire's mother had left him on several occasions. They lived in a high-rise block of flats in a very rundown area of Newcastle. Mick was now a casual labourer on building sites. He'd gone bankrupt and lost the fencing business. He was a member of the National Front and known to the police; he was often seen standing on picket lines.

They were sitting around the kitchen table tucking into a meal of sausage and mash when Mick, who was wearing a grubby vest, stopped and bent his head sideways. He had sandy hair and thick ginger stubble; his arms were festooned with tattoos. "Did I hear something? There it is again."

"Eat your supper, Mick."

He picked up a can of beer and put it to his lips. Suddenly, the baby started to cry, and he stood up.

"What the hell is that?" He jumped up and rushed upstairs and the women looked at each other with fear in their eyes. The mother started to pick up a plate.

"Look, there's going to be a big explosion any time now and all hell will be let loose. I think you better get to your bedroom before you get hurt; you know what he's like when he loses his temper: he's out of control and I won't be much help."

Next moment they heard a roar and shouting upstairs and then the baby shrieking.

"Look, I'll hold his attention and you slip upstairs. Lock your bedroom door."

They heard heavy treads on the stairs. "Where is she? Where the hell is she?" he said, rushing into the kitchen red-faced, looking wild. "That bloody girl needs sorting out." His eyes had gone wild. He was loosening his belt. "I know what she needs is a bloody hiding."

"Stop that, Mick; if you lay a finger on her they'll lock you up again."

"My God, where is she, the slut? She wants teaching a lesson. How could she, and a black baby. What's my mates going to say? They will be laughing at us in the club. Where the hell is she?"

"I sent her to bed. We can talk about this tomorrow."

Mick suddenly came off the boil, opened the cupboard, took out a bottle of whiskey and flopped into a dirty old couch. "God, I need a drink. I feel bloody awful. If I get my hands on that filthy bitch I'll kill her."

After consuming half the bottle, he started shouting and swearing. There was a heavy knock on the door and a voice shouted, "Tell him to put a sock in it or we'll call the police."

Finally, after consuming most of the bottle, he drifted off to sleep. Madge, his wife, tiptoed up the stairs quietly and tapped on Claire's door.

"Look, pet, I think you better go. I've never seen him in such a state. I've been saving a few pennies; you take it. I know he will turn physical tomorrow. I hope that's not him moving around. Look, get ready. I'll pop up when we have the all clear. For God's sake, don't stay locally because his mates will find you."

After getting the all-clear, Claire tiptoed out, praying the baby would not wake up. She left the house in the early morning, struggling with the carrycot and a suitcase.

o o o

Todd was slowly getting on top of his farming activities, but Vicky was concerned that they were always struggling to keep in the black. They were sitting around the supper table. "I think we need some professional advice," said Vicky. "I sometimes wonder, have you got too many balls in the air."

"Yes, you're probably right. I'll have a word with Rod; he always tells me not to specialise. Still, the pig cooperative is at long last on a sound footing. That partnership with Drysdale's Meats certainly helped. The Christmas turkey sales went well, although we had to give the final batch away at a loss. Still, I managed to put the profit into an emergency account."

"Tell me, Todd, how many farmers have we got in the cooperative? I believe you told me it was somewhere in the region of 42."

"No, the numbers have slipped back to 35. Really, I need somebody on the road to coordinate all the activities and sign up new members, which is not easy, and really we do not generate enough capital to afford a manager. I have been looking around. The ideal chap would be a retired farmer, but really they don't want to do all the travelling. Still, the grain business is making healthy returns, although storage as always is my biggest problem."

Vicky was sipping her wine. "Tell me, where are we regarding that river pollution thing and possible prosecution and, more importantly, have you fixed the slurry tank?"

"Yes, I had it emptied and intend to repair it today."

"I imagine we will be prosecuted by Callington Estates."

"No, the estate sold their fishing rights on a 10-year lease to River Tours, a leisure company. Look, I'll get onto Neil tomorrow; he is handling the case, but it seems to have gone rather quiet. Last I heard he had passed all the documentation regarding the insurance cover over for a second opinion; he told me that it was all very technical and we need to take advice from a specialist in insurance law."

Vicky looked worried. "Keep me in the picture. If we lose this it could break us and we would become bankrupt."

Todd was now looking grim. They said it would take them five years to bring back the fishing yields to full strength and they are seeking damages of £325,000. Mind you, I think they have pumped up the figures but, darling, leave it with me. I'll give Neil a ring tomorrow, but I think he is waiting to hear from a QC regarding the legal opinion."

Todd could see Vicky was fretting and tried to change the subject. "When are Rod and Gloria getting married?"

"I told you yesterday: they slipped away to a registry office and got married last week, but they are going to have a grand party when his parents get back from Italy."

"Well, how do Marilyn and George feel about it?"

"I don't know, but I think they have come to accept Gloria; she says she wants to start a family and Rod wants to get back to real farming."

As they were talking, they heard a noise upstairs and then a loud squeal. Vicky jumped up quickly and ran up the back stairs. Todd stood, picked up the wine bottle, pressed it to his lips, and emptied it. He then picked up the plates and put them in the dishwasher. Next moment Vicky carefully descended the stairs with little Heather in her arms, who looked around with those large brown eyes and was cooing all the time. "She keeps falling out of bed. I think we shall have to put her back in the cot. Thank goodness she did not wake up Charlotte or Simon."

"When does Simon go up to St Michael's school for the interview?"

"Do you ever listen to me? I told you three times: it is the day after tomorrow. I'm just a little concerned; he's a bit moody. I think it is because he has not heard from his dad. I was very impressed with the school when they showed us around." Little Heather was soon snoring quietly in her mother's arms. Vicky whispered, "I will put her in our bed tonight." She slowly ascended the stairs whilst Todd tidied up the kitchen.

Finally, the day arrived for Vicky to take Simon over to St Michael's for his interview with the headmaster. She was met by his secretary. "Now, you had a tour of the school. I'm so sorry but the head's running late; he would like Simon to see the admissions officer. The headmaster likes all new pupils to be screened first." After 20 minutes and with no sign of Simon, Vicky was ushered into the head's office. He was very young; he looked in his early thirties, with quite a boyish short haircut and was certainly good-looking.

"I've got Simon seeing my admissions officer and sitting a few minor tests. He comes with a glowing testimonial from his teacher but because he has not sat the common entrance we like to check his attainments, but more importantly to see if he has the necessary abilities to cope with our scholastic syllabus."

Vicky smiled. "I am sending him here to prepare for his future life and we do hope the syllabus is not just aimed at university entrance but will prepare him for the broader challenges of life."

The head, David Cassel, smiled. "Yes, I can see where you're coming from, but you must appreciate that higher education is an essential step in helping our pupils to achieve their goals. Now, are there any questions you would like to ask?"

Vicky opened her notebook. "Well, yes; how old are you and how much teaching experience have you had?"

The head smiled. "Well, really all this is in the school prospectus but I am delighted to answer your questions. I am 38 years old, went to Manchester Grammar school and then on to Oxford and got a first in the Greats. I then had a short service commission in the Royal Navy followed by a teaching spell in a prep. school and have been here two years. I started here as a housemaster and still try and get into the classroom to teach Latin and Greek."

He smiled. "I feel I'm being interviewed but this is all very refreshing. Now Mrs,"

"Oh, please call me Vicky."

"Then you must call me David. Now, I must ask you a few questions about Simon."

Vicky sat up straight. "Well, yes, I'm really his adoptive stepmother; his actual adoptive mother was my eldest sister Heather and she was killed in a car crash; his father Edgar never really recovered fully from his loss." Vicky then told the headmaster about her family and spoke about Simon's interests.

"Well, Vicky, I think Simon is a very lucky boy to have you and your husband and to be living on a farm. But, really, I am wondering if this would be the right place for him. I appreciate initially he would be a day pupil but later we would expect him to become a boarder. Now, the fees are touching £18,000 per annum; would his father be able to cope?"

"Yes, his mother was very comfortably off and Edgar set up a trust fund for his son."

"Well, really, before I admit him I would very much like to meet his father. I did a spell of teaching in a prep. school for eight years and I am all too aware of the pressures we place upon our pupils."

Vicky put her notebook away and looked up. "Incidentally, are you married with a family?"

"Very much so. I've got two wild daughters who are away at St Margaret's in Exeter and they are a real handful." Suddenly the phone went. "Yes, please bring him along."

Simon suddenly appeared, looking pale and very tired. After 15 minutes with the head, whilst Vicky sat in the outer office, Simon and the head re-emerged. "Look, Vicky, please leave this with me. As I said, I would like to meet Simon's father, but I will come back to you in the next week with my decision."

They then drove home. As they sat in the car, Vicky spoke. "Well, how did your interviews go?"

"Well, the tests were quite easy, but that teacher was not very friendly. The Headmaster, Mr Cassell, was good fun. I liked him. He is keen on cricket and he told me he went to a primary school."

o o o

Todd had a busy morning sorting out a consignment of pigs for two farmers. He was making an appointment to see a contractor about laying a waterproof skin in the slurry tank and dealing with a grain order from a national pet food distributor.

He managed to speak to his brother-in-law, Neil. "Yes, Todd. I got on to the QC over the phone; he has studied the insurance policy and feels reasonably confident that you are covered. I am awaiting his written report and then I will write to you accordingly, but I will be much happier when I hear back from the insurance company."

"Thanks, Neil. Please send me your account. I would like to try to keep up-to-date."

"It will be very reasonable but the fees from the QC may be a different story. Even so, they have been quite positive, which is rare; they usually sit on the fence."

"How are you all? How is Caroline, and the baby?"

"Fine. Caroline is blooming, and our little son Oscar is now walking. Sadly, dad is not well; he is due to go into hospital soon for a range of tests. Look, sorry, I must go. I've got a client waiting. I'll ring you tonight."

Vicky was getting the children's high tea when she had a call from Robert Stansbury, the proprietor of the shop which handled the wedding arrangements. "Vicky, am glad I caught you; it's just that my head of Department told me that Renée Kingdom has been admitted to hospital. Look, I don't know any details; it's just that when I rang the hospital the ward sister was very unhelpful. Renée was due to meet two brides in the shop this morning and she didn't turn up, which is so unlike her."

"Thanks for letting me know. I'll get on to the hospital, but I might ring her niece first."

"How's Todd?" Vicky remembered they had played rugger together in their youth and had been friends.

"Look, have a word: he is here." They had a chat. Vicky was amused to hear Todd laughing.

After feeding the children, they seemed to be extra lively. Vicky tried ringing Renée's niece with no success and then the hospital, who were not very forthcoming. "Look Todd, I'm going to drive to the hospital. I will get back as soon as I can, but if I am held up put the children to bed and see that they wash properly."

Eventually Vicky got to the district hospital and spoke to a young nurse in a corridor which contained private rooms. "I'm sorry, but she does not want to see anyone; she's had a very disturbing experience."

"What do you mean by that?"

"Well, the police were involved; it would seem that she has been physically assaulted."

"Good God; by whom?"

"I'm sorry, but I do not know any of the details. The police are carrying out an investigation."

"Look, she's been like a mother to me. I can't leave here before I see her."

"I'm sorry, but that is her request." She was a very young nurse and was very sympathetic. "We are short of staff. Now I must rush over and see three patients of mine in another ward. Look, I have not seen you, but she is in Room 2C."

Vicky tiptoed down the corridor and softly knocked and slowly put her head round the door. She was in for a severe shock. Renée was sitting in an upright chair looking out of the window with her back to the door.

"Please go away. I don't want to see anybody." She turned her head and saw Vicky. "Please, please, go away. I don't want you to see me like this. Please, I feel so ashamed," and her voice broke. She started to cry. Vicky could see that she had no dentures in; she had bruises on her face and a badly cut lip. She looked very old and frail as she sat in her dressing gown in the upright chair. Vicky ran over and threw her arms around her. In no time they were both crying together.

"Renée, darling, I can never leave you; you have been like a mother to me. I just want to be with you." Suddenly, the door flew open and a stout fierce-looking woman appeared in a dark blue uniform. She was obviously used to exerting authority. "Mrs Kingdom, is that woman bothering you? I don't know how she got in but,"

"No, no, please let her stay; she is a very, very dear friend."

"Well, I have turned away a numerous number of your friends and,"

"Thank you, matron, but this is a special friend. Could we have some tea please?"

She looked up. "Vicky, darling, thank you for coming. I realise you must be busy with your family." Renée started to dry her eyes.

"Don't worry about my family. Todd can see to them. I just wanted to be with you."

Renée started to cry again. "I never thought he would behave like this." Her voice broke. "I have given him so much, so much money; he wanted more. I thought he loved me." She started to speak very quietly in gasps as if she was fighting for her breath. "Why, why, do I always bring out the worst in men?"

"Look," said Vicky, looking very serious, "you are certainly not going home to an empty house; you're coming home to me."

"I couldn't do that. You've got a family. You don't want an old woman like me."

"Look, you're coming to me when you leave here and there is no argument. Don't worry, I will soon put you to work. I could do with another pair of hands."

"Vicky, darling, are you sure?"

"I certainly am. It has been decided. Now, is there anything you want from home?"

"No, I'm fine, but I would like to look in and pick up a few things and check all the services when I come out. Vicky, you are so kind; having you it's like having a daughter, which I always wanted." Tears started to well up.

Vicky blushed and kissed her on the forehead. "Is your denture broken?"

"No, it's just difficult, but the doctor said I will heal up very soon. The police want to take a photo: what a cheek. I refused them. How could I, looking like this? What would my friends say?"

Vicky smiled; it was obvious that Renée did not realise the police wanted the photo for evidence of the assault. As they sat munching biscuits and drinking tea, Vicky was about to ask a question when Renée held up her hand. "No, darling, sorry – I can't talk about it. I just feel ashamed. What do they say? There is no fool like an old fool."

As they sat back talking about the various brides and excited mothers, the young nurse came in with a tray. "I have your sleeping pills here. The doctor felt it would help you to relax and get a good night's sleep."

Vicky finally left and arranged to speak to the consultant the following day. By time she got home it was getting late and everything was still. She looked in on the children; they were all fast asleep. She found Todd asleep in the kitchen in the armchair with half a bottle of whiskey on the table. She switched off the TV and he woke with a start.

She then explained about Renée's assault, and he agreed. "Of course, she must come here; she has been such good friend. I would like to know who is responsible. If I could get my hands on them I would soon sort him out."

"No, that's dangerous talk. Leave it to the police, but the trouble is I don't think Renée will press charges, but we can talk about that tomorrow, when I hope to bring her home. I must warn you, she is very depressed and feels ashamed for what has happened, so let me broach the subject. I don't want you charging in and upsetting her."

Todd nodded. "Incidentally, I had a call from Neil reference the pollution of the river." He stood and stretched. "I'm feeling all-in so we'll have a chat about it tomorrow, but it's all becoming so involved; things are never as simple as you first imagine."

o o o

So, Bob's big day had arrived and after an early start and a long coach ride the Godstone players finally walked out onto the East Lee pitch. It was in perfect condition, cold and dry. The crowd was touching 6,000 with two large stands overflowing with supporters. It was by far the biggest crowd of the season and they came to the pitch bursting with confidence. Their star home forward Wilf Mannion was captain; he was thickset, short, only 5 feet two, the highest scorer in the league. Both teams came out holding the hands of small children, and after the captains shook hands the coin was spun and the ends were chosen. They took up their positions for the first half. The ref. studied his watch then blew his whistle and the East Lee match kicked off.

The first half was a complete disaster for Godstone United; they only had two shots at the East Lee goal. Their opponents played with complete assurance and had a team of experienced and seasoned players. They tapped the ball around the park and their man-to-man passing was immaculate. The visitors lost their shape and their confidence and were hemmed in their own half. It was very much one-way traffic and they came off at half-time losing 2-0. But it could easily have been 5-0.

Bob had the players in the changing room at half-time. Suddenly they saw another side of Bob. "That was a bloody disgrace. I've seen 10-year-olds play better football. You were utter rubbish. There was no aggression or commitment; at times it looked as if you were giving the game away. I've never in all my time in football seen such a shambolic display. I felt utterly ashamed of all of you and sorry for all our supporters who had made sacrifices to come up to be with you. What the hell happened? There was no shape in our set pieces and all our planning seemed to have gone out of the window. In fact, it was a bloody disgrace. But it's not too late. I don't mind losing, but only after a fight. Now what you next do is get out there and get stuck in. I want you to fight for every bloody ball and, for god's sake, where the hell are the two players marking Mannion? I'm surprised he didn't score more goals; you certainly gave him plenty of space. Now, the next 45 minutes are the most important of the season, so get out there and prove it." The players looked at Bob with respect. They did not speak. There were no excuses. He sensed the message had got through. "Right, now, off your arses and prove yourselves: 45 minutes – you've got to create history."

They ran back onto the pitch with a purpose. At the sound of the whistle they tore into the opposition. They had three free kicks against them in the first 10 minutes. They fought like tigers for possession and drove back the opposition but seemed to falter when the goal was in sight. But they plugged away and then one of their set manoeuvres came off: a long ball was hammered across to the left-wing where it was collected; the player quickly crossed and the reserve centre forward, Nat Lofthouse, who was six feet two, came hurtling down the pitch, rose up and headed the ball neatly into the corner of the goal. The goalkeeper was at fault: he should have raced out to cut off the cross. This seemed to set the Godstone players on fire, but all attempts were in vain. Then suddenly out of the blue a long ball was hit down the middle which caught the defence off guard and the left-winger raced in, took possession and took three strides and hammered the ball into the goal. It hit the upright and slithered over the line. The crowd went mad. There was dancing and bellowing. Wilf Mannion was shouting at his players. Suddenly East Lee started to attack with a real purpose. One shot hit the crossbar, another glanced off an upright, then Mannion received the ball, turned and hit it into the corner of the net, but the goal was disallowed: he was offside. All the Godstone players and supporters breathed a sigh of relief; it finally looked as if it was going to be a draw when the referee was looking at his watch to blow the final whistle. Then suddenly out of nothing and in the final minute of the game the right winger robbed the ball off the left back. He raced down the wing and crossed into a crowded goal mouth. The goalkeeper rushed out, jumped up high, leaning backwards, and caught the ball but stumbled, dropping it in a melee of players. It was kicked, ricocheted against two players and eventually entered the goal. The Godstone supporters all went bonkers;

nobody heard the final whistle. The players ran to the touchline, grabbed Bob, lifted him up, then ran across to the corner where all their supporters were shouting with joy. Ted Drake and Don Rowbotham came down from the directors' box and congratulated all the players, who eventually sauntered back to the changing room to shower and change for their journey home. They were all in great form. Johnnie Mortimore, the supporters' secretary, booked up for the coach to stop at a five-star hotel; his paper was paying for a Champagne dinner for all the players. Wilf Mannion came across and congratulated Bob. "What did you say to them at half-time? They were a changed team. I thought we were going to win five nil, but it's a funny old game. Well done."

Bob finally got back rather late and very tired. He did manage to ring Rosemary with the good news. He arranged to meet up with the players on Monday morning for a light training session and to listen to the draw for the next round of the FA Cup.

Chapter 8

The three gunmen looked very threatening, wearing black balaclavas and dark clothing, and pointing their hefty pistols at the bed. Two of them were well-built but the third villain was quite small; he leaned down and pulled back the duvet. Hilary rolled off Claude. They were both fully exposed. The short thug grabbed a handful of her blonde hair. She screamed in agony but he yanked her out of the bed. She was completely naked, showing her sturdy, plump body with big breasts and prominent bottom, and exhibiting a pronounced black forest of pubic hairs. "Come," said the little gangster in a hoarse whisper. "Where's the safe?" Hilary was now screaming. The gunman smacked her across the face.

"No one will hear you; this place is soundproof." She continued to shout as he grabbed her hair and dragged her screaming out of the bedroom into the hall. Claude sat up and tried to get out of bed; he too was stark naked.

"Stay," said the gunmen. Claude continued to try to get up but was hit on the shoulder with the butt of the gun. He could hear Hilary crying out as if in pain; she was shrieking at the top of her voice. There was a loud bang and then all went quiet.

"What the hell is he doing with her?" shouted Claude.

The two gunmen looked at each other. "Go find out if they found the safe and, you," said one of the gunmen, pointing at Claude, "lie on your stomach and don't move." He rolled over. "Put your hands behind your back." He then felt a sickening blow on the back of his head and suddenly passed out.

It must have been 10 hours later when he felt the sensation of cold water on his face. He slowly came round to find a group of people looking at him. Three were police officers, heavily armed, and the rest looked like senior staff.

They threw a towel around him after cutting the binding holding his hands. "You better get dressed, and then we have to talk."

"Where is Hilary? Is she okay?"

"Sorry, buddy; the news is not good." The tall, slim white police sergeant spoke. "She's been sent off in an ambulance to City Central. She is not good."

"Well, what happened?"

"You don't want to know," he said with a broad New York drawl. "Those animals have had their way with her."

"What the hell do you mean?"

"Just what I said, man. She is hanging on by a thread."

"Good god, those bastards! We've got to catch them."

"Don't we know it; we have had a call from the President's office this morning and the FBI are very much in the picture. Go and get cleaned-up and dressed; there are a lot of questions we must ask you, and we want you to try and remember everything."

Claude still felt shaken. He was seen by a doctor and given the all-clear, but he had a splitting headache and felt queasy. Eventually, he sat down with the two police officers and explained the events which had taken place.

After a gruelling two-hour interview, which was carried out by a senior FBI officer, he eventually got back to his hotel. The police had given him permission to leave the following morning to catch his flight to Heathrow.

"I would like to look in and see Hilary before I go."

"Sorry, Sir Claude, but she is not up to it at this moment. She is unconscious and on life support; her injuries are very serious and it's doubtful that she will pull through. Look, I have pictures of her but,"

"Let me see them."

He passed the photos over. Claude was in for a big shock. There were three pictures of her laying semi naked on a bed. She was unrecognisable; she had been butchered, possibly with a blunt instrument. Both eyes were closed, with bruising, and there were cuts across her head; also red blotches all around her neck.

Claude swallowed. "My God, what savages could treat a woman like that?"

"That's not all; she had been savagely raped and has a bad tear in her vagina due to frenzied activity, and we have collected semen from both her anus and her cervix. It was as if she was being attacked sexually by two predators. That poor woman has gone through hell. I've been a member of the New York Police Department for 20 years and, really, this is one of the worst cases I have seen. Yes, it's horrific, but we have their DNA and I am quietly confident that we will bring these villains to justice. The small guy I think we know. We are not sure, but the crime is very similar to a recent crime he committed. He is Mexican and we are very busy at this moment looking for him."

"I imagine this will be all over the papers tomorrow."

"Well, it will get out, but Washington have stepped in and put a temporary news embargo on this crime. Hilary Hilton has a lot of friends on Capitol Hill; she is a great American idol with all the right connections."

"Thank goodness, but I do appreciate it will eventually get out. I am the chief general manager of the third largest bank in the UK, the London and Edinburgh, and the time delay will prepare me for the storm of adverse publicity."

The FBI agent who had taken over the investigation looked like Broderick Crawford, a big bulky man with no hair and a broken nose and he often smiled. "Well, Sir Claude, it has been a pleasure meeting you. We all feel very sorry for your misfortune but we hope it will not put you off coming over to visit us again. In fact, I've just come off an assignment as part of a team protecting your Prime Minister, a really great guy. I hope you have a safe journey home. If there's anything else you should remember please communicate with us. I don't think we will want you again."

Finally, Claude slipped out of New York and after a quiet journey where he caught up with some much-needed sleep he arrived at Heathrow airport. It was late afternoon; the hired car met him and he was soon entrenched in his apartments at Holland Park studying his post, after which he spoke to his wife, Pat, who was staying with her sister Rosemary.

"Darling, you're home; I've been missing you. I do hope all went well. I will quickly pack up my things and be with you. I'm so looking forward to hearing all your news."

Pat finally got to the flat and threw her arms around him. "I missed you so much and I hope you are not going away for a long time." Claude felt very guilty; he could see he had a lot of explaining to do, which was not going to be easy. They had a quiet evening and Pat did most of the talking, telling him about Bob's recent success as an assistant manager at Godstone United. She also mentioned having spoken to Rita, Edgar's sister and how worried they were that Edgar had not been found.

It was the following day when all hell was let loose. They had two papers delivered. Pat liked to read an up-market tabloid, the Daily Dispatch, whereas Claude read one of the heavies. He picked up her paper.

"It has been reported that Hilary Hilton, one of America's favourite icons, was seriously ill in hospital, having been assaulted in her New York apartments with Sir Claude Dibbs, chief general manager of the London and Edinburgh Bank." He realised that all the national papers would be screaming with similar reports. He continued to read that the UK's chief banker, Sir Claude Dibbs, who had played a leading role and had led a team of delegates on a

trade mission with the Prime Minister, was also present in Hilary Hilton's quarters. He learnt later that most of the tabloid reports went over the top with pictures of the apartment, pictures of Claude and Hilary, and even a photo of their recent visit to Eastbourne. Claude took in a deep breath and pushed the paper to one side as Pat came into the kitchen in her dressing gown.

"You look sad, darling," she said, slumping into a chair. "I can understand you must feel exhausted. Still, you're home now and you can rest."

Claude thought, *it's now or never*. He pushed the paper across the table. "I think you better read this."

"Why, darling? I do hope you're not going away again." She picked up the papers, read the article with rapt attention, and tears started to well up in her eyes. "How could you? How could you?" Slowly, tears were running down her cheeks. She pushed the papers to one side.

"How could you?" Her voice broke into despair. "You have broken my heart. I had so much love and respect for you, and now this." She was now screaming with grief, and then she suddenly jumped up and rushed into her bedroom, slamming the kitchen door.

Claude sat back. *I asked for that*, but he was also at the same time thinking about Hilary. He could not get her scarred body out of his mind. After several abortive attempts to speak to Pat, he decided to try and reschedule his day and come home in the afternoon. By then he hoped she would be a little more amenable.

Claude finally slipped into his office. After a brief word with Roy, his chief clerk, he turned his attention to a backlog of paperwork. He studied a long detailed report from his number two, Christopher Barrington, but his mind was not on the job. He decided against his better judgement to ring up the hospital in New York and try to get an up-to-date report on Hilary's condition. The pictures of her bruised and broken body haunted him.

o o o

Vicky was working on a wedding dress trying to get it ready for the bride's fitting the following day when she had a call from the police. "I am Inspector Jimmy Johnson. Now, it's nothing to worry about, but I would like to interview your boy, Simon."

"Well, what about?"

"Please, Mrs Hosegood; he's done nothing wrong, but it is just to help us with our enquiries."

"Well, what enquiries are you talking about?"

"Look, I am sorry, but this is a rather sensitive matter. I can be with you tomorrow morning when I can explain it so much better."

"I am now very intrigued. Can't you give me some idea what this is all about now?"

"No, I'm sorry, but I'll be with you at 11:00 am tomorrow morning. Please don't worry; Simon is not in any trouble."

Todd came in for lunch with a big smile on his face. "I just had a call from Neil reference the pollution of the river; I think at long last events are moving our way. It would seem that the NFA have been liaising with the river authority and have traced bacteria being discharged by that poultry farm into the river."

"You mean Braunton Chickens?"

"Yes, that's the people. Neil feels confident that they will accept our claim."

"Why have they had a change of heart? They have kept us waiting and have not been very helpful. Still, it's a big weight off my mind."

"I think the NFA has put pressure on the Three Cities insurance company where they placed the business. Still, it is all looking brighter, but I will be glad when this is over."

"Listen, Todd. I had the police on the phone this morning. They want to interview Simon, but did stress... now, what was he called? Inspector Jimmy Johnson; he did say Simon was not in trouble in any way and is going to look in tomorrow at 11 o'clock."

Todd picked up a bottle of beer and then paused. "Yeah, I want to be there when they interview him but, you're right, it seems very odd. I wonder what it is all about."

"Well," said Vicky, diving into the Aga for a steaming chicken casserole. "You hear so many stories about boys' boarding schools, but let's wait until tomorrow. Sorry, but I keep thinking about Renée. I shall certainly miss her. She has passed over all the business to me. She'd had enough, but I will need to get help, what with bringing up a family – that's a job in itself... No, I have not heard from Rod. I believe Gloria is due to have the baby any time. He'll make a wonderful father. I gather that since the sudden death of his dad he's had to try to keep an eye on his mother. Incidentally, I must chase up Chope's MD. What was he called? Fred Bromley; he was very interested when I spoke to him over the phone about opening a bridal hire business and said he would get back to me after he has spoken to his directors. I'm sorry to leave Stansbury's but they think it's a doddle. I was surprised when they would not renew our lease. They are in for a big shock: finding skilled seamstresses is not easy."

They kept Simon home from school. He was now 14, a tall boy with pale blue eyes and a ready smile. He was adored by his two cousins, Charlotte and Heather. The small one would follow him around all day, which amused Vicky. Inspector Jimmy Johnson arrived in a small private car. Short in stature, he had a head of grey hair and dark penetrating black eyes. Todd and Vicky led him into the kitchen. "Look, may I speak to you both first?"

"Yes, please do; Simon is in his room." They sat around the kitchen table with mugs of coffee.

"Now Mrs..."

"Oh, please call me Vicky."

"And it's Todd."

"Well, Vicky; this is a very delicate matter. We've been approached by two sets of parents. Their sons have made complaints that the headmaster David Cassell has acted in an inappropriate way and has made sexual advances."

Vicky looked grave. "What does that mean?"

"Well, to put it as delicately as I can, it would seem he has touched their private parts."

"Surely not; he's a young happily married man with two young daughters."

"Please, Vicky, believe me; I spend all my time having to investigate these sorts of complaints. It's possibly not on the increase but cases of this kind are coming to our attention far too often."

Vicky put down her mug. "Well, where did all these things happen?"

"I gather with one in a shower cubicle and the other after lights out outside a dormitory."

"I can't believe it; he's not the type. He's already started to turn the school around."

"How do you mean?" asked the inspector, taking out his notebook.

"Well, the numbers were sliding, and all the parents seemed to be moaning, but now they seem to be much happier and the numbers are increasing, and I would say the school is on the up."

"Look, Vicky, I take on board all you say but I spend all my time dealing with these crimes. I'm part of a national investigation team dealing with this problem all over the country and you will be surprised at some of the convictions. Now, I think it's time I spoke to Simon, and I hope I have dealt with all your concerns."

Simon eventually came down with a quizzical look on his face.

"Simon, you've done nothing wrong so please relax, and what we discuss is strictly confidential; please only talk about it with your parents but nobody else, and I mean nobody. Now, Simon, I have complaints from two boys saying that the headmaster Mr Cassell took inappropriate advances towards them."

Simon coughed. "Sorry, what do you mean?"

"Well," said the inspector, "they are complaining that he touched them; yes, they said he touched their private parts."

Simon sat up straight. "No, that can't be; Mr Cassell's not like that. He takes us for games, and who are these two boys saying this?"

"Well, Simon, if I tell you then this must be our secret; if you want to help him then you must not tell anyone. One of them is Ian MacDougall and the other is Nigel Beaton. What do you know about them?"

"Well, both have been in trouble. MacDougall stole a boy's watch and was fined and gated, and Nigel Beaton, he ran away twice and broke into somebody's house and is now in disgrace. So, I know they don't like Mr Cassell, and they are always in trouble; that's why they said it."

Jimmy Johnson continued to scribble in his notebook. "You don't like those boys?"

"They are juniors and I am a prefect. Beaton is always in trouble and never does what he's told, but you're right, I don't really like them, and Mr Cassell is a super chap. He takes us on outings and for games."

Todd and Vicky sat quietly and refrained from asking any questions.

The inspector put his notebook down and looked at Simon. "Are there any questions you'd like to ask me?"

Simon scratched head. "No, but I hope he does not get into trouble. I know he can be very strict, but he's helped me a lot."

Jimmy Johnson put his notebook in his briefcase. "Thank you for giving me all your time." He quickly stood up and picked up his briefcase.

Vicky spoke. "How long will these enquiries take before any action is taken? Naturally, we will be very worried and so, I imagine, will Mr Cassell."

"Yes, I can appreciate your concern. I hope to have made a final decision at the end of next week and I will then communicate with you immediately. Now, sorry, I must get on; I have more people to see but please, please keep this to yourselves."

Later in the week, Vicky was in the kitchen sorting out the supper. "I had a letter from that Fred Bromley, the boss at Chope's dress shop, sending me a formal document with very similar conditions we have with Stansbury's. I'm quite excited, but I must push this onto Neil."

"What a shame; I spoke to Neil this morning and had great news: the NFA are at last making the right noises and will support our insurance claim. They are also mounting an action against the Braunton poultry company who has also been polluting the River Barle. Really, the water authority could not have been more helpful. So, thank goodness it all looks like things are going our way, but I shall only be fully satisfied when I have their cheque in my hands."

"How much will that be for?"

"That's a good question. Of course, we have to pay an excess but I believe the final figure could be as high as £335,000. Still, let's change the subject."

"Oh, before I forget, I had a phone call from Renée this morning, and she seems to be fully recovered and certainly enjoying staying with her niece in Norwich. Reading between the lines, I think she will eventually move down there permanently. She's the sort of person who will make friends wherever she goes. My God, I shall miss her, but she is coming home next week to sort things out. Incidentally, I got a feeling she rang Fred Bromley; she's a real friend. I think the operatic society has missed her. She was the honorary vice-president and I gather there are two prima donors there who have caused friction in the society, but of course Renée is the peacemaker. She's still the principal shareholder in the business, but she has given me some shares."

"What's that mean?" asked Todd, reaching for his coat.

"Well, simply, I get a very good salary – I'm paid on piece work and then I share in the profits. But don't worry, darling; I know Renée would never take advantage of me. Incidentally, I heard from Bella yesterday; it seems she hasn't settled in Sidmouth and wants to come back. I think between you and me that marriage is going through a rocky patch. I have not heard from Rod of late and I believe he's busy looking for a job. I think he has had an offer from a firm of Taunton land agents; they want him to open up a new office in Dorchester."

"The poor chap; he is going to be very busy, what with setting up this new farm, which I gather he's leasing from Somerset County Council, and then setting up a new office in Dorchester. He will certainly have to employ a farm manager or get some help."

Vicky looked at the clock. "You better get off and pick up the kids, and also pop into Tesco's. I've got a shortlist of essentials they need."

Both the girls were at the convent and seemed quite happy. The elder, Charlotte, was coming up to 15 and was placid like Todd. She was starting to blossom into a young lady. Little Heather was now shooting up. Both the girls adored Simon, who was now very involved with his school activities.

Todd picked up the shopping list. "Before I go, I've been thinking of leasing 40 acres at the home farm to a South Malton potato company to grow spuds. I know my sister will not be very happy, but they pay a good rent. We would lease the land for three years. Really, it is difficult to farm land 10 miles away single-handed."

"That sounds great, but I think it should be reviewed after a year so you can get out of the deal if there are problems. Oh, I forgot to tell you, I am going up to the parents' evening at the convent to discuss with the careers teacher Charlotte's future. I could use her here, but I know she's not keen. Mind you, she could learn. Still, we need to be firm with her, and don't you get involved; you're always spoiling her. You're far too soft and her future is very important. Look, we can discuss this later." Suddenly, Vicky went red in the face. "We've got to have this sorted out, and certainly not in front of Charlotte. Her future is one of my chief worries. Still, you better get going, and don't forget Tesco's."

That night as they sat in bed, Todd was trying to read the paper, but Vicky was like a human dynamo and never seemed to switch off. "Simon has been asking if he could go down and stay with Rita. I know he gets on well with Freddie and, of course, they are off to Australia soon. I expect he will want to go out and visit them when they have settled."

"Yes, I had a call this evening from Inspector Jimmy Johnson; you know – regarding those allegations by those two boys. He said that the headmaster David Cassell was completely innocent. They finally broke down and admitted it was a pack of lies and I gather the school expelled the boys.

Sadly, one of them has a mother who finds it difficult to cope, but the other has a very cross father. Still, it's all over, but he did say that he did not believe the story from the start. He thanked me for our help in interviewing Simon and asked me to thank him. He was very impressed with his openness." Todd switched off the lights and rolled onto his side. He was soon fast asleep, whilst Vicky lay on her back pondering the events of the day.

o o o

Pat experienced a whole range of emotions after studying the tabloids reporting on Claude's indiscretion. She felt angry and depressed and that she had lost her self-respect. She quickly picked up a small suitcase and crammed it with some of her clothes and shoes. *Claude is the last man I want to see*, she thought. *I must get out of here. I must get away and start to think.* After checking all her cards and her cheque book, she rang for a taxi. Her mind was in a complete spin. *No, I shall go back to Devon, the one place I was always happy.* She had a fleeting memory of her dear dad and then in no time she jumped into a taxi heading for Paddington station. She spent the journey looking out of the window and noted some of the old familiar stations of Westbury, Castle Cary, Taunton and Tiverton; it brought back potent memories of her father and mother. Her dear father worked as a farm hand and brought them up. She remembered him cutting her hair and repairing her shoes. He was a wonderful dad, but sadly her mother had a drink problem and ran off with a flashy Irishman.

Finally, she arrived in Exeter and dragged her case out of the town station across the road to the Grand Hotel. She booked a room for three nights under a fictitious name. Finally, she locked the door of her room, stripped off and sank into a bubbly hot bath. She slowly started to come to her senses but was still feeling bitter and angry. She finally took the important decision to seek out Edgar; he had always been the real love of her life, never far from her thoughts. Now she wanted to discuss her problems with him. *I am sure he will understand.* But where was he? The last time she had seen him he was not well. Her mind flitted back to her last visit in his office after the request from Maggie. He certainly was looking run down and very dishevelled, needing a shave and smelling of whiskey. She suddenly felt a warm glow when she remembered him kissing her and whispering, "I shall always love you." She closed her eyes and sank lower in the bath. There was a blissful sensation in her vagina. *No, no,* she thought. *I must get out before I get carried away. I must take a hold of myself.*

She briefly thought about Claude. *He can now start to worry about me. I've been taken for granted for far too long.* Finally, she rang Rita, Edgar's sister.

"Rita, is that you?"

"Pat, where are you? We are all sick with worry. I have had Rosemary on the phone."

"Look, you can tell them I will contact them when I have had an opportunity of sorting myself out. I was wondering, have you had any news of Edgar? When you speak to him please send my fondest regards. I would be grateful if you would give Rosemary a ring and tell her I am okay, but for the time being I just need some rest and peace. I am going to turn my phone off for now."

"Funny you should ask; Edgar rang me last night. For the time being, he's rented a cottage just outside Salisbury. I think he is now starting to feel better and has already made a few friends. I think he had a tough six months, the final straw being that poor girl hanging herself; then he had to attend an enquiry but, yes, he sounded quite chirpy on phone."

"Sorry, Rita. I have not asked after your family?"

"They are all fine. Freddie is now up at the comprehensive and is doing well but little Colin is a slow learner. However,

I've great news – Doug has been shortlisted for the archdeacon job in Western Australia. He deserves a break; if successful he will start there in six months' time. We are so excited. It will be a wonderful opportunity for the boys, but I will keep you posted. Now, what shall I tell them? They are all so worried about you. Can't you give them a ring?"

"No, that would be fatal; just let them know I am okay and will be back in a few days' time."

Pat finally put down the phone, feeling a little excited. Just the thought of Edgar seemed to wake up her hormones. *God,* she thought, *I want that man; in fact, at this moment any man, the way I feel.* Then she took hold of herself and realised she must control her carnal desires. Suddenly, she felt hungry and looked at her watch. *I must get on else I'll miss dinner.* She put on a smart little party frock, and her make-up, noticing her hair was going grey. *I must make a hair appointment tomorrow and have the works. I've got to keep my standards up.*

She took the lift down and approached the restaurant, which all looked very quiet. Ahead was a man in his early forties. He approached and took down her room number. He had a slight accent. "Yes, we are very quiet tonight but are expecting a full house on the weekend. I prefer it when we are busy." He showed her to a table in the corner of the room. There were only two other tables occupied.

"Where do you come from?" she asked.

"Oh, I am Joseph, and from Germany. The restaurant manager is off sick, so I have had to stand in. Now, can I get you an aperitif?"

"Yes, I'd like a gin and tonic."

"Here are the menus."

"I think I'd better avoid a starter; as you can see, I don't need it."

Joseph smiled. "I think you look good."

She looked up, beaming. "I am Pat, and this is my only meal today."

In no time, she was tucking into a tasty fish salad and quickly polished off her G&T. Joseph reappeared. "Would you like wine?"

"Yes, a glass of white would be nice."

He produced a half bottle of Chardonnay. "This is with the compliments of the house."

As she was finishing her meal, she noticed Joseph sitting nearby on a table by himself. She waved him over. "Come and join me. I like to have company when enjoying a meal." In no time, Joseph joined her, but a little voice was telling her to be careful; he looked too innocent and they were always the ones to watch.

"Yes, I am the assistant director of the hotel, but I live in Torquay, so I have a lot of travelling... Yes, it's part of a large group but I am leaving at the end of the month and returning home to take charge of a big American Lodge in the Black Forest." They continued to chat. "Yes, we've got a busy weekend: a wedding on Saturday – relations of a local MP, a gentleman called David Penhaligan, quite a big political wedding, and then the veterans' car rally at the county showgrounds, but most of the drivers are staying here." He then gave Pat a searching look. "Pat, I don't wish to be nosy, but are you running away from something? You look tense. Would you like to talk about it?"

"Certainly not, but tell me about yourself."

He spoke with a pronounced accent. "Well, my father was a university professor, lecturing on international law, and mum was a nurse. I have a sister who is older and lives in Munich and is married to a soldier, and they have a son."

"Have you got a wife?"

Joseph smiled. "Yes, of course; my wife has just returned to Germany with my little daughter and I am due to join them at the end of the month." They continued to chat about the hotel and the luncheon club which Pat had been a director of.

"Well, Joseph, it's been a long day and I'm ready for bed."

"Just have one small glass of wine."

"No, but thank you. I shall sleep like a log tonight."

"Pat, I hope things turn out good for you, and if there's anything you need just let me know. If you ring 800 it will come directly to me." He smiled. "It will be a pleasure to be of service if you need anything."

Pat blushed; she could clearly see what he was hinting and quickly stood up. "Thank you, Joseph, and good night." He quickly stood and smiled and kissed her hand.

As she finally slipped into bed she thought of Joseph. He was certainly a good-looking guy but was probably very skilled in seducing ladies. She had heard that in some hotels waiters offered extra services to older women who often paid. *No*, she thought, *I am not into a one-night stand.* The thought switched her off. She was soon fast asleep, when she was suddenly woken up by the phone. "Pat, Joseph here. Hope I did not disturb you, but I've got a bottle of brandy and I thought we could share it."

Pat was quickly wide awake. "Well yes, Joseph, you did disturb me. I was fast asleep, and sorry I don't like brandy."

He quickly broke in. "I'm sorry. I'll let you get to sleep and say goodbye because I am off tomorrow but will be back on Saturday if you are still with us. Good night."

She felt she had been a little short but realised he was after just one thing. *He'll probably spend Saturday night servicing one of the guests.* She suddenly felt sorry for his wife. *Well, first thing tomorrow I will give Edgar a ring and hope we can meet up before I return home.* She drifted off to sleep with only one man in her thoughts.

Chapter 9

Edgar was startled by the light shining in his face.

"Who are you?" He was thinking quickly about some form of defence.

"Sorry to disturb you. I am the estate manager, and we've had two break-ins over the past month."

"Well, I am Edgar Collins and I have taken over this cottage for six months on a shorthold tenancy."

"Sorry, I didn't know you were coming in so soon. I've just come off leave. The office told me it was next week. They have had a change of secretaries and I don't know this new one, but she seems to get her facts wrong. Sorry to disturb you. I expect we will meet up over the coming weeks."

Edgar had a good night's sleep. He got up early and, after a cooked breakfast, he felt energised. *Right, I must ring up Vicky and arrange to go up and see Simon, then ring Bennington School and speak to Ian Hogg and see how they're getting on. I must have a word with Maggie; I expect she is worrying about me.* He felt very guilty about Simon. This started to make him feel depressed. *Maybe I better go and see Dr Mary Marshman; she was very sensible and could give me some sound advice.*

He switched on his phone and was startled to see a call from the Reverend Tom Owen, the vicar whom he had known many years earlier in Surrey and had recently seen in Salisbury. "Edgar, how are you? I tried ringing recently but to no avail."

Edgar mentioned he was staying in a cottage on Lord Marchant's estate. "Yes, I know where you are. I'm preaching near there this morning, standing in for the parish priest nearby who is ill. Why don't you come along? The church service is at 11.00 and then maybe we could have some lunch here. My daughter Jennifer is married to a farmer and staying for a few days. She likes to try and fatten me up, so we will get a tasty lunch. Sadly, the vicar, Roger Reeves, who is quite a young dynamic chap, is in hospital. His wife has asked me to lunch afterwards but I have refused her kind offer."

"Yes, I would very much like to come. All being well, I'll see you later." Tom explained how to find the chapel and they agreed to meet up later. Edgar then got through to Ian Hogg.

"Edgar, how are you? We've all been worried about you, but so glad you're fine. Poor old Dick Loxton has not been well. Yes, most of the pupils came back after Carol's terrible accident. Only two education authorities withdrew their children but since then we have received applications for a further five pupils. Leonard Holdsworth, the Inspector, rang to speak to you. He has been a good friend and the Department of Education wrote a supportive letter, I think possibly due to Holdsworth's recommendations. Also, that medical officer – what's she called? Hilary, yes Hester Hubbard; she rang to speak to you. All the children are very excited and looking forward to half term in a week's time. We'd love to see you sometime. Incidentally, we now have four pupils attending the local comprehensive and so far all is going well."

Edgar breathed a sigh of relief. "So pleased everything is going smoothly. I will try coming up, possibly during the school holiday. I don't want to cause any unnecessary excitement."

"Oh, incidentally, Holdsworth did say he is retiring next year. He was also interested in the trustees and what skills they have to offer. But, most importantly, do ring up Maggie; she has been on to me three times to find out your number. Naturally, she is very worried. Sorry, Edgar, but I must go and get the church parties ready."

"That's all very interesting; which churches do they go to?"

"We use four denominations and they all take a great interest in the children: The Methodist Church, the Catholics, the C of E, and a group go to the Congregational church. You know my philosophy – get the kids out, and we are slowly building up some strong links with the various Christian groups. Sorry, I must rush. I'll give you a ring later. Take care."

o o o

"Rita, is that you?"

"Edgar, where have you been? We have all been worried sick about you. So where are you now?" Edgar explained his whereabouts and his breakdown. He was surprised how understanding she was.

"Look, you know you are welcome to come here and stay any time. I know the boys would love to see you. Freddie is growing up and now attends the senior school. He is quite bright but sadly Colin is not very academic. Look, I've got a piece of good news: Doug has applied for the position of Archdeacon in Western Australia."

"I've heard of it, but what exactly is an archdeacon?"

"Well, it's quite high up; he will be one step down from being a bishop and will be working directly for the Bishop of Western Australia, organising all the parishes, appointing clergy and so on."

"That's wonderful."

"Don't get too excited; there are five archdeacons out there answering to that bishop. But we are all so excited. We have to go up to Lambeth House for the final interviews. I gather there are two other vicars who have been shortlisted. If he is successful it will be a wonderful opportunity for the boys. I'm so thrilled. The trouble is, Doug's not at his best at interviews; he's never very good at selling himself. Still, we will just have to wait and see and cross our fingers."

The last phrase amused Edgar, coming from the wife of a vicar. "Look, sorry, I've got to get off to church. I'll give you a ring later."

"Thank God you are alright, and do ring up Maggie; like us all, she is very worried, so put her mind at rest."

"Look, I must rush. I will try and ring you tomorrow."

He was about to go and jump in his car when the phone rang. "Henry Marchant here. Would you like to come up for a drink?"

"Thank you, but I have been invited out for lunch."

"No matter but, before I forget, at the end of the month I have a get-together with some members of my old regiment. You must come and join us. We usually go to a pub. They are a rather noisy lot, not quite Elizabeth's scene. Look, I'll contact you nearer the time. Still, have a good lunch. Bye."

Edgar eventually found the chapel. It was rather off the beaten track in the small hamlet of East Chariton. The service had started. It was packed. He was handed a hymnbook and sat on a small pew at the rear of the church. Tom Owen, tall and gaunt with a small grey beard, was taking the service. They sang heartily and the sermon was preached by a young cleric wearing the vestments of office. He found the sermon to be boring. It was read from a prepared address, after which they withdrew into a large room attached to the chapel where he was handed a glass of wine.

Tom made his way over. "Thank you for coming. I am really retired but as you can imagine I never have a free Sunday. We also have the retired Archbishop of Canterbury in the congregation; he lives close by. He likes to play a low-key role and only gets involved on the big occasions. But first come and meet my daughter, Jennifer, who is staying with me for a few days."

Tom brought over his daughter Jennifer, a very plain lady in her early fifties, quite tall with powerful shoulders and dark grey eyes with no make-up. "So, you must be Edgar; dad always enjoys picking up the waifs and strays. I like to get down at least once a month to try and feed him and give his house a tidy up. I live in Cornwall just outside Truro. My husband has a bulb farm and I am an administrating officer at Truro Hospital. But, tell me, how do you know dad?"

Edgar was explaining how he knew him in Surrey when Tom suddenly reappeared with the ex-Archbishop, Dr Richard Gilpin. After brief introductions, Tom and Jennifer slipped away, leaving them together. Edgar found Dr Gilpin to be friendly, but his eyes were scanning the room and Edgar felt he was not particularly interested. "Yes, I live quite close by and I advise the Trust. You are possibly not aware, but this chapel was taken over by the parishioners and they established a trust and, of course, from that day it's gone from strength to strength." He suddenly touched Edgar's arm. "I am awfully sorry, but there's someone over there I must speak to. It's been a great pleasure speaking to you, Edgar; I hope we will meet up again. He was tall and fat with a florid complexion, as if he had been dining out too often.

Edgar was quietly sipping his wine and looking at the company when a short, fair-haired lady winked at him from across the room. The next moment she was by his side, holding the hand of a little boy. "Hello, I am Christine. I am the vicar's wife. Unfortunately, he is in hospital. He went in for a routine operation then suddenly there were complications. I've got two men in my life: my husband and my little boy William. She looked down. The boy was about six years old and seemed utterly bored with the proceedings. "And you? Have we met?"

"Sorry. I'm Edgar, an old friend of Tom's."

"Oh yes, he did mention you might be with us. Where are you living?"

"I'm renting a cottage on the Hannington estate."

Christine smiled. "Yes, we all know Henry and Elizabeth Marchant; he is a delightful chap, but I don't know his wife very well."

Edgar smiled. "I suspect you have a very busy life."

"Well, yes, at this moment I am trying to dodge one of my parishioners, but you are right, I'm an unpaid curate. Damn, she's seen me; I better head her off – it's back to work. So nice meeting you. I am sorry you're not coming over for lunch but no doubt we shall meet up again." She then bustled away holding little William's hand, who was trying to pull her in another direction. He was a dear little chap with dark hair and large brown eyes and very smartly dressed.

They finally slipped away to Tom's small semi-detached in the next village where they had a marvellous Sunday lunch of roast chicken, bread sauce and all the trimmings. Jennifer was a contrast to Tom. She could be very outspoken, so unlike her father. She had no children and was the deputy general manager of Truro General Hospital. He learnt later that she was quite bright and had come down from Oxford with a Maths degree then married Michael who had a daffodil farm in Cornwall. He learnt later they were complete opposites; he was a simple Cornishman whereas she was very bright and ambitious. As he drove home, he thought about the day. Jennifer certainly did not like Christine. "She's always flirting with the men. You can't see it, dad. She puts on that innocent act, and you know there have been a lot of rumours about her private life." Edgar smiled. He liked Jennifer, but she certainly could be very outspoken.

o o o

Rosemary was delighted Bob had suddenly taken on a new lease of life since being involved in football management, but was worried about her sister Pat who seemed to have aged and was making a slow recovery after the hydrocephalus operation. Then the final blow was her husband Claude's indiscretion which had suddenly soured their relationship. Rosemary's little son Freddie was a quiet little boy and, like Bob, had a placid disposition. As they sat finishing the evening meal, they continued to chat. "The catering business company is attracting more upmarket business, in particular the weddings, which are quite lucrative. Naturally, they want value for money and some of these mums can be difficult, to put it mildly. It's hard work trying to run a house with two children. I am thinking about selling my shares and pulling out. The constant problem is staffing; we have tried to put up their wages but with many of them it is just pin money."

"What about your two directors? Surely they can carry some of the weight."

"They are good friends but really have no contacts and could not take charge, but are useful helping with the luncheons. I have been thinking about appointing a general manager if I pull out. I can't just walk away; who will buy my shares if it goes down the chute? If the worst comes to the worst, I'll leave my shares in the business, but I've got my eyes on our wine waiter to act as a general manager. He is quite keen, but the trouble is all the waitresses fancy him and really I need somebody to crack the whip. Still, that's my problem for the moment; I'll keep my thoughts to myself. Tell me, how's the football going? Sorry, I do rabbit on."

Bob drained his glass. "Did I tell you that Godstone United have offered me a full-time contract at the end of the month?"

"Oh, that's wonderful."

"I'll be a part-time fund manager."

"What does that mean?"

"Simply, I will be out on the road speaking to various organisations and individuals trying to get more financial support for the club."

"You've got no experience in that line of business. Surely you've got directors who are much better qualified and possibly have more contacts?"

"No. Really, I am quite looking forward to the challenge. We are in a desperate position and I think the club is just hanging on. This next month will be make or break. If we can win our next cup match then we will be in the money. Still, a lot depends on this tie. I did tell you tomorrow we are meeting in the members' bar to see on TV who we will be facing? The place will be packed; some of the press will be there. The big clubs will enter the draw for the next round so we will all be sweating we get an easy match, so we are still there to play the big boys."

Suddenly they heard a noise. The door opened and Freddie wandered in half asleep. He was soon in his element, settling in his father's lap, and looking very mischievous. Rosemary leaned over to pick up a plate. "Before I forget, did that Johnnie Mortimer catch up with you, and who is he?"

"He's a great guy: the sports editor of the Godstone Herald. He was a Premier League footballer but retired early. I think between you and me he got suspended."

"What does he want?"

"Oh, he's the secretary of the supporters' club and helps us in all sorts of ways. He's a local boy; he went to the grammar school. He wants me to open the new Tesco store."

"Will they pay you?"

"No, I don't think so, but the club will be paid a fee."

"You're becoming a showbiz star."

"I'm not interested; my job is to win matches and the next game is probably the most important game in the club's history."

Rosemary smiled then picked up Freddie who by this time was sleeping soundly. She then put him back in Bob's lap. "You better carry him up; he's far too heavy for me."

As Bob carried him up the stairs, he spoke softly. "I've got to be in two places at once tomorrow. I have got a tricky job supervising the electrical installation of a new workshop at JS Marine; it's all precision work and some of those builders can be, well, let's say they need constant supervision. Then I've got to get over to the supporters' bar for the FA draw. I gather that we might be on the telly."

"When am I going to see you?"

Bob looked at his watch. "I'll do the school run and get back later in the day. The draw should be over by 1 o'clock. Maybe you'd like to come over and join us."

"You must be joking. I've got two luncheons to organise and try to make sure that we are fully staffed. Getting enough people is a real pain. Yes, I am determined to appoint a manager. I might look around. Maybe that wine steward, but then possibly he is too young. Some of the girls never leave him alone. He is married with a little girl. Still, that does not make much difference with some men. I shall be busy ordering the food and trying to inspect the premises, checking the cooker works and so on, but I will catch up with you later in the day."

They were soon in bed. Bob lay on his side and was fast asleep in no time. Rosemary felt disappointed; her hormones were restless and she kept thinking about the wine steward. He was tall, with black hair and dark broody eyes. They could see he was well endowed; he always wore tight jeans. No wonder he was popular with the ladies.

Bob had a very busy morning and finally arrived at Godstone Football Club to find the supporters' bar packed. He had spent the morning sorting out the position of an electrical installation on a workbench.

On arrival at the club, he was mobbed by the supporters and players. A drink was put in his hands. Loudspeakers were hanging from the walls and a large TV screen had been hung up, courtesy of a local TV shop. He noticed the presence of TV cameras and there were members of the press who he recognised. He was jostled as he tried to drink, and the entire crowd were very excited, all talking at the same time. The bar was heaving with people and next moment he had Johnnie Mortimer clapping him on the back. "Well, matey, this will make or break the club. Before I forget, there are three groups who would like you to come and talk to them in the near future. Still, we can talk about that later. Suddenly the noise quietened down; the television was on. Bob could see there was a small group with jackets and ties, but the majority were wearing anoraks and overalls. Suddenly the announcer came over loud and clear.

"We are now going over to Lancaster House, the headquarters of the FA, to witness the draw for the FA Cup." The officials were introduced and then went through the procedure of taking small balls out of a tumbling container and shouting out the numbers and the clubs they represented. It seemed to go on forever. The crowd were getting restless and then they heard Godstone United was drawn to play number five Blackwater Rangers. Cheering broke out.

Johnnie looked excited. "We've drawn one of the weaker teams, and a home tie."

Bob turned. "They are new to me. What do we know about them?"

Johnnie smiled. "Leave it to me, but you are going up to see them play next Saturday so that you can plan a strategy. Look, I better get up on the bar and say a few words. You heard that poor old Ted Drake was admitted to hospital last night; he's been going downhill the past few months, so you'll be in charge, but we're all here to help. Anything you need, just let me know. Hang on, I must go. I can see Don Rowbotham, and he is not very well either; he certainly could do with some good news."

The next moment, Johnnie Mortimer was standing on the bar. There was a loud boisterous cheer. He raised his hands and slowly the noise quietened. "He is going up in the world," he heard a voice say.

"My dear friends, we are nearly there, thanks to your help and support." There was a loud cheer. "But more importantly, thanks to the players and to Bob." There was a loud roar of agreement. "But we're not quite there; just one last big push and we can do it. I am about to have meetings with the committee to, quite bluntly, try to raise more finance so we can get the team away together for a few days to a training camp before we take on Blackwater Rangers. Of course, it will all depend on funds, and we also need to get teams of workers to brighten up this place. I feel ashamed of the bar and a lot of the ladies have been complaining about the toilet facilities. Still, we're all aware that this next cup game is possibly the most important in the club's history." Suddenly there was complete silence. "Now listen, I want you to drag along all your pals, relations and all your kids to support us. I feel quietly confident that with them all behind us we will win. Now, one final thing. I can see Don Rowbotham; he has not been well and has had open-heart surgery, so I think we should all thank him. He has been a great benefactor to the club. Let's have three cheers for Don."

Bob was interviewed by one of the national papers and then with Johnnie they spoke to the BBC sports editor. As he was leaving, he had a brief chat with Don Rowbotham who commiserated on Ted Drake's illness. "I have known Ted for over 30 years and he has been a great pal, but we can all see the results over the last few years have been abysmal, so if we stay up and win the next match the job will be yours – good luck."

Bob finally got home after looking in at JS Marine, a research engineering company working closely with the Royal Navy. The builders had completed the heavy-duty workbench ready for the installation of electrical junction boxes. He checked through all the specifications and came away feeling relieved.

He finally got home to find Rosemary putting the children to bed. He took over in the bathroom, washing Freddie, and then he put him into bed and read him a story. They were soon in the kitchen eating their supper.

Rosemary was in good form and had had a very successful day; the next two functions would be fully staffed, all the food had been ordered, and she had quickly visited the venues. As she was speaking, the phone went. "It's for you, Bob – a Mrs Lofthouse."

"Hello, Mrs Lofthouse. I am sorry to hear that, but you say it's only temporary. It sounds as if he has eaten the wrong thing or has been drinking."

"I got him to go to the surgery this evening and the doctor has given him a prescription to stop the sickness but I am a little worried; he is very easily led and rather thick with that Jimmy Greaves, who spends all his time drinking and chasing after the girls; he's a bad influence. Mind you, that Jimmy Greaves has no home life. His father is in prison, although they say that's not his father. The mother is quite frankly a tart. They say she has a different man every night. I heard she was seen in the Red Lion with two young West Indians; she was virtually legless, and her company had only one thing on their minds. I have a friend married to a policeman and he says that pub is full of vermin; they say she is never short of money. I think she's probably on the game."

"Look, Mrs Lofthouse..."

"Oh, please call me Nelly."

"Well, Nelly, I will read them the riot act. I have already warned the team that if they step out of line they will only get one warning and then they are out."

"Oh, thank you. I know that Nat thinks the world of you and I'm sorry to say my husband is far too soft; quite frankly, he spoils him."

"Well, thank you for ringing. Nat and Jimmy are two of my most talented players but, don't worry, I shall give them a final warning. You only want one rotten apple and it can affect the whole team. Just leave it to me."

Rosemary was in good form and looking forward to the first function, which was a wedding. The guests were always appreciative and well behaved, whereas some of the all-male business luncheons could get out of hand, due to heavy drinking.

Bob smiled. "Freddie was funny this evening. He never stops asking questions, which at times can be very tiring."

Rosemary lifted her glass. "Why? What did he say?"

"Well, he was asking about the birds and bees."

"What do you mean the birds and bees?"

"Well, he was asking how babies came into the world. I thought he was rather young for all that."

"He's got a very enquiring mind. Still, what did you tell him?"

"I told him they came out of mummy's tummy, and then he was asking how did they get in there."

"So what did you tell him then?"

"Well, it became rather difficult, so I mentioned that dads use their Willie."

"My God, did he understand that?"

"I think so because as I was drying him he looked down at his Willie and complained that it was very small and would it grow and be big like mine."

"My word, that certainly was a very informative bathing session. What happened then?"

"Well, I tried to divert the subject and next he was asking how it was that he was white and some of his pals were coloured. I must say I felt quite exhausted by the time I put him into bed."

"Yes, his teacher says he is very bright and at times she has to curb his questioning."

Rosemary stood up and stretched. "Well, I feel bushed. I am off to bed."

"I am just going to watch the news then I will be with you."

"Oh, darling, forget the news. Come to bed. I want to see how big your Willie is when it's blown up. Your sex lesson has made me feel fruity."

Chapter 10

Claude was very conscious that his horrifying experience with Hilary had now hit the tabloids and was common knowledge. A colleague in New York reported that news of the assault was now being widely circulated. Hilary Hilton was an American icon with all the right connections; her Godfather was the late president, Dwight Eisenhower. In her youth she had been pretty wild but turned over a new leaf when she became president of a worldwide children's charity, Enfants Sans Frontières. The American public were hungry for news of her, but she had quietly bowed out from public life and did not court the media.

Roy Tibbles, his chief clerk, politely brought it to his attention: 'British banker assaulted in New York. American idol butchered with her Brit Lover.' There was very little mention of it in the 'heavies'. Claude winced. *Well,* he thought, *my hands are tied.*

"Yes, Sir, you cannot block the story; it is factual and..."

Claude took off his glasses. "Yes, Roy, I thought that would be the case. Still, there is very little mention of my name."

"Well, I'm sorry to disillusion you, Sir, but you are mentioned in most of the papers and we have had a handful of calls from the media asking for a statement."

"Yes, you're so right; it's all wishful thinking on my part. Now I've got to face up to this crisis. Before I do anything else I better ring my wife. She was in a dreadful state when I left. I should have dealt with this matter before. God, this is not easy; just give me 20 minutes then we better prepare a statement for the press."

Pat answered her phone. "What the hell do you want? I've just had a call from one of my pals who worked in the soup kitchen with me. Of course, everybody knows about it. Now they are all talking about me. How do you think I feel? I seem to have lost my self-respect, and after my recent illness I've lost my confidence." He could hear her crying, and suddenly her voice broke. "How could you do this?"

"Darling, I was going to mention it."

"Don't 'darling' me; you've broken my heart. How could you? I thought you loved me."

"Look, I'll cancel all my appointments and come home so I can be with you."

"You're the last person I want to see, and when you get home you'll find me gone, and I hope you rot in hell." She then slammed down the phone.

Well, thought Claude, *I probably deserved that. I better see Roy to reschedule my diary and try and get on home.* As he was studying his appointments, he took a phone call from Sir Peter Lipton, the Chairman.

"Sir Claude, I have just read the gutter press. It was brought to my attention by my secretary who enjoys being titillated. Now remember, I and the board have the greatest respect for your professional abilities, so for God's sake don't let this problem worry you. Keep your head and it will all blow over in three days. Just make a prepared statement for the media, and I suggest take a few days off to let everything settle down. Finally, if there's anything I or the bank can do please don't hesitate to ask."

Claude decided to ring Rosemary. As he lifted the phone, Roy put his head around the door. "I've got three urgent calls, Sir, but I will endeavour to keep them at bay."

"Rosemary, Claude here. I imagine you've heard."

"Oh, yes. I am worried about Pat. She's still not herself. I think I will try and get hold of her, but I have a very busy day."

"If you would, I'd be most grateful. I just gave her a ring and she was naturally very distraught. I will try and reschedule my day and get on home."

Claude got back to his clerk. "Roy, I want to reorganise my diary for the next three days, just to let things settle down, and I hope to try to repair some of the damage."

"Well, Sir, a statement to the press is needed urgently, and then we can open your diary and implement the necessary changes."

They had just finished when Rosemary came back. "Claude, I am at your place. No sign of Pat. It looks as if she's taken a suitcase and some clothes and really disappeared. I will try ringing a few friends but, really, I suggest you come home immediately and ring the police regarding missing persons. I'm just sorry I must rush, but I will look in later in the day."

Finally, Claude got away from the office, after having a brief word with Christopher Barrington, his number two. Look, I shall be away for three days. I have reorganised my workload and have prepared a press statement but if there are any problems please ring or have a word with Sir Peter."

"I do understand, Sir, but by the end of the week everybody will have forgotten about it."

Claude finally got home; there was no sign of Pat. He tried ringing some of her friends with no success. He noticed some of her drawers were open, items of clothing missing. He then rang the police and spoke to the department dealing with missing persons and gave a description of her and stated she was in poor health and he was very concerned about her safety.

He had brought home a large quantity of work, but just could not settle. His mind was all over the place. He was cross with himself and worried about Pat, and then his thoughts turned to Hilary with her serious injuries. Against his better judgement, he decided to ring the hospital in New York to enquire. He finally made contact with the hospital. They were very tight-lipped so he decided to ring her daughter, Jane.

He finally caught up with her. She had a rich American accent. "Sir Claude, thank you for ringing. Yes, mum is slowly picking up. She's been taken off the life-support but, really, it was a very near thing. She was conscious last night but full of drugs and I don't think she recognised me. It's all been so upsetting but thank God she's pulling through. I'll tell her you rang when she comes down to earth. At the moment we are all living under a dreadful cloud."

"Have the police made any arrests?"

"Oh, yes; they have caught one of the villains, a little Mexican, and seem to be confident they will catch the rest of the gang and bring them to trial. If you can get over, we would love to meet you. I know mum was very excited about your visit. At the moment we're all holed up in New York. I want to take mum home to LA where she will quickly make a recovery. She's got lots of friends but really she's quite lonely and, of course, dotes upon my little daughter. I will keep you in the picture, when we have some news."

Claude was worried about Pat. She had just simply disappeared. He tried some of her friends again and constantly rang but her phone was switched off. Late in the afternoon, Rosemary looked in and noted the clothes which she had taken. She invited Claude to go back with her but he politely refused.

Claude stayed at home, kept his head down and turned off his phone but kept his private line open. After a day with no news he was starting to get worried.

o o o

"Edgar, is that you?"

"Pat, how lovely to hear you. I wish you were here. I often think of you. But, still, where are you? Whatever are you doing in Exeter? I am not far away; for the time being, I'm living near Salisbury. I've taken over a cottage on a rather a grand estate, but would love to see you. Why not come up on the train? I could meet you at the station."

They had a brief chat about Pat's family.

"Now, more importantly, Edgar, how are you?"

"I'm feeling much better. You probably heard I had... well, let's be honest, I had a bit of a breakdown, but I'm now feeling better. Running a school was, quite honestly, getting too much for me. I enjoyed it. Still, what about you?"

Pat suddenly felt she could not talk about her problems.

"Look, Edgar, I must go, but I'll check the times of the trains and speak again or leave a message. I am so looking forward to seeing you."

Pat suddenly felt on top of the world, and then she thought, *I better ring Claude and think about going home, but that can wait,* She dreaded the thought. *Right, I'm going to spoil myself, and have my hair shampooed and a pedicure and look out for a smart dress; I must look my best for Edgar. God, I so want that man; just the thought of him makes my body ache.*

The day flew past. After leaving a message for Edgar, she went out and had her hair dyed and styled, and bought two skimpy dresses. She got back footsore and jumped into a warm bath with a G&T and started to feel very relaxed. The picture of Edgar turned her on. She could feel her hormones racing around out of control. *I must restrain myself before I do something silly.*

There was no sign of Joseph, the restaurant manager whom she had met the previous evening. The place was very busy. There was a noisy gang of girls shouting and laughing; it looked like a hen party. She gathered later that one was due to get married and they were certainly out to have a good time. There was possibly a mother,. who looked very subdued. Pat was finally served by a young man with an American accent. "Yes, ma'am, I am from New York. Yes, it is great here, but I miss home. I'm living in a small town called Crediton with my pal who works in the kitchen. I'm Brad. Are you ready to order?"

After tucking into roast chicken with all the trimmings and a glass of wine, she read the local paper. She could see that two girls were being very noisy, and noticed one of them patting the waiter's bottom. She observed him go and speak to the restaurant manager who went and spoke to the table; they then quietened down. Brad came back and collected her plates. "Yes, they are very noisy and have been making rude suggestions. Still, my shift's coming to an end and I can get off home. Most of the time this job is okay but, sorry, is there anything else I can get you?"

Pat selected a sweet to be followed by coffee. "And, yes, I'll have a brandy."

Pat watched the party and was amused when one of the elderly ladies stood first, which seemed to be a signal for all of them to move. They left in high spirits and suddenly the room became quiet.

Brad, the waiter, approached. "Now, do you want anything else?" he asked, smiling. He was slight of stature with a warm friendly smile and with a perfect set of white teeth. He had a dark complexion with large brown friendly eyes. "If there is nothing else, I will go and get your bill for you to sign."

"I should imagine you'll be glad to get home, I hope you have a quiet night and are able to catch up on some sleep."

"I wish, the night porter is off sick so I have to cover his duties "It's typical; my pal who works in the kitchen gets paid more than I do and works shorter hours. Still, if there's anything you want, I mean anything, just give me a ring," he said, winking.

Pat finally rolled into bed feeling sleepy and excited at the thought of seeing Edgar. She had left a message that she would be at Salisbury station at 12:10. Her sleep was disturbed by a window blowing in rain. She found it difficult to close so she rang the reception and Brad, the American, arrived after a soft knock on the door.

"Can you help me? I can't seem to close the window and the rain is coming in."

He smiled. "Is that all you want?"

"Certainly, just fix the window please, and then I can get some sleep."

He then stood on a chair and after much exertion managed to close it.

He was smiling as he stepped down, and then, without warning, he slipped his arms around her and pulled her to his body. They had a long warm kiss which she quite enjoyed.

"Now, stop that. I am not a piece of cheap meat. I have been spoken for."

He stood back, smiling. "I think you better go. This hotel is not safe for a single woman. Sorry, but I don't find Devon ladies very friendly, and that gang tonight were over the top and very silly."

"I'm sorry to hear that, but I think you better go, and thank you for fixing the window." He quietly moved towards the door, looking a little sad. He must have been in his early thirties and was wearing a white shirt and close-fitting jeans. She finally got back to bed and was soon fast asleep.

She heard a noise in the early hours and opened her eyes to see a figure sitting on the side of the bed. She sat up; it was Brad.

"Whatever are you doing here? You better go before you get into trouble."

"I just couldn't sleep, and I had to come and see you."

He leaned over and kissed her softly on the lips. She fell back onto the pillow and he embraced her passionately.

Finally, she moved her head to one side. "Look, you must go. I am a married woman." She did not have time to finish when, the next moment, he slipped into bed and was kissing her passionately. She tried to push him off. "If you don't go, I shall scream." She felt his lips cover hers and his light body rolled on top; it was then she realised he was naked. There was a little voice in her head telling her to scream but she could feel the sensation of his manhood as it was teasing that magic spot. The thrill was overwhelming. She started to feel relaxed. *I've been waiting for this; damn the lot of them.* He continued to tease, which aroused her, and before long they were locked into each other's bodies. She whispered in his ear, "Have you got a rubber on?"

"Yes, I take precautions." Then suddenly, with no warning, he thrust deeply. She could feel his warm breath on her cheek. He had skilfully placed a pillow under her bottom; the sensation was heavenly. Slowly, they rocked together. He seemed to explode very quickly.

"Don't stop now," she groaned. "I'm nearly coming." He continued to make love gently and then the world seemed to stop; she had the most glorious orgasm. She could feel her pent-up juices flooding out. It was utter bliss and then that little voice full of recrimination. *You silly girl, you were saving yourself, and now what have you done.* She lay back exhausted but contented.

She rolled onto her side facing him and continued to stroke his body. "Tell me about yourself, I can't go off to sleep for a while. How long have you been working here?"

"It must be about six months. Finding a job down here has not been easy and, to be quite honest, the locals don't really like foreigners. Mind you, saying that, working in a hotel at nights brings in a lot of unexpected invitations."

"Yes, I met Joseph, and he was very suggestive."

"You don't have to worry about him; he is gay. We've got clients who come here so they can spend the night with him. Yeah, a lot goes on at night in this hotel; it's all very secretive. We've even got a few coppers who use our facilities and bring their lady friends. Then, of course, we've got a few of the ladies who are looking for a good time and usually have no money."

"What, do you mean prostitutes?"

"Well, shall we say on the borderline, usually looking for a good time and earning some money; they are not very choosy."

"You surprise me; I never thought of that sort of thing happening."

"Lady, you don't know the half. Everything's got a price, and that includes sex; it's the biggest selling commodity. Even tonight I was propositioned by two of the ladies on that table. In fact, I quite like the older one. I think it was one of the mothers. She gave me her phone number. I heard she just got divorced. But these sex encounters never last long and really I am saving up to go back home. Well, Pat, I better slip away. Must get down and open everything up. I've got a busy day: two big functions; there's a wedding in the cathedral and they are due back here for the wedding breakfast at midday. I gather it's the MP's sister, and then tonight putting on a big carvery for the vintage car people. They have got a big show on in the county grounds and most of them are staying here."

"Gosh, that's a lot in one day."

"Yes, I know, but we are told that the hotel business is very competitive and I gather it's only by putting on these big events that we make any real profits. Of course, we live in an area surrounded by restaurants and hotels so it's always a struggle. Still, darling, I must be on my way, and I hope everything works out for you."

As he leaned over and gave her a long, warm, lasting kiss, she thought, *I wish he would do it again; it was utter ecstasy.*

"Wait a moment; I must go to the loo."

She jumped out of bed, running naked into the bathroom, grabbing her dress and handbag. She could feel damp juices on the inside of her leg. She dried herself quickly, brushed her hair, had a quick spray and then slipped on some clothes, and opened her handbag and took out £50. She returned to Brad who was now pulling on his trousers and fastening his belt.

"Brad, please doesn't take offence, but please accept this and buy yourself a little present."

"Ma'am, I couldn't take it. You're a real beauty and I shall often think of you when you're gone, so please."

"I insist. Take it for my sake. I shall probably never see you again and you brought me joy when my confidence was at low ebb." After a long warm kiss, they separated. She pushed the roll of notes into his shirt pocket and suddenly he was gone.

She sat at the dressing table looking into a mirror and felt life was really worth living. The thought of seeing Edgar, although very exciting, had just waned a little. *What did Brad say? I shall often think of you. I bet he says that to all of his conquests. He was a nice boy, very gentle, but I certainly can never come back to this hotel. And to think I paid him. I feel ashamed,* she thought, smiling to herself. *But I enjoyed every moment, all so dangerous and exciting, but now I must see Edgar.* She then jumped into the bath and relaxed in the warm soapy water and could still feel that exhilarating sensation of his foreplay and then having that divine orgasm. The water started to cool, so with great effort she pulled herself out of the bath, dried herself, feeling a little numb but tingling with excitement.

o o o

Pat finally packed her case, paid up her account and dragged her case across the road to the station. In no time, she was in Salisbury, arriving later than expected, and there was Edgar, darling Edgar, waiting at the end of the platform. He was starting to look older and he was leaning on a heavy stick. He was wearing an old Parker and a battered hat but he had those large blue eyes and that lovely smile. Just the sight of him made Pat's heart melt. She felt warm and excited. *Now don't do anything silly,* she heard a voice telling her; *you've got a husband to think of.*

After a warm embrace, they moved towards his car. She continued to pull her case. "I've got a friend coming over for supper. I thought you could help me, and I will take you back when you're ready to leave. He's Tom Owen; in fact, Claude and Florence were in his parish. He thought very highly of Florence and took her funeral service. He lives just down the road in the village of Chilmark. But, Pat, I must warn you – the cottage is very basic and it has only the essentials."

Pat smiled as she feasted her eyes on Edgar. *I won't t be able to keep my paws off that man tonight. What's wrong with me?* "Who owns the cottage?"

"It's on the Hannington estate, the home of Lord and Lady Marchant. He's a super chap but she's a bit of a cold fish. He's ex-army so we've got something in common. You might meet him tonight. I did invite him in for a drink if he can make it."

The cottage reminded Pat of the farm cottage where she was brought up – very basic, cold and damp, but to be with Edgar was all that mattered. She was soon in the kitchen. "Now, what have you got in the way of food?"

"Well, let me see. I've got some sausages and bacon and eggs, potatoes, baked beans, soup powders, milk beverages, some wine, a large bottle of gin."

"What time are we due to eat?"

Edgar put on the kettle. "Plenty of time, so let's sit down and have a cuppa, and tell me what you have been doing since we last met."

"Well," she said after he had related his problems. She found it difficult to talk about Claude's indiscretion. "I'm going to have a wash and brush up and then prepare a tasty supper."

"Can I help you?"

"No, but thanks; cooking is the one thing I enjoy."

As she was in the kitchen she heard the front door and voices. "Good of you to come, Sir."

"Oh, please: it's David." He was tall, with a large sandy moustache, grey eyes and a toothy smile.

Pat came into the hall, where she was introduced to Lord Marchant. "He's kindly brought us a bottle of malt whiskey, which I'm sure Tom will enjoy." They sat round the coffee table. Edgar had lit the fire. All seemed to be very homely. It was not long before Tom arrived, tall, a little bent over and now in his early eighties. They sat together sipping the malt, which seemed to relax the atmosphere.

Finally, Lord Marchant looked at his watch. "I must go in a moment to the one to be obeyed," he said smiling.

He had quizzed Edgar about his army service. "Yes, I had spells in Aden, Egypt, Cyprus, and Ireland and finished up in Germany, which was a very cushy number. But, to be honest, I was not good enough to get to the top. I came through the ranks."

"That's no mean achievement, but promotion in the guards was very much helped with family connections and being in the right place at the right time."

They continued to chat about military affairs. "I came out a half colonel and then was offered a job in Whitehall with promotion, but by then I'd had enough and I got back to running the estate, which had deteriorated, but with my wife's money and some hard work we are slowly getting back into shape. We've got a stretch of salmon fishing which seems to attract all my friends but does need constant maintenance so I have decided to lease it to a sporting company; they can have all the headaches. We had Princess Anne here last month and, contrary to what I'd heard, found her to be jolly good company. My wife got on well with her, and my wife can be very outspoken."

Tom Owen sat quietly supping his malt with a twinkle in his eye. "Yes, I'm due to move down to live near my daughter. This is the time when your children get their own back," he said smiling.

In no time, Lord Marchant stood, shook their hands, and was gone, and two minutes later his wife was on the phone. "Has he left?"

"Yes, he just left."

"Oh good. We've got a dinner party here and all my guests are due shortly; he's never here when I want him. Now, I must sort out the drinks."

"Sorry, that was Lady Elizabeth Marchant; she's a bit of a dragon."

As Edgar and Tom chatted, Pat disappeared into the kitchen. In no time, she had put together a simple wholesome meal with a chilled bottle of wine. Tom talked about his work. "Sadly, I have not seen Sir Claude, but remember fondly his wife Florence who was a tower of strength. I believe she a staff inspector with the Department of Education and I gather very highly thought of." After an enjoyable evening, they finally drank their coffees in front of a log fire. "I must not touch anymore, and I shall have to drive carefully."

After the farewells, Pat popped into the kitchen, quickly cleared up and got back to find Edgar sleeping soundly in the large armchair. The fire had burned through and the room was quite chilly. She noticed him stir. "Would you like a coffee or something?"

He opened his eyes, smiling. "I feel as if I'm having a wonderful dream and I know it cannot last." He stood up and stretched and then suddenly grabbed her and soon they were in each other's arms, kissing tenderly. "I made your bed up in the spare room. Sorry, the mattresses are rather hard, but if there is anything you want, give me a shout." She finally got to bed and looked around. It was all very basic cheap furniture with a cheap stained carpet. It possibly had not been decorated for years, and the bed was certainly hard and damp.

She eventually got out of bed and padded across the hall and entered Edgar's room. He was snoring vigorously on his back, so she slipped into bed and nestled into his warm body. He suddenly woke up, put his arms around her, and pulled her close, and they drifted off to sleep. *God*, she thought, *what can I do to bring this man to life?* But it was to no avail, so they slept in each other's arms.

Over the breakfast table, they had a chat. "You know I respect you, Pat, and would never take advantage of you."

But Pat had other thoughts. "Surely you read the papers about Claude being involved with this other woman. It was all very hurtful and suddenly my respect and confidence seem to have taken a hard knock."

"Pat, darling, stop feeling sorry for yourself. Yes, he has hurt you, but two wrongs don't make a right; he is, as you know, basically a good man, and you've got to learn to forgive. I know it's not easy, but have you thought about how worried he is? Look, if you're not forgiving, it will drive him away for good; you taught me that. Love is very fragile and should not be taken for granted but needs to be nurtured."

"Yes, you're right. I will ring Claude after breakfast, if I can catch him. It will be difficult, certainly not easy. Edgar, I'm so pleased to have found you, and thank you for taking the time to put me right and not taking advantage."

Chapter 11

Philip was experiencing a wide range of emotions. He still had a soft spot for Claire but knew any reconciliation was now impossible. He tried to bury himself in work; he had few friends and really no hobbies and had been hopeless at sport, which just did not interest him. He was now quite comfortably off, had leased his mother's house to a lady solicitor, but felt very despondent and was also losing interest in Wadham Developments.

"Look, Philip," said Maggie, "I can see you're not yourself, but you've got to snap out of it. I think you know your problem: you need a soul mate. Life is so lonely when you do not have a companion to share your life. I know your mother Joan could be difficult. She did not like me but, really, I can see you're missing her. Now, this is a long shot, but have you ever thought of joining a dating club or going on a singles holiday? But again, be on your guard or you may land up with another Claire, and that's the last thing you want. Some of these dating agencies can be very expensive and attract some very unreliable clients who are just looking for a rich partner."

Finally, Philip booked a singles holiday with a well-established travel operator to the Costa del Sol. He was very disappointed, although they were all very friendly. In the group there were 12 men and five ladies. He was amused when talking to a male member who divulged he was 72 and looking for company. The only girl he was interested in was snowed under with invitations. He got back home eventually, thinking *that was a waste of time.*

Maggie was very interested. "Don't rush it; you've got plenty of time."

"Well, I am thinking about joining a dating club on the Internet, but I hear so many stories that I am a bit hesitant."

Maggie smiled. "I'm glad you're not too disillusioned but leave it for a while. I know you'll find what you're looking for. Now listen, I've got one of our contractors says he's got a difficult client, I think a police officer, and he's complaining the house they purchased is not built according to the specifications. I did speak to Sally and she assures me that the plans she sent to the solicitors are the ones which were approved by the local authority."

"Okay, give me all the details and I'll look in at seven this evening, and could you arrange for the builder, Alan Harris, to join us?"

"Thank you, Philip. I shall not be in tomorrow, so I'll deal with this other matter; we have received an approach to sell the eight sites in South Reigate.

"Yes, it's the builders, Michael Hynes. I believe he's back in the driving seat. I gather he bought back a large tranche of shares. I've spoken to Sally and she asked for more details. She's always got her ear to the ground. She heard they wanted to do a trade-off to include a cash payment. Look, I'll get onto this today and try to speak to Mike Hynes direct, but the trouble is these people are so evasive. Still, leave this in my hands. I will leave you to get along this evening and speak to the policeman. You'll find all the details are in the enclosed folder."

That evening Philip got over to Shackleford just outside Godalming to an old farmhouse which had been divided into two units and could quickly see that there was a variation with the conversion which had not been fully recorded by the building inspector. He knocked on the door at 7.30 p.m. but there was no sign of Alan Harris, the builder. A tall thickset lady in her early fifties came to the door, looking very harassed.

"Yes, yes. I was expecting you at seven. I am busy feeding my kids. I had a message from a Mr... yes, a Mr Harris, I think. He apologised but could not make it. Well, you better come in; look, give me 20 minutes."

The house was very untidy with children's toys everywhere; he could hear them screeching in the background.

"Can I have a word with your husband?"

"That will be difficult because he's in Australia."

"Well, I came to see him reference the misunderstanding regarding the plans."

"He's in Sydney; he ran off with some young bimbo, a real tart, and I have not heard from him since."

Philip could hear the children making more noise and the mother was getting to look very harassed. "Look, just let me get my kids to bed; they are tired and I can hear them fighting." She finally came back after half an hour. "Sorry to keep you waiting. Look, I'm Barbara, and you?"

"Sorry, yes, I am Philip. I am an architect. I work for Wadham Developments and we employed the builders. I have studied your grievances and really we are studying two sets of plans, but what exactly are you unhappy about?"

"Well, you can appreciate, having two young sons, I want the sitting room and dining room to be one big room, and I thought the dividing wall would contain an open access between the rooms instead of having to go into a corridor. There are two other small points but that is my main bugbear."

"Look, I can see where you're coming from. Now, really, it's not going be a particularly expensive job, assuming we only make an access to move from one room to the other. I can see that we can do this quite cheaply. Look, leave it to me, and I will get onto it. Possibly we could carry out this work in two- or three-weeks' time. It's going to be a dusty job; you will need a lot of dust covers. Look, to avoid any ill feeling, my company, Wadham Developments, will pay for this minor conversion."

Barbara stood up with a large smile on her face. "You are so kind. Can I get you a glass of wine? I certainly could do with a drink. I love my children dearly but there are times when I feel like murdering them."

Philip stood. "Thank you for the offer, but I must be on my way. I will contact you in a week's time, but I will have to check with the builders first."

Barbara came forward and shook his hand. She was quite tall with broad shoulders and short dark hair and with large matronly bosoms and a pronounced bottom. As they shook hands he could smell her scent. "Thank you, Philip, for coming over. I shall look forward to seeing you." She had large green eyes and a small turned-up nose. In fact, Philip thought she was quite attractive. "Now I must go and see to my two sons; sadly, they're missing their father and reaching the age where they need a man in their lives. Still, that's my problem. I shall Look forward to hearing from you, Philip," she said with a twinkle in her eye.

Philip kept thinking about Barbara. He had not heard from Claire and felt he must make some provision for the child; he finally made contact with Madge, her mother.

"Sorry, Philip; she did not stay here long, and moved out, but really I don't know where she's gone. I did love her little boy, Winston, but Micky, as you can imagine, was not happy and went berserk. He has these almighty tempers, and felt it was a personal insult. But you say you have not heard from her. I am worried. I must not panic. She never rang me when she ran away in the past, so I thought she was with you. I'd better get onto the police. This is so worrying. She's really a kind-hearted girl. If I get any news I'll let you know."

Philip finally met the builders at Barbara's house. He quickly appraised the work and gave them a date; the work should be completed in two days. "Sorry, Philip, but I must rush. I've a meeting with the planners and they don't like being kept waiting." They shook hands and he was gone.

Barbara looked at Philip. "You in a rush? Stay on and have a sandwich."

"I'd like that, but where are the children?"

"They are at school; it's the only time I get a breather, and it's nice to have lunch with some company."

o o o

Claude Dibbs was at home wading through a long list of security problems. He was studying the housebuilders, Michael Hynes Constructions. The bank had been closely involved with the company for over 20 years and had recently granted them a loan to buy back a large tranche of their shares. His mind floated back to over 20 years ago when Mike Hynes was a jobbing builder. He came over from Ireland where his father was a farmer, one of a large family, and lodged with some distant relations who had a garden centre. He led a gang laying the concrete raft for houses. One of the builders he contracted for was in difficulties, so he took a handful of building sites in lieu of monies owed and quickly became an established builder. Through hard work and ambition, he started to build up a successful business, and then his biggest break came when he bought a 70-acre site but he could only build on 25% because the main line from Waterloo to Reading made it uneconomic to bring all the services to the cut-off area. He then entered into negotiations with British Rail and they, for a very substantial payment, closed the line from Saturday night until Monday morning so he could excavate under the line and install all the services. It was a great success and the company then went public and suddenly Michael became a paper millionaire.

Three years ago, the company started to suffer from a slump in the housing market and poor management. A faction of the shareholders was trying to vote him off the board. He finally bought back a tranche of shares and became the principal shareholder and turned it back into a Private company. The bank was now seeking a timeframe concerning repayment of the outstanding overdraft.

Claude then raced through a list of companies and could see that a high volume of retail businesses were experiencing trading difficulties. Christopher Barrington was dealing with these problems; it was now his brief. He was a sound general manager, softly spoken, but could be sarcastic. Claude felt at times he was too ruthless in closing down lines of credit.

As he was about to retire, the phone went; he picked up his mobile. A soft voice spoke. "Is that you, Claude?"

"Yes."

"Hilary here. How are you?"

"Hilary, darling, it's lovely to hear you. Thank you for ringing. I just can't stop thinking about you. I feel so responsible for what happened."

"No, no, it was my fault and really I should have thought about your dear wife and should not have taken advantage of you; it was all wrong."

"Dearest Hilary, I love you, and I'd do anything for you, and after what I saw of your injuries I have never in my life felt so depressed and guilty. I just felt helpless."

"Claude, there was nothing you could do. Don't make this difficult for me. I am ringing to say goodbye. Our affair will only cause suffering, particularly to your close ones, and I certainly don't want to break up your family, dearest darling. I rang to say I shall miss you. This is breaking my heart; the thought of losing you is causing me so much pain but I cannot go on like this."

"Hilary, dearest, I'm sure we can work out something. I want to be with you."

"Sorry, I must leave. This is so agonizing. I just cannot go on. I feel so miserable. Must go."

He could hear her crying and then the next moment the line went dead.

After a stiff brandy, he thought to himself, *I should not be drinking; certainly, it won't do my ulcer any good.* He went to bed but couldn't sleep. All he could think about was Hilary. Next morning over breakfast he thought, *I shall be 64 at the end of the month. I must pull myself together and try to make peace with Pat. I know I have hurt her deeply. God, my life is a bloody mess.* He had heard from Rosemary only the day before that Pat was well and would be returning home in the next two days. He then took a call from his chief clerk Roy Tibbles who started to outline a long list of assignments requiring his attention.

"Roy, I will be in today. Yes, I appreciate my in-tray is now overflowing. I'd like to see Christopher Barrington at 11.30; it's about time I got back into the driving seat."

"Right, Sir. We are missing you, Sir, and shall look forward to seeing you later this morning."

Sir Claude that afternoon was sitting in at a meeting of the general managers. They were discussing staffing levels when he had a violent pain in his abdomen. He excused himself and took some painkillers and then finally made an appointment with his doctor, John Ritchie. After a tiring day, he finally arrived in the early evening at his consulting rooms in West London, feeling rundown, exhausted and experiencing pains in his intestines.

"Right, Sir Claude, slip off your shirt and lay on that couch. After 20 minutes, when he had thoroughly examined him, Claude put on his shirt. "Yes, it's as I thought. I'm not going to pull any punches. I have been warning you for a long time regarding that ulcer. Quite bluntly, you are a sick man. As I thought, it has burst and is causing havoc with your digestive systems. You will need to see a gastroenterologist; I will make all the arrangements."

"I've just come back from a conference in the States and, really, I'm trying to catch up on a mountain of work. I just haven't the time, but I could get away for a consultation."

John Ritchie held up his hand. "You must realise this is very serious. You are a sick man. I am going to make arrangements for you to be admitted to St Mary's Hospital tonight and they will perform an endoscopic procedure which should give us some indication of the problems."

"Is this really necessary? Really, I am so busy."

"Yes, that is part of the problem; like many of my clients, you never take your health seriously until it's too late. You're overdoing it. You're obviously very tired, you look very anaemic and really you need a good long rest. I do appreciate your problems, but really this is a matter of life and death and what with blood in your stools, the palpitations and tiredness and pale skin, you are heading for a serious breakdown. I want you to report directly to St Mary's Hospital. My worry is if this is peritonitis it could lead to sepsis, and then we'll have a risk of a multiple breakdown of organs."

"Right, John. I got the message. I will pack a bag and report to St Mary's, but I must make a few brief phone calls."

"Sir Claude, leave all the arrangements to me. I shall certainly feel happier when we have you in hospital with a clearer picture."

Claude paused from adjusting his tie. "One final question: from what you're saying, this sounds as if I shall be out of commission for quite a time and, really, I must prepare my directors so they can cover my absence. The obvious question: how long is this going to take?"

"Well, that's a difficult one to answer, but to play safe I think we must be thinking of three months. Of course, it could be shorter but, really, from my experience, bearing in mind your condition and your age, it's not a procedure we should rush, and you will need a sensible period of convalescence. I will look in and see you tomorrow after all the tests have been assessed and give you a report on all our findings."

They parted on amicable terms and then Claude spoke to the Chairman, Sir Peter Lipton, who was very sympathetic. "Now, don't worry; Christopher Barrington seems to be coping. The board feel that the company is in safe hands."

Then he spoke to his chief clerk, Roy Tibbles, to prepare him, and finally he rang Rosemary.

"I am so sorry, Claude. Is there anything I can do to help? We are all hoping that Pat will be back tomorrow. As soon as I hear from her I will tell her of your problems."

"Rosemary, dear; how about you? Isn't your baby due soon?"

"Yes, in a month's time and I'll be glad when it arrives. We are very busy at work and hoping to appoint a catering manager to take some of the pressure off me. Mind you, Pat is always a tower of strength."

"Yes, I've been reading about Bob and Godstone United; it must be exciting."

"Well, yes and no. The trouble is, he does not have any peace. Still, he is enjoying himself, but the next match is the big one. Claude, I must go. If there's anything I can do, just give me a ring. Unfortunately, nobody knows where Pat is. I will speak to Rita. Take care. I hope to see you soon."

He finally spoke to Barrington, who was very supportive. "I do hope you'll be back with us soon, Sir, but I will endeavour to continue to adhere to your policies, which I have always fully supported."

Claude liked him; everything was in black and white. He was not popular with his peers, but Claude found him to be loyal and devoid of any ambition, a rare quality with a general manager.

He finally arrived at St Mary's Hospital and unpacked his belongings, including John Gresham's latest novel. He was immediately subjected to a long series of examinations and his whole body was X-rayed. It was during the night; he had settled down after a cup of cocoa, when he had a call from Pat.

o o o

Bob suddenly felt he was really in the thick of it. He resigned from the very loose partnership which he had set up with two electrical pals, which in a very short time had gone from strength to strength. He was now employed at Godstone United as the assistant trainer and fund manager; he was never busier, and Johnnie Mortimer, the supporters' secretary, never gave him a minute's peace and had him shunted from pillar to post. He even had to give a short address to the Women's Institute. He was surprised how interested they were. He attended the mayor's dinner in the Guildhall where again he was called upon to say a few words and so it went on, but his principal job was to cajole, coax and try to improve the playing skills of Godstone United. They had played one away game before the cup match, which they lost. Bob could see they had taken it badly and needed a boost to their confidence. He felt this was a mixed blessing; they had been getting a lot of attention in the community and this had gone to their heads. He stressed that Waterstone Wanderers were playing in the Liverpool Central league and were two divisions higher, although he did not point out they were near the foot of the table. Bob had a chat with Johnnie Mortimer, who scratched his ear. "Well, what would you suggest?"

"I've got a pal who plays for Brighton United and they have invited us down for the day to train with their team. I would like to take the boys down there for a day and a night, possibly to stay in the luxury spa hotel. It would be useful for a bonding session."

Johnnie was a tall chap in his mid-fifties and still had a lot of contacts in the game. He had refused numerous offers, what with his job at the Godstone Journal and writing sporting articles for two of the nationals. His wife also had a dry-cleaning business and he often helped out, so he was quite comfortably off.

"Okay, Bob. I can see where you're coming from and that it's now or never. It will be a waste of time trying to get a loan from the bank, but I have salted away a small emergency fund which we can tap into. I have also organised a boxing evening next month, which is often very lucrative. Quite frankly, trying to sell to our punters the night away in Brighton for the team would be a waste of time; still, you sort out the costings and come back to me."

Bob finally got home feeling quite exhausted and found Rosemary looking very depressed. She rushed over and flew into his arms in a flood of tears. "Darling, darling, what's wrong?"

"I smacked Freddie this evening. I have never known him to be so obstinate." She continued to cry. "You're never here when I need you. I'm fed up with the luncheon club; I never have enough staff and half of them are a waste of space." She broke back into tears. "And I am missing Pat; thank God she is on her way home."

Bob pulled her close and kissed her on the forehead. "I promise I'll be home tomorrow night to bath Freddy." Finally, Rosemary settled down over a glass of wine. Bob spoke to Freddie, who came in and kissed his mother.

The following evening, Bob got home early to find Rosemary back to her old self. "I had some wonderful news. I had a call from Rita; Pat had rung and she is okay and hopes to be back in a day or two. Then I had a call from Steph in New York, full of the joys of spring. I can never keep up with all her boyfriends, but she wants to come over and visit us. I did not mention Pat and her problems. I hope that will all have blown over by then. Sorry, darling, about last night. I just felt things were getting on top of me, what with Pat. I am thinking of making the wine waiter general manager, but I might put an advert in the local paper under a box number and see what comes up. I have got certain misgivings about him. Still, darling, what sort of day have you had?"

Bob finally managed to slip away for the night with the team for the training session at Brighton United. They trained with the Premier team and they were certainly put through their paces. They quickly realised their shortcomings and received some very sophisticated coaching manoeuvres. They enjoyed the night at the spa hotel and much of the feedback was very positive. They finally got home relishing the thought of the big match at home on Saturday against Waterstone Wanderers.

The big day arrived; it was wet and foggy, not conducive to a fast game of football. The ref. inspected the grounds and passed them for use but he was not happy with the playing conditions. Bob had taken possession of a loan-signing from Brighton, Billy Steele; they wanted to see him stretched. He was a quiet, slightly built boy of 17, with the skills of holding the ball, but his early promise had not materialised. He was a Scot from Glasgow, very homesick and wanted to go home. Bob was pleased to see that Jimmy Greaves had taken him under his wing. Bob decided to bring him on in the second half but wanted to concentrate on some of the manoeuvres which had been practised at Brighton. He felt more comfortable with the whole team; they seemed to be very enthusiastic and up for the big game. The national papers sent down reporters to interview members of the team but the spotlight had been focused on Bob. He also received numerous calls from old colleagues wishing him success. Rosemary cancelled her ladies' luncheon so she could be on hand. She was surprised when he was mobbed in the local high street.

He had an early call from Billy Steele's landlady that he had been up half the night with an upset stomach which she thought might be down to nerves, but he so wanted to play. The local primary school provided the young pupils to accompany the teams onto the field. Waterstone Wanderers were a bit of a mystery. Unfortunately, Bob was unable to get away to see them play, but had received a report on their playing strengths. It would seem they were a defensive outfit and lacked penetration in attack; they had recently signed a new trainer who was starting to turn things around.

The ground was packed with 5,500 brightly dressed noisy fans, a record gate. Eight coaches had come down from Liverpool full of over excited supporters. Sadly, the manager, Ted Drake, had just come out of hospital and was convalescing at home. Johnnie Mortimore, the secretary of the supporters' club, was everywhere; he organised a special area for the press and TV cameras; he produced a glossy programme chronicling the history of the club and set up additional catering facilities and increased the size of the bars. He was very conscious of the club's finances. He put up a hospitality marquee for the club's patrons to entertain their guests.

Finally, there was a crescendo of applause as the teams holding the hands of the children walked out onto the pitch. After all the formalities of handshakes, and the spin of the coin, the ends were chosen. It was a very damp dull day with no wind and a sticky surface.

Godstone United felt confident but they were in for a big shock; their opponents flew into them and in the first 15 minutes they saved a goal off the line and conceded two corners. Then suddenly out of the blue a pass was neatly pushed through the middle, quickly picked up by a Waterstone forward who ran 20 yards, avoiding two late tackles, and pushed the ball into the corner of the goal. Except for the shouts of elation from the visiting supporters, there was a stunned silence. The unexpected goal gave the visitors the edge. Godstone seemed to lose their shape and lacked possession. But as the half wore on they started to find their feet and Bob decided to bring on Billy Steele. After a slow start, he started to stamp his authority on the game. As they approached half-time, the visitors put a man to mark him and tried to starve him of the ball. He was small, pale and slightly ginger-headed; he held onto the ball and his accurate passing started to cause problems. They soon became desperate; two players were shown yellow cards after they upended him.

Half-time came and went and suddenly the games came to life; a straight ball was pushed through the middle by Billy Steele and picked up by Greaves on the halfway line. He skipped past two defenders and was about to shoot when he was tripped by a sliding tackle from a desperate defender. A penalty was immediately awarded and Greaves, who never lacked confidence, strode up and placed the ball in the back of the net. There was a tumultuous celebration; all the supporters suddenly came to life. The noise was deafening. Neither side looked as if they were going to score. Extra time was played, and it looked as if the match would be decided by a penalty shootout. So the match was petering out, a mist was descending on the wet and sticky surface, when suddenly there was a flare-up on the other side of the pitch. Johnnie Mortimore stood up and focused his field glasses. "It looks like somebody has been thumped; yes, one of the players is on the ground with a bleeding nose and there is a melee around him. Oh Christ, the supporters are flocking onto the pitch. I must get to the address system and get them off the pitch; this could turn nasty." Johnnie quickly made an announcement over the tannoy system telling all the supporters to get back off the pitch or else the match would be stopped and both clubs could be faced with expulsion and heavy fines. Gradually, they retired to the stands and peace was slowly restored. The Godstone player was given a red card and sent off; it was Jimmy Greaves, and finally the match continued. There were only five minutes to go, and the score was still standing at 1-1. The whistle blew. Both teams dropped onto the pitch exhausted. Bob learnt later that one of the Waterstone players kept upending Billy Steele and Jimmy felt the referee seemed to close his eyes to these offences, so in a fit of madness he ran over and punched the offending player in the face, splitting his nose.

"Well, it was unfair; poor little Billy was being fouled every time he got the ball. You can't stand by and let your mates be pushed around like that, can you?" Jimmy had a reputation of being hot tempered with a very short fuse. The local policeman, Sergeant Osborne, was a member of the supporters' club and had in the past helped to keep him out of trouble.

Bob did not have time to look into the fracas but was now preparing his team for the penalty shootout. Suddenly all went quiet. The referee approached the two captains; they tossed a coin and decided upon ends. It was a very tense moment; some of the crowd were covering their eyes. Again, it was level pegging at four goals each. Nat Lofthouse strolled up to take the fifth penalty. He hammered the ball straight at the Waterstone goalkeeper, who misread the kick and dived to his right. The ball hit the back of the net. So, the visitors placed the ball ready for their fifth attempt at goal; the ground was damp and slippery. The Godstone goalkeeper was very young but had played a blinder; he was due to leave the club to take up a sporting scholarship in Ireland, and so here it was, after 2 and a half hours, it would all now depend on this final kick, or would it?

The Waterstone penalty-taker was a bag of nerves; he took a long run and was about to kick the ball when, cruelly, he slipped and miskicked the ball. It reached the goal at half speed. The goalkeeper had no trouble in stopping the attempt.

The crowd went crazy. There was shouting and dancing. Suddenly all the pumped-up tension was released. It was all so disappointing for the visitors, who in long sessions of the game looked the better team. Rosemary turned to Bob. "Look, I must get home and take Freddie with me; he is getting to look very tired, so don't be late."

Johnnie Mortimore was in his element. The programme sales, the catering caravans and the bars all seemed to be doing a roaring trade.

Bob paid a visit to the changing room, congratulating all the players, and being splashed in the process. He finally had a brief chat with Jimmy Greaves, who had a terrible league record and was well known to all the referees. They all felt he could go a long way if he could control his temper. "Well, you know you will be hauled up before the FA disciplinary committee and be fined and banned from playing for possibly the rest of the season. There is a danger the club could be fined and disqualified from the FA Cup, meaning that Waterstone Wanderers could be awarded the match. Then, of course, you must realise you will be brought before the club's directors and your contract might not be renewed."

They were standing in the corner of the boot room. Jimmy stood with a bowed head. "Sorry, boss. I don't know what gets into me, but that bloke had it coming; he kept fouling and tripping up Billy, and the referee was bloody useless."

"Look, Jimmy, that's no excuse; you just can't take the law into your own hands."

"Yeah, you're right. I feel I let down the team."

"Well, you know the form; you could be fined and suspended. I am hoping the club doesn't get punished. Look, I can see you're upset. Get off home, have a quiet evening and stay out of trouble. Naturally, we will do what we can for you. Now, where is Billy Steele? I must have a quick word with him."

Chapter 12

Pat, with a heavy heart, decided it was time to get home; if she stayed much longer she would come under Edgar's spell. She could see that he had been through a rough patch. She had a shock when she got a message from Rosemary to say that Claude had been admitted to hospital with peritonitis.

"Look, I am about to come home. Yes, I'm feeling a lot better. Now, don't worry, but could you put a pint of milk in the fridge, and I could do with a loaf of bread. I must go and check the times of the trains."

"I am so glad you're feeling better. I can understand how you felt, but I think Claude needs you. I couldn't get a straight answer from the hospital. I'll give you a buzz tomorrow morning. Now I must go and check up on the arrangements for the next the luncheon... Yes, we are quite busy, but the margins are still narrow, and I am about to appoint a functions manager. Still, all news when I see you."

Edgar drove her to the station. It was very painful to bid him farewell. He had and always would be the great love of her life. There were tears in her eyes as she kissed him goodbye. He held her close and whispered in her ear, "I shall always love you. I wish it could have been different." As she looked out of the window and waved, she thought, *what a sad figure; how he has changed.* He had lost a lot of weight, his hair was now very thin and, if anything, he looked rather scruffy, but he had those beautiful blue eyes and a wonderful smile.

Well, she thought, *it's about time I got back home and put my life back together.* The news of Claude's admittance to St Mary's Hospital came as a big shock. *It's funny how one can love two men in different ways; still, one has to make a final choice.* She thought of her wedding vows, for better or for worse. As the train pounded towards Paddington, she started to make plans. She decided to try and get out of London back to the country again but not too far away from Rosemary. Then she would insist on more holidays; she had always wanted to visit Venice, and she would like a larger home so they could entertain friends.

Pat finally got home feeling tired, but any hostilities towards Claude had disappeared. She realised he had been a good husband but for the latest episode, so the first thing she did was to ring the hospital. It was now very late, and she spoke to a junior houseman. "Let me see; just give me a moment. You said Mr Dibbs? Sorry, Sir Claude Dibbs. I am not familiar with the case." After a few minutes, he said, "Yes, I've located his medical notes and the report states he is seriously ill and suffering from peritonitis. He has just been put in the life-support ward so all his bodily functions are being monitored, but ring tomorrow; the surgeon, Mr John Baxter, can give you an up-to-date report on his progress. I'm sorry to terminate this conversation but I shall be in hot water if I discuss this case, so please ring tomorrow. Good night."

Pat put down the phone. She looked at the post and decided to leave it. She went to bed feeling guilty and depressed, and had a restless night but finally drifted off to sleep dreaming of her childhood, the life on the farm in Devon. They were so poor. She was broken-hearted when her mother, who was like a big sister, ran off with a flashy Irishman, but they were a little better off when dad got a job on a large farm in Surrey. She was finally woken by the phone.

"Is that Lady Dibbs? This is St Mary's Hospital, and I am the surgeon, John Baxter, dealing with your husband. We have been trying to communicate with you over the past three days. I am pleased to report that Sir Claude had a very satisfactory night and we are taking him off life-support. He will be transferred to a private room. He has been seen by the gastroenterologist and we have carried out a series of tests using an endoscopic procedure. I have already carried out a small operation, which has stopped the internal bleeding. In brief, the linings of the stomach are splitting and he has a mild case of peritonitis. Look, I don't want to dazzle you with medical terminology, but we are worried he may develop sepsis, so I will need to carry out further investigations and remove some of the cancerous tissue in his stomach. Look, I am sorry, but I am just about to go into the operating theatre, so please make an appointment with my secretary for tomorrow then we can discuss this in more detail. I shall be operating on your husband in the morning."

o o o

Vicky was worried over the insurance claims regarding the pollution of the River Barle and the damage which had been inflicted on the salmon stocks. "Yes, I had a word with Neil. He expects a decision any day from the legal people, who will give their final opinion, but when he spoke to them recently they were very positive. He has also suggested I liaise with the River Authority. I gather they have carried out a survey on all the inlets which enter the River Barle to check for any additional pollution such as that poultry factory which, of course, was set up in the last six months. First, I really must pop over and see my sister Norma; she's always having a moan. Now she's living in the farmhouse she is complaining the garden is not large enough. I must get on. I do miss Rod; he could always see a job before it arose. I'm thinking of looking for an older man who is reliable and can take some of the pressure off me."

"I don't know what you're moaning about; you try running a house, bringing up a family and being a seamstress."

"Sorry, love. How's Renée?"

"I don't think very well. Really, very lonely. Yes, I know she's got a lot of friends but it's not the same. I think she is going to sell up and move down to Norwich to be near her niece, Susan. I shall miss her. She's slowly passing the whole business over to me and, really, I've got more work than I can cope with. I put up my prices last month and it has not put off any of our clients. It's certainly more lucrative than making curtains. These brides, and the mums, seem to want everything. Incidentally, changing the subject, Simon wants to be a weekly boarder next term; he says there are lots of things going on when he's not there. I know the girls will miss him; they both worship him. I better have a word with Edgar. I'm glad he's been found, but I've no idea what he's doing. I will try and ring him tonight and invite him up."

As Todd went into his office, he shouted, "I heard that Bella's coming back to live in the Manor next month; she's been in contact with Mrs Watts and asked her to come back for two days a week."

Vicky was opening up her post. "Oh goody, another cheque. I seem to be bringing in more money than you. I've taken on a young girl. I felt sorry for her, but she certainly can't cope with the difficult stuff. Really, I need an experienced seamstress, but they are impossible to find. Sorry to go rabbiting on.

"Yes, I heard about Bella. Still, I am pleased that Simon is happy. I heard that the numbers have been going down and this new head David Cassell who has just been appointed seems to be turning things around. He's quite young and rather dishy. I am so glad those accusations by those two boys were dropped. I gather he played rugby for Scotland."

"Really? What position?"

"How should I know? But I gather he's only been there two years and already things are picking up. Simon asked if he could bring two pals to stay for the weekend. Naturally, I said yes, but told them to bring their sleeping bags; the girls will love to see them."

"Before I forget, I didn't tell you I got the National Farmers' Association rep. looking in on Friday."

"What does he want?"

"They carry part of the insurance on the farm and I want to pick their brains. They also asked me to come and sit on the livestock committee to advise on pig breeding. I gather they're getting a lot of problems and are very short of experienced pig farmers. And don't forget next month: it's the county show and I'm showing some livestock, but I'm not very hopeful; the competition will be stiff."

Todd got up. "Well, I better go and pick up the girls. Thank goodness Simon's school has a parent close by."

"Yes," said Vicky, throwing the envelopes in the bin. "I must buy her a present at the end of term and try to help out." *Incidentally, I must give Renée a ring. I hope she is not seeing that awful man; he should be locked up. The trouble is, she is far too soft. I'll ring her tonight.*

Just after Todd left, the phone rang. It was a bride enquiring about her trousseau and asking for additional changes. *God,* thought Vicky, *these brides can never make up their minds.* The phone then went again. "Hello, Edgar here."

o o o

Renée was feeling better. She was lying naked in bed with Carlo. He was sleeping soundly, and she could feel his hot breath on her shoulder; it was so exhilarating. She thought back to her husband, Arthur, who was utterly useless, with a small weapon, but it never stopped him chasing the girls. *But then,* she thought, *he was spending my money. God, however did I get here again after the last tryst with Carlo when he became physically aggressive? I must be mad and must be careful.* He had come knocking on her door late at night with flowers and perfume and was tearful and made wild promises; she just could not turn him away. Suddenly he moved and opened those large sad brown eyes, and then he smiled. Just the sight of him made her heart melt. He was not good-looking but was tall, slim and certainly well-equipped. Renée felt aroused. He suddenly came to life and hopped out of bed. "Sorry, love; must go for a pee."

She lay on her back anticipating the joys of lovemaking and thinking of how they fell out; it was over buying a house together. She could hear the flush and suddenly he appeared and jumped into bed and ducked under the duvet. She could feel him exploring her body; she could feel him sucking her vagina. It was excruciating, it was heavenly, and then he suddenly moved up her body and she could feel him sucking her breasts. Her nipples went hard and then their lips touched, and it all happened. He was astride her. She had opened her legs and could feel his large penetration. It was joy of joys. He moved slowly. She could not remember having felt such ecstasy and then he dug deeper; this she found to be painful. "Slow down; you're hurting." But he continued to pound away. She bit her lip. He groaned; he was quickly coming to a climax. She suddenly felt pain and very sore and her libido seemed to wane, and then she felt all his hot juices flooding into her body but sadly she felt disillusioned and was now experiencing acute soreness. She rolled onto her side, regretting that she had allowed him into her bed; it had finished up being a disappointing and painful experience. He was soon on his side, snoring. In a flash, she could see him for what he really was: a selfish man only interested in his own personal needs and gratifications. Really, there was no future continuing this relationship. *This*, she thought, *was a big mistake. I really must get him out of my system, rid myself of him.* Her memories went back to when he knocked her around because she refused to buy a house for them to live in. *This is not going to be easy but I really must end this affair.* She had nearly a quarter of a million tied up in property and land which she never spoke of, but he had gone through all her private papers when she was out one evening and unfortunately he seemed to be in the picture. *I think I will try and appoint an attorney so that I need a second person to countersign my cheques. Yes,* she thought, *Vicky would be the most honest and sensible person to approach just in case I am put in a difficult position. Now, how do I get rid of that man? I shall have to think up some ploy.*

Early the next morning, showing no affection, Carlo quickly dressed. "I must not be late. I just started a new job."

"What job is that?"

"Oh, working for an insurance company. It's great. I am my own boss, on a very low basic wage, but the commissions are good."

"Well what do you insure?"

"In the main, household items – you know, Hoovers and fridges, TVs, computers; you name it, and we will insure it."

"Do you make an appointment?"

"No, it's cold selling. It's all going very well but, the trouble is, I got to wait a month before I get my commission and the basic wage is a joke."

Hello, thought Renée, *I know what he's after. I shall be ready.*

"Sorry I can't see you tonight; I've got some meeting with my solicitors to sort out my divorce. My ex is behaving like a cow; she took the house and now she's trying to take me to court for some outstanding maintenance. I tried to explain but, God, it's all getting me down. Then I got another part-time job in a pub; well, it's a sort of nightclub, but I'll be with you the following night... Oh, the job. Yes, I have to do the cleaning up. Bloody awful place; it is filthy, and we get some nasty types hanging around. The police seem to look in most nights."

Finally, Carlo left. *Now,* thought Renée, *I really must get that man out of my life.* She was kicking herself for allowing him back. She was about to ring Vicky regarding her predicament. She was also thinking of pulling out of the bridesmaid hire business and handing over the day-to-day operations to Vicky. She reached for the phone, when her niece, Susan, rang who was now recovering after a long session of chemotherapy, sadly. She lived in Norwich and rang to ask Renée down. She was back at work on a part-time basis and feeling better. After a long chat with Susan, she put the phone down and rang Vicky.

"Vicky darling, I just rang for a quick chat... Yes, I'm feeling much better... Oh, Carlo; he's the one I wanted to talk about. I think we should meet up this week, and there is one other thing on my mind."

"Well, now you've got me very intrigued."

"Look dear, I am getting old and I want to hand over the bridal hire business to you and just help out at special events and presentations. I will give you more shares and pay you a basic salary but if you're not happy..."

"No, no, I'm more than happy. Yes, you're right; we'll meet up and discuss the arrangements." They made a date to meet at the end of the week and parted on the friendliest terms.

Then Renée dealt with some general enquiries regarding a huge wedding; she was finalising dresses for four young bridesmaids. She made her way over to the shop to meet a bride's mother who had suddenly put on weight and needed urgent alterations to her costume. Renée used two other ladies to make alterations but had to spend time checking their work. The business was certainly thriving. She was in two minds whether to sell up. She had offers but they wanted her to stay on. Finally she made her way over to Stansbury's to see the bride's mother.

o o o

Carlo sat in his car and watched for Renée to leave. He knew she had an appointment and he was waiting for the opportunity to break into her bungalow. He knew there was no cleaner that day and the part-time gardener was on holiday. In no time, he slipped along her short drive, quickly found the key and was soon inside the building. The original mansion had been pulled down and there were now 12 bungalows in the old orchard.

Now, where has she hidden her cash? She had briefly mentioned that on occasion some of the fathers like to pay cash to avoid tax receipts and she gave them a big discount. Carlo quickly tore into the sitting room, ripping all the pictures off the walls, lifting the carpets, slashing open the soft coverings, but to no avail. After half an hour, he had moved quickly but with no success and he was now getting very agitated. Finally, he tackled the kitchen, where he struck lucky. It was under the kitchen sink; he noticed the floorboards were loose and he prized them up and there it was: a large biscuit tin. He pulled off the top and it was overflowing with bank notes.

By now he was sweating. He needed the money urgently to buy a fix. Unknown to Renée, he had been sacked by the Commonwealth insurance company – that silly woman had invited him in and given him the glad eye. When he took her up, she suddenly turned nasty, started to scratch him, so he smacked her. She complained to the insurance company and he was immediately dismissed. They did not want it reported to the police; this would avoid any adverse publicity. Having already served time for handling stolen goods, he realised he must be careful.

He found a large canvas holdall and emptied the notes into it and then quickly slipped out of the back door. Before he left, he placed a plug in the kitchen sink and turned on the taps. He thought that would flood the property, which might divert the attention of the police and destroy any evidence. As he slipped back to his car, he quickly realised the police would be looking for him, so he decided to ditch his old car and go to ground. *But I must get some dope.* He drove to a block of flats in a seedy part of town where he knew he could buy a fix; the thought of it excited him. He then decided to make his way to a row of deserted houses which were due to be knocked down for redevelopment; the trouble was, it was a meeting place of all the 'down and outs' and one needed to sleep with one eye open. The police knew of its whereabouts but showed no interest, so after ditching his car he was soon camped in a filthy little kitchen amidst rubble and dust with a bottle of cider, some bread and cheese and an envelope of white powder.

o o o

Renée was taking the measurements of the bride's mother's dress when the phone went. "Vicky here. I've got to come into town. Can we meet up for a coffee?"

"What a lovely idea. I shall look forward to that."

They were soon seated in a corner teahouse, smiling at each other.

Vicky picked up her coffee cup. "Now tell me all. I'm all ears."

Renée took a deep breath and opened up. After 15 minutes Vicky put down her empty cup. "Look, I can see you're very upset and I am here only to help."

Renée had a tear in her eye. "Darling, you're so kind. I have been a damn fool, but it will never happen again."

"I am not going to say the obvious, but if that terrible man comes near you again you must go to the police."

"Yes, yes, you're right; that's what I should have done. I know he's trouble and only after one thing, and that's my money. In fact, I think I'd better get home and check the house. I suddenly feel that I am not safe. I have been planning to go down to Norfolk to see my niece, Susan. Look, tonight I'll make a list of all the outstanding work and accounts and send them on to you. I will also write to my solicitor in the next couple of days and send you a copy."

Vicky squeezed Renée's hand. "Just one thing: how did you come to meet that dreadful man?"

"Well, it's rather a long story, but in a moment of madness I joined a very exclusive dating agency through a friend who is a member of the operatic society; she had met a very nice gentleman. So I went along with her idea and had dinner with three nice old chaps who had lost their other halves; they were all very dull but very kind. The trouble is, the exciting men are often the dangerous ones. I also came to realise that most of the clientele were poor but looking for a rich partner and, of course, this is what happened to me. I met Carlo; it must be six months ago. To start with he was very tender and thoughtful, although he never seemed to have any money. He disappeared for a time and then, like a bad penny, he's came back. We had a very unpleasant argument; he wanted me to buy a house in our joint names, which I refused. Still, I don't want to talk about it. I have been a complete fool and should never have seen him again."

Vicky frowned. "Now, don't worry about a thing; we can sort out everything when you get back from Norfolk, but do send me a copy of all the outstanding accounts and I will chase them up."

They finally kissed and Vicky drove to pick up the children.

Renée made her way back to her bungalow with a heavy heart. As she approached, she could see water was running out from under the front door. She flew inside to witness a complete disaster. The kitchen and all the downstairs rooms were under water. She splashed through to the kitchen and turned off the taps. She surveyed the drawing room; all the pictures had been ripped off the walls, the soft furnishings had been slashed. In fact, the place looked as if a bomb had hit it. Tears came into her eyes. *No, surely it can't be him; he would not treat me like this after all I have done for him. Well,* she thought, *there is only one thing I can do. I'll have to go to the police.* But she quickly made her way into the kitchen, which was under water, and leaned down under the sink. The boards had been displaced and she felt for the large biscuit tin and immediately knew it had been stolen. She stood and splashed her way out of the house and rang the police. They sent round a patrol car. By then the flood was starting to subside. In no time, she was in the police station making a statement. She came clean with them and felt the only person she suspected was Carlo Jones, if that was his name. She had very few details, but they recorded all the facts, including the insurance company he worked for. She then inspected the book of mug shots of known petty criminals but with no success. Finally, she went home and, after the police left, packed a case and spent the night in a local small hotel. The proprietor was a member of the operatic society of which she was an honorary vice president. Renée spoke to Vicky that evening, feeling very depressed, and broke down over the phone. They arranged to meet up at the bungalow the next morning and then she decided she would drive down to Norfolk for a few days. She spoke to her niece, Susan.

"Auntie, I can't wait to see you. I've been looking forward to this for a long time. Yes, I'm feeling much better and back at work only part-time." Renée did not mention her problems. The short chitchat made her feel so much better.

After a very hectic morning meeting Vicky and the domestic cleaning company at the bungalow, she gave Vicky some personal valuables for safekeeping then had a final word with the police and left them with her address. Vicky was very supportive. "Look, Renée, leave everything to me; we will soon put your house back together. I will change the locks, so don't worry about a thing, and I'll give you a ring and we can sort out all the business details when you get back."

o o o

Pat felt depressed. She unpacked and sorted out the post, which she placed on Claude's desk. She was just about to go shopping when Rosemary rang. "Look, could you do me a favour and come over and see to Freddie? I have just appointed a manager; he was the wine steward but, really, I think I moved too quickly."

"Yes, of course, I would love to come over, but I must look in and see Claude first. Don't worry about a thing. I shall enjoy looking after Freddie."

She had a marvellous afternoon. Freddie was a bright little chap and never seemed to stop asking questions. Rosemary got home late afternoon, tired but said the luncheon party for the East Cheam WRI went down well, although she was determined to appoint a new manager. "Yes, I made a mistake with the wine steward. Really, he is not up to the job, and the girls take advantage of him and, what with the baby due next month, I really must move quickly. Yes, I have him on a trial period, so my hands aren't tied."

"Now let me cook you a tasty supper."

"Would you? I'd love that. Bob is hoping to get home at seven. He's got so much to tell you. In fact, he's become quite a celebrity. I have to keep bringing him down to earth. Look, why not stay the night?"

"No, I must get back. If you are stuck, you know where I am. Now you go and bath Freddie and I'll get on with the supper."

There was no sign of Bob, so they decided to carry on. It was 10.30 p.m. when he finally made an appearance, looking very sheepish and smelling of drink. "Sorry, darling," he said, stumbling through the front door. "The chairman, Don Rowbotham, wanted to take us out for a drink and it was very difficult to say no. As you are aware, Ted Drake, the manager, is retiring at the end of the season and he has offered me the job. He also told me the club is on the market." Rosemary's eyes were now blazing.

"I'm not bloody interested. I've been slogging around all day and was expecting to have a nice family supper together. Quite frankly, I'd rather have you back as an electrician; at least you worked sensible hours instead of coming home half pissed."

"Darling, I'm doing this for you and Freddie so that we've got some future."

Pat knew Rosemary when pushed had a nasty temper and could be quite vicious. She moved towards the door and stretched for her coat. Rosemary jumped up. "Pat, you don't have to go just yet."

Pat kissed her. "I've got a lot to do. I will ring you tomorrow, but I must ring the hospital."

"Thank you," said Rosemary with tears of anger in her eyes. "He's so soft," she said as they parted at the doorway.

Pat shouted goodbye to Bob and made off home in her car. As she drove, she thought, *it's good at times to clear the air*, and then thought about Claude. *I must now try and mend the bridges, but he has got to give up that woman.*

o o o

Claire decided to make her way to London; she had a couple of pals who lived in Romford. She finally got to the station and when she went to buy the ticket she choked, "God, how much?" She was now in a spin and could not think straight.

"Look, miss, if you bought that a fortnight ago it would be much cheaper."

She finally laboured with the carrycot and the case onto the train. It was crowded with football supporters. An elderly man gave up his seat then made his way to the bar. After a long and uncomfortable journey, they arrived at King's Cross station. She was sitting in a café trying to have a cup of tea and feed Winston, when she looked up to see a fat woman with dyed blonde hair who caught her eye and smiled. In no time, the woman came across and spoke. "What a lovely boy, you seem to be lost."

"Well, I've got a close pal who lives in Romford, but for the moment I'm looking for a bed for the night."

The eyes of the woman lit up. "Maybe I can help you; my husband and his brother have a small hotel in Clapham. Well, it's really a boarding house; they help out Social Services for distressed families, that sort of thing."

Claire put down the bottle. "To be quite honest, I'm a bit short after the ticket from Newcastle."

"Don't fret; we can sort out a cheap rate for the night. Look, my hubby is coming over to pick me up. Why not come back with me and then you can make your way to Romford tomorrow."

Claire hesitated. "Well, yes, that would be a great help."

"What is your little boy called?"

"He's called Winston, and I shall be happy when I can settle him down for the night; it's been a long difficult day."

"Look love, I'm Beverley, and my man is Kennedy. I can see him coming," she said, jumping up. Suddenly, a tall West Indian of mixed parentage came bouncing up, smiling broadly with a gold front tooth and a goatee beard.

He then threw his arms around Beverley and kissed her full on the lips, squeezing her waist. She flustered as she pushed him away and gave Claire a half smile. "He is a real romantic," she said. She must have been in her early fifties, with chipped nail polish and wearing a dark coat and baggy trousers, whereas Kennedy looked to be in his early thirties, tall, muscular and wearing a white sweatshirt and jeans. She then explained to Kennedy, who turned his attention to Claire; she suddenly had that feeling that she must be careful. It was the way he looked at her and smiled. *No, I am not interested*, she thought. *I must try and put my life together.*

They were soon on their way to Clapham in a dirty noisy old van. Kennedy seemed to spend most of the journey squeezing Beverley's knee. "I've been missing you, baby. I wanted you so badly." Claire felt embarrassed and tried to break into the conversation.

"Look, I only want a bed for the night. I'll be no trouble and will be gone tomorrow."

"Look lady, you stay as long as you like. You have a good time, and you'll have lots of company. In fact, you'll have a great time; you just leave it to me."

Suddenly Claire was in two minds but decided to remain and view the accommodation. Winston was becoming very restless.

They finally arrived in a very run down and depressed area with large Edwardian buildings with dustbins standing outside most of the houses and an array of dirty children playing in the street. All the properties in the square had seen better days. Certainly, this was not what Claire had expected. They went up a short flight of steps. Kennedy carried the carrycot, waking up Winston, who started bawling.

Claire could quickly see she had made a big mistake; it was a glorified slum. It was dirty, smelt of cannabis and pee, there were prams, toys and cardboard boxes in the hallway and a group of noisy kids chasing up and down the stairs. Finally, Claire was shown to a small room on the first floor. There were no washing facilities but a bathroom down the corridor.

"Be careful when you light the geezer. You'll need a £2 coin; it can be difficult." She looked around the small bedroom with the stained carpets and soiled wallpaper. It was all very basic, just a single metal bed and a chest of drawers, and there were wire coat hangers on the back of the door. Claire suddenly felt depressed. *Surely things can't get worse.*

Beverley looked in. "I'll bring you some supper later. Sorry, but the lock on the loo door is broken, so be careful. I got a nice bit of quiche left over with some veg. and I'll see if I can find you a glass of wine." The thought of the quiche certainly did not excite her. *But tomorrow I shall be off. Another night here is the last thing I want.*

She hardly touched the light supper. It was disgusting, and the wine was sour. After putting Winston to sleep, she finally got into a damp bed with a lumpy mattress and tried to get off to sleep. It was a very noisy house, with frequent shouting and the sound of music, but she did finally get off. It was in the very early hours when she was awakened on hearing a key in the lock. The door slowly opened to a dim figure; by the half-light she recognised Kennedy. He looked naked except for a pair of boxer shorts. Claire sat up in bed, very frightened.

"Look, if you don't go I will scream."

"Baby, baby, I want to give you a good time. You'll love it. I've got some mates who want to meet you."

"Get out before I start to scream."

"No, no, don't be like that. I don't want to hurt you. I thought we could have a good time."

"Look, this is my last warning; if you don't go now I promise I'll scream."

The next moment he hit her across the face with the back of his hand. She fell back, cricking her neck.

"Look lady, let's be friends. I don't want to hurt your baby."

Suddenly the threat of Winston being harmed sent Claire into a spin. She started to think quickly and a desperate plan evolved in her mind.

By now Kennedy was pulling down his boxer shorts exhibiting a large erection in the half light. "Look, you lay on your back and then we can have some fun, cos I wanted you when I first saw yer."

Claire spoke softly. "Look, if we have sex, I want to be on top; you lie on the bed and I will come on top of you."

"Okay lady, but you finish on the bottom and then you can give me a blow job." She could smell his sweaty body and the alcohol on his breath but, unknown to him, she had a long pair of sharp scissors in the drawer of the bedside locker. The plan was now taking shape and she was determined to see it through.

The thought of dear little Winston was in the back of her mind. She was soon riding up and down. She could hear him grunting. "Quicker, baby quicker Holy Jesus, this is heaven." As she came down, she reached over and picked up out of the drawer the large pair of scissors and opened them up. Then, holding them up in both hands, she came down with all the force she could muster and drove the scissors into his chest. They seemed to hit a rib, so she wriggled them and they sunk deeper into his body. He suddenly roared, pinched her bottom and, after a deep groan, went still.

She got off his motionless body. He was now unconscious. *No,* she thought, *I just don't want to know. No man takes advantage of me.* She looked in the corner and little Winston was sound asleep snoring quietly. Claire dried herself and, after all that happened, felt quite calm.

The door slowly opened and Beverley's head appeared. Claire put on the light and then Beverley came in and let out a loud scream. Kennedy was lying on the bed with blood all over his chest and the handle of the scissors standing erect. "What have you done to him? He only wanted some fun; he likes a threesome. What am I going to do without him?" She then screamed out in agony and the next moment the room seemed to fill up with a host of people scantily dressed; it all seemed surreal.

In no time, the police arrived and Claire was arrested. She spent the night in a prison cell after giving a detailed explanation to a lady police sergeant. Social Services sent over an officer and took Winston away to a children's home.

"What I can't understand is, if he raped you, why were you on top? It doesn't seem to add up. What did you say? He threatened to bring in some pals? You were hardly defending yourself, and who is the father of your little boy?" So Claire explained to the lady police sergeant about Winston and the rape by Kennedy and she seemed satisfied.

"Well, Claire, I believe part of your story. We all know of Kennedy. He has a record and is wanted for questioning regarding a serious assault on an old lady. He's nothing more than an animal. Look, I am going to support your testimony, but your little boy sadly will be placed in a care home with Social Services for the time being, but you must appreciate this is a manslaughter charge so you will receive a custodial sentence, but all the extenuating circumstances will be taken into account.

Chapter 13

Christopher Barrington had taken up the reins of chief general manager whilst Claude was off sick. He was tall and slim with a head of grey hair and had dark brown eyes. He was avoided by his peers due in part to his sarcastic manner. He was slowly making his presence felt and immediately started to implement Claude's innovations, in particular the risk assessment team. He studied a complex report, which in the main would speed up the decision-making process. He set up an experienced team under Lawrence Davies to implement these changes. He then dismissed two general managers and an assistant who Claude felt were not up to the job; they did not want a sideways move so he retired them on a full pension. Then he overhauled the areas of responsibility for senior managers but continued with the monthly executive meetings where all the general managers could be cross-examined. This had been started by Philip Beaumont and when Claude chaired the meetings it became very lively; he could be very outspoken. In fact, they all dreaded these meetings.

Barrington then turned his attention to reports from three highly respected economic research organisations warning of a serious decline in financial growth. The bank paid good money for these reports; they were untainted and in the past were found to be surprisingly accurate in assessing the long-term economies of the major trading nations. He underlined in green ink areas of concern and passed them over to the Wealth Management Adviser. He employed a small research team known as the 'Think Tank' and wanted a report on their observations, with particular reference to the bank's fiscal policies.

Barrington had a very busy first month. He addressed the AGM of the Shareholders Association in the Great Hall in

Westminster; there were 450 delegates and in the main it went off smoothly. This was due to the Chairman, Sir Peter Lipton, who was excellent on these occasions; he had a slight Brummie accent and a tall commanding presence. He was called on to make a report on the past year's trading position and then fielded questions. Sir Peter was very adept and quickly silenced a small hostile group of shareholders, for which he received some applause. He then invited the guest speaker, the assistant governor of the Bank of England, to address the meeting. It all passed off smoothly, helped with a finger buffet and a glass of wine.

Barrington called in the reports from the legal department concerning the bank clerk who had complained that her manager, Ken Sturtridge, had tried to rape her. She was threatening to take legal action and, after studying all the reports, in particular from the security officer, Gareth Jones, and a firm of barristers, he decided to dismiss the claim. It would seem from their testimonies they were in collusion. He wrote a pungent note to the Manager of the legal department dealing with the matter.

There was a buzz in the City that a small Scottish bank, the Perth and Mallaig, had to be bailed out by the government with a large loan, and a building society based in Runcorn with 23 branches was in acute difficulties. He asked his security officer for more details.

Barrington was very secretive and a mystery. It was known he was a bachelor and at any of the bank's social functions he was usually absent. It was reported that he had an elderly mother who was an invalid and needed a full-time nurse. He had allowed this rumour to circulate, but his mother had died five years previously. It was not known that he had a darker side to his life; he was a member of an exclusive art club which was a front for a mixed culture of adults involved in an extensive range of erotic activities. The police knew of their existence, but they had some very influential members, including a senior police officer who was able to cover their tracks. To protect their members, they employed a gang of thugs who were on occasions used to carrying out clandestine duties. The Art Society had access to a wide catchment of accommodation across the south-east. He was very thrilled the society was holding an exhibition of fine art with a talk in the house of the President, and a party was to follow at a local hotel. It was all very low-key and open only to members. He was so excited. He had just changed partners and had met Jeremy at an open evening to welcome possible new members. He was an ex-public schoolboy in his early thirties, married with two children, and had a drink problem and some very expensive habits. He had just been dismissed from an exclusive City firm of land agents because he frequently arrived back in the afternoon smelling of drink, and this was becoming common knowledge. After three warnings, they decided reluctantly to dismiss him. He was now looking for money. In short, his life was in a mess, with debts everywhere and no income. His wife was threatening to leave and take the children. He had attended a range of clinics to combat his drinking problems but, sadly, he always 'fell off the wagon'. Jeremy was quite tall and had been good-looking but was starting to age. He was losing his hair, his eyes had lost their sparkle; he carried stubble on his chin, and was starting to look scruffy. Barrington felt sorry for him and decided to see his tailor and introduce him as his nephew and fit him up with some smart clothes.

As he sat in the back of the hired car, he thought about his last partner, Michael, who had become difficult and demanding. In short, he was trying to blackmail him. Sadly, it was time for him to be warned off, but he did have a great shock when he went to visit him in hospital. He had spoken to the chairman, an old Polish Jew with a chain of betting shops who had a very unsavoury reputation, but he quickly pushed those grim pictures from his mind and became excited at the thought of meeting up with Jeremy.

He cast his mind back to the early days and his great love, Edward. They had known each other for 18 years. They met when he was in his late twenties. He was engaged but his fiancée ran off with another man, much to his satisfaction. Edward was an accountant, married, with a grown-up family of two sons; the elder was only two years younger than himself. They met up twice a week in a small flat which Edward owned the lease on but suddenly it all came to an end when he was swiftly admitted to hospital after a serious bout of heart attacks; he was 78. It was a very sad moment when his wife left them together to say their farewells.

He was so looking forward to the National Art Society autumn event; they had arranged a talk on the historic gardens of the Italian lakes. There was quite a good attendance and, after a noisy start, with all the kissing and hugging, they had an interesting presentation then retired to a local hotel. There must have been 25 in the group. They were all very conservatively dressed and arrived in mixed groups but quickly joined together as long lost friends, with the usual shouting. They sat together to enjoy a sumptuous dinner served with a variety of wines; nothing was spared. It was starting to get late when the guests slipped away in their hired cars.

"Would you like to come back for a nightcap?"

"Yes, why not; that certainly was a magnificent dinner. Your members live well," said Jeremy, slipping on his old anorak.

They finally got back to Barrington's rented apartments, the top floor of a small exclusive block of flats.

"I am so glad you enjoyed the evening. We must do this more often," he said as he hung up Jeremy's anorak. "I am just going next door to put on something less formal. I must take off this monkey suit," he said, untying his bow tie.

"Look, I won't be a moment. Do have a drink; you'll find everything you want in the cocktail cabinet, and I've got some rather upmarket cocaine, but am careful: it is pure."

Jeremy was soon snorting the white powder and, after a large whiskey, started to lie back, but was in for a big surprise when after half an hour a well-dressed lady entered the drawing-room. She had long blonde hair, was beautifully made up, wearing a close-fitting red blouse and a short miniskirt and high heels. Jeremy was dozing on the couch when he awoke and quickly sat up.

"Hello, stranger. Just call me Angela." She had a very soft voice and slid over to him, wrapping her arms around his neck. She kissed him on the lips. Jeremy looked amazed.

"Now," said Angela, pressing her body into him. "I know you have got problems; let's sit down and you tell me all about them."

They continued to drink and snort the white powder off the back of their hands. Jeremy let forth with all his anxieties; his wife had just left him with his two children and had run off to her mother. "Yeah, I got unfairly fired; the office manager is always tight. In fact, we do a lot of our business in that pub and, yeah, they still owe me some commissions, which I'm chasing them for. Been a bit under the weather of late; my ticker's been playing up and this worry doesn't help. I get so depressed and I haven't got anybody to help me," he said with tears in his eyes.

Angela leaned forward and squeezed his knee. "You've got me now. We'll soon get you better, darling." He could smell her fragrant perfume and leaned over and kissed her on the cheek.

Finally, laughing at nothing, they slowly dragged themselves into the adjoining bedroom and climbed into a large double bed. They were scantily dressed and in a dopey state of intoxication, and in a matter of minutes they were both out for the count.

Barrington woke with a start and sat up. He had a dry, ill-tasting mouth and a splitting headache. *I am too old for this.* He looked across to Jeremy, who was lying on top of the covers not moving. Suddenly, he felt something was wrong. He tried to shake him, with no success. He jumped out of bed and rolled him onto his back and tried some artificial respiration, but he felt cold and he knew Jeremy was dead, stone dead. *My God, what the hell shall I do?* He looked at his watch; it was nearly 4 o'clock. He started to flap. *I must do something; this is the last piece of publicity I or the bank wants.* He wracked his brains and the only person he could think of was the chairman, Peter Abrahams, the old Polish Jew who he disliked intensely.

"Yes, what do you want? Do you know what the time is? It better be bloody urgent as I am just about to put the phone down... A body – did you say a body? Look, you better tell me, but make it quick."

After a very brief report, Peter Abrahams quickly took the lead; he was a man not to trifle with.

"Yes, I can see the problem; this is a job for the Black Tigers. Now, listen to me carefully; you must move swiftly. They will come and remove the body and dispose of it, but you must realise this is a very expensive exercise. It will cost you in the region of £20,000. Now, in a moment, put the phone down and I will ring them. Time is important before people get about. Now, there are no names, all money payments are in cash and this conversation has not taken place. I'm just introducing you to a business colleague... Yes, I want you to resign from the art club and not to communicate with any of our members; it will be better for all concerned. Now, goodbye; you won't hear from me again."

The phone suddenly went dead but much had been achieved. Barrington had a gut feeling this problem was not going away.

Twenty minutes later he had a call from a man with a strong Polish accent. They arranged to meet near the lift at the rear of the flats; he would bring a transit van and an invalid chair. A price was agreed over the phone, the final figure being £30k, all payments to be made in cash, no names or receipts, and payments made in three stages. He readily agreed to these terms.

Two men arrived wearing white uniforms and the operation proceeded efficiently. There was no conversation but they seemed to speak to each other in Polish and were gone within 15 minutes.

Barrington's mind was now reeling. *I must make a plan. He will be reported missing in no time and then the police will be knocking on my door and possibly searching these premises.* He decided later in the day to ring the domestic cleaning company and arrange for them to carry out their weekly clean but, on second thoughts, he decided he would instruct them to give the apartment a 'spring clean'. Then he made a methodical search and found a sock and a handkerchief belonging to Jeremy. He disposed of the remaining cocaine and cleaned all the surfaces with an alcohol cleaning agent. As he sat back drinking a cup of tea, he could not believe how swiftly these events had taken place. After due consideration, he decided it would be prudent to go into work and carry on as normal. He continued to ponder his predicament and realised his biggest mistake was disposing of the body and if this came to the notice of the police it would be prison. So he decided not to lie about his private life. Yes, he had a wardrobe of ladies' clothes and some strange friends and, yes, Jeremy had come back for a nightcap and then left after ringing for a taxi, but this was not an offence.

Barrington finally locked up the flat, including the two locks on the wardrobe door, and made his way home to his house in Golders Green, and after a shower and a light breakfast was collected by the hired car and made his way to the London and Edinburgh, where he was now busy as the acting Chief General Manager.

He was soon in the thick of it. His in-tray was snowed under with work; he started off with a string of new initiatives to be discussed by the strategic planning committee. He had a meeting with the executive committee of the shareholders which included General Harding. They were becoming very vociferous and threatening not to support any of the present directors in the next bout of elections by putting up their own candidates. He also wanted to monitor a shortlist of large companies who were in difficulties to see if they were adhering to the remedial structures set up by the bank. It was late in the day, which had been hectic; General Harding had been very outspoken. He was just packing up his desk when he had a call from New Scotland Yard.

o o o

Pat finally was able to see Claude in hospital; she felt very apprehensive. She had a session with Mr John Baxter, the surgeon. He was very optimistic in his prognosis but emphasised that Sir Claude needed a strict diet and should avoid any unnecessary stress. Pat entered his room and found him dozing in an armchair. He slowly looked up and smiled. She flew over and embraced him and was so shocked to see how ill he looked. He was pale, gaunt and seemed to have lost a lot of weight. He looked up with a tear in his eyes. "Sorry, Pat. I feel I've let you down." His hands were shaking; it was so unlike him. Pat sat on the side of the bed and held his hand.

"Oh darling, I was wrong to run away like that; still, let's put the past behind us. The big thing is to get you better, but there is just one promise I want from you: I can't go on if this were to happen again. Promise me that you won't see that woman again, although I can't really say that I've been an angel of late but,"

"Yes, yes, Pat. I promise. She has already broken off our friendship." He picked up a glass of water and had a gulp.

Pat leaned over and kissed him on his forehead. "Now let's change the subject. I had a long chat with Mr John Baxter, such a nice man. He hopes at the end of the week, if you're feeling better, you should come home." Claude started to nod his head. She could see he was very tired, as if he was under heavy sedation. As she spoke, he closed his eyes. The next moment, his head lolled onto his chest and he slipped into a light sleep, just as the nurse looked in.

"I think we better get him back to bed. If you could just give us a few minutes, I will give you a call."

Pat eventually left the hospital feeling very sad. She could see that Claude was ill and would need a lengthy period of convalescence. She had a guilty conscience and decided to look over and see Rosemary and possibly be on hand for the next few days. She could make herself useful. Rosemary was about to enter hospital to have her baby which was due any time. Pat felt she must be careful. There was a ripple of tension between Bob and Rosemary. They both had careers which seemed to clash. She could see both points of view but was fully aware that it would be dangerous to get involved.

"Pat, of course, I would love to see you. I'd be so grateful if you could come over. I seem to be up to my neck with seeing to Freddie, making sure the luncheon club is fully manned. In fact, I felt like chucking the whole thing in last week, and that wine manager is a waste of space, utterly useless. And, you know, he is married with a young family and I heard he is carrying on with one of the waitresses. Still, I'm just about to appoint a new manageress. I've got a very good lady lined up; she is not cheap, but she won't put up with any nonsense. The trouble is, it's difficult to find reliable staff, and some of these young waitresses seem to be sex mad."

"Rosemary, leave it all to me. When is your next function?"

"Yes, in two days' time, in a church hall in Redhill. It's a 40th wedding anniversary, all very low-key, just a few drinks and a finger buffet."

"Well, that seems like a doddle. I can see your new manageress will have no difficulties."

"Incidentally, did I tell you that Steph is hoping to come over from New York next month? She is now married and wants to start a family and can't wait to see Freddie."

"Look, I'll be over later this evening... No, after supper; I don't want to get in the way."

"No, no, you'll be a godsend. I think I'll be going into hospital soon, any day, and really Bob's got a lot on his plate... Yes, he seemed to be enjoying being the acting manager and, of course, the fundraiser; the players always ringing up. He's become a long-suffering uncle but he loves it, although I do get a bit browned off with some of the demands they make. Still, I mustn't bellyache. Look, I'll see you later. Don't bring anything; the house is full of food. Sorry, I never asked how Claude is."

"Not too good but I'll explain all when I see you."

Pat enjoyed helping Rosemary, who could have mood swings, and with the advent of the baby became very short tempered. She was now dashing between the hospital and Rosemary; it was so nice to be wanted. She felt sorry for Bob who was now trying to be a dutiful husband, and had to bite her tongue when Rosemary started to be difficult. Dear Freddie was a joy; he had Bob's passive temperament. He was getting on well and shooting up, and started to take an interest in football. Bob would take him down to watch the Godstone team practise and to the matches; he became the unofficial mascot and all the players doted on him.

Then finally Rosemary was rushed into hospital. Bob was in the middle of a training session with Freddie but he dropped everything and rushed to the hospital. Pat went in the ambulance and it all happened so quickly in the back of the ambulance on the way to Reigate hospital. A dear little girl was born with very little effort; she just seemed to pop out and in no time was in Rosemary's arms. They were both crying with joy. The baby was soon making its presence known with a powerful pair of lungs. Rosemary looked up at Pat with tears in her eyes. "I want my baby named after you; you have been more than just a sister, really. You have been a mother to me, the mother I never had. They both continued to cry in each other's arms; with little Pat nestled between them.

Rosemary looked up. "I'm sorry I've been a bit of a cow of late."

Pat squeezed her hand. "Now don't worry, but try to make it up to Bob."

"Yes, I know, but now I've got a complete family with two little mouths to feed, I will turn over a new leaf." Pat decided not to offer any advice; it never went down well and probably she wouldn't take any notice.

Bob rushed into the hospital wearing his tracksuit, closely followed by Freddie. He soon had Rosemary in his arms, kissing her. He was over the moon, and then was handed little Pat. He kissed her softly. There were tears in his eyes as he looked down at Rosemary.

"I'm so proud of you; I've never felt so happy."

Chapter 14

Edgar felt he was sliding into a rut. The days, then the weeks, were sliding past. Both Lord Marchant and Reverend Tom Owen tried to talk some sense into him, but he seemed to have lost his way; he'd abandoned his sense of purpose. Vicky was worried, and his son Simon avoided him when he came up to stay. Edgar was starting to let go and was neglecting his personal hygiene. Although Henry Marchant looked in to see him, Elizabeth, his wife was more outspoken. "For God's sake; don't invite that man in for another supper. He stinks and always seems to be drunk. Someone needs to give him a good talking to."

"Yes, I agree. I'll have a word with Tom Owen. He has a very outspoken daughter, Jennifer, who I met briefly. I think she would get him to pull up his socks."

Edgar started to turn off his telephone so no one could communicate with him, but early one afternoon he heard a loud banging on the front door and opened it to see his sister, Rita, and with no more ado she brushed past him into the cottage. "My God, you look a mess. Why the hell do you keep turning off your phone? I've been trying to contact you over the last three days, and look at you. Quite honestly, you look like a tramp, and this place, it stinks. It's about time you gave it a clean-up and emptied these bins." She stepped into the kitchen still slightly out of breath. "This food looks to me as if it's on the turn. It's about time you washed up and swept the floor. I've never seen you in this state. Whatever would Heather say if she could see you like this? She would be thoroughly ashamed." She continued to lecture him. "You've got no excuses. We all have had our problems. I've certainly had enough crises in my life. It's about time you looked at yourself. At the moment you're no use to anyone and…"

Edgar suddenly had an opportunity to get a word in. He was standing rather unsteadily, having consumed a quantity of liquor. "Yes, I know; you are right and when I am sober I feel ashamed of myself. Thank you for coming over. I must try." He started to stutter. "Yes, I must try and give up the drink. I have not felt very well of late and I don't want to be a nuisance to anyone."

"Right," said Rita, taking off her coat and rolling up her sleeves. "You are coming home with me. I'll soon put you on the straight and narrow, but before we go we must tidy up this cottage. I feel ashamed to leave it in this state, so first throw all this old food into the bin and take it out, then you can sweep the floor and I will start on the bedroom."

"Incidentally," said Edgar, picking up a mouldy loaf of bread, "how are the job interviews going for Doug's appointment in Australia? What was it? To be an archdeacon? I remember you were all so excited and..."

Rita was bustling towards the bedroom. "He did not get that appointment. Look, I'll tell you later, but he is still going to take up a position out there, possibly as a rural dean. Let's get this place licked into shape and then I really must get home; we have choir practice tonight and I must see to the boys."

After 40 minutes the place looked cleaner and the smell of the polish made it feel more habitable. Edgar packed a case, left a note, and they were soon in Rita's car speeding back to Hampshire.

Edgar soon started to pick up, staying with Rita and her husband Doug, who was a quiet chap, very dedicated and hard-working, and the boys Freddie and Colin were delighted to see him; they soon had him in the park playing football. Rita sent him off to buy a set of clothes.

He soon became quite popular in the parish, helping to run the book stall at the church fete and giving a hand painting the kitchen in the parish hall, and helping to cut the grass in the graveyard. The boys always wanted constant attention; the younger one, Colin, was a slow learner and he spent much time helping him with his reading; the elder boy, Freddie, who was three years older, was bright, and Rita had been hoping to get him into New Milton high school, but her plans were changing by the day.

Edgar rang Lord Marchant, who was very friendly. "Yes, we have missed you. It's great that you haven't touched a drop. I attended the regimental dinner recently; it went down well. In fact, it got a bit out of hand so we all stayed the night, but really I must follow your lead. Oh, incidentally, I had a call from Tom Owen; do give him a ring – he was very concerned about you."

Edgar suddenly took on a new lease of life. He came to respect Doug; although he lacked any personality, he could see that he was highly regarded by his parishioners. He made contact with Philip and was sorry to hear that his mother, Joan, had passed away. He also learnt that Maggie's husband was in hospital. It would seem that Wadham Developments was not too heavily involved in building projects but was busy buying and selling sites. Sally Bridgeman, the agent, had built up a large land bank; she had purchased sites on spec. and Philip, the architect, was skilled in obtaining planning approvals. It would seem that Wadham Developments was progressing very smoothly. Edgar still owned 51% of the shares, the other directors being Maggie, Philip and Sally Bridgeman. He decided to sell his shares and gave the directors first refusal; they jumped at the opportunity. He spoke to his solicitor, John Phillips, and instructed him to draw up the contracts and send them on to his bank, after which he arranged to drive Tom Owen to Scotland to a 'retreat'.

Edgar returned to Hannington Cottage feeling like his old self. He collected Tom Owen for their journey to the sanctuary on the Isle of Mull. He was starting to look very frail. They made the drive north and spent a night in Carlisle. Finally, they reached Scotland and took the ferry across to the Isle of Mull to the Abbey of the Sacred Heart. Tom had been very good company; he could be very witty and had over the years added to his income by his writings under a pseudonym. They arrived hungry and tired but met the Abbot, who seemed to lack any sparkle, but he discussed the work of the community and finally they bowed their heads for a short prayer. After a very basic meal in an empty refectory they were then shown to their rooms; it was all very Spartan, with stone floors. They saw two monks with bent heads sneaking along a corridor which was very dimly lit and rather depressing. Edgar was in two minds about leaving and finding alternative accommodation and taking Tom home at the end of his stay. There were three services and two meals a day, but it was all very basic. Edgar felt very tired so decided to stay the night and review the situation the next day.

o o o

Rita was getting excited about the big move to Australia the following month. Although Doug had just missed out on the appointment of Archdeacon near Perth, they had been approached to take over the living of a small parish in north-west Sydney. They were now busy making plans, packing essential clothing and making arrangements to have the furniture collected and put in a container for the big move. Rita was still teaching part-time and was discussing the move with Doug when the phone went. She picked it up.

"Tom, nice to speak to you. Edgar has often spoken about you. Are you still up in Scotland? That must've been a long journey... Sorry, did you say dead? No, you must be wrong." Suddenly tears came to her eyes and she started to cry. "It can't be true; surely not Edgar. He was staying here only last week." She gulped. The tears were running down her cheeks. "My darling Edgar is dead. It can't be," she shrieked out with grief. Doug jumped up and took the phone. Rita continued to cry and scream. "No, no, it can't be. Whatever will I do?" she shouted.

Doug spoke to Tom. "Whatever has happened?"

"Look, I am sorry, but Edgar was found dead in his room this morning."

"Oh no, whatever happened?"

"Well, the police are here but it would seem he took an overdose of sleeping tablets and then had a mini stroke which caused heart failure, but all this needs to be confirmed."

Rita was crying softly. She suddenly jumped up and rushed out of the room, slamming the door. She flew up the stairs to the bedroom. Doug could hear her screaming with grief.

"Edgar was so fond of you both and often spoke of Rita."

"This is terrible news. Rita and Edgar were so close. Goodness, we will miss him. My two sons worshipped him. Look, sorry, I must go to my wife; she needs me."

"Just one final thing; if you could communicate with his friends I would be most grateful."

"Yes, yes, I'll see to that. Sorry, but must go."

Doug quickly ran up the stairs to find Rita lying on the bed sobbing. She spoke in a halting manner. "Whatever happened? He left here so well and happy. Look, ring up my school; I just can't face teaching this afternoon, and then I'll give you a brief list of calls, but you must ring Pat. They were so fond of each other." She then burst into tears.

"Shouldn't we wait for some formal confirmation before we embark on telling everyone?"

"I don't know. I can't think straight, but ring up the police; they should know."

They finally got official verification from the West Scotland Constabulary. Poor Rita was looking drained. She kept breaking down.

"Darling, go and lay down and then I will ring Pat and then Maggie."

Pat picked up the phone. "Lovely to hear from you, Doug. Rita did mention you may be going to Australia with the church. I bet the boys are excited... What was that? You got some bad news about Edgar? What are you talking about?"

"Yes, I am sorry, but it's Edgar."

"Well, what about Edgar?"

"I don't know how to put this, but he is dead."

"Did you say dead? I only saw him, what, three weeks ago, and he looked fine."

"Sorry, but he had gone up to Scotland with the Reverend Tom Owen to stay at an Abbey on the Isle of Mull for a few days."

"Yes, I know Tom, but you must have got this wrong. Oh my God, if it's true, I've lost one of my dearest friends. I know it can't be." He could hear her starting to weep. The news suddenly seemed to sink in, and the cries became louder. "Edgar, Edgar, whatever's happened?" she spoke in desperation. "Whatever happened?"

"We have had it confirmed by the police. It's all very vague, but he was found in his room at the Abbey of the Sacred Heart; it is a retreat for the clergy to give them the opportunity for peace and meditation. I do know of it; it's all very primitive." By now Pat was crying softly.

"Is your husband there? Can I have a quick word with him please?"

"Yes," she said suddenly, shouting.

Doug had a short chat with Claude Dibbs. "I am so sorry. He was a real friend. He came to my help when I had some problems. Look, if there's anything I can do..."

"No, I think Pat needs you, but if I do have any problems I will come back to you, if I may."

Doug then turned to ring Vicky, who was out. He then rang Maggie, the secretary of Wadham Developments. Edgar still owned 51% of the shares, which he was in the process of selling to the partners. She was very shocked but said she would inform all his friends.

o o o

Vicky was devastated and was worried how she was going to break the news to Simon. He was now attending Downton College. He had performed well in the entrance exams but had been interviewed by the school prior to being offered a place. The competition had been fierce, and a quarter of the pupils came from overseas. Vicky decided it would be sensible to speak to him at the weekend. He had grown in confidence and physically had shot up and was nearly six feet. He was very popular with all his mates, and enjoyed the new environment, had a wide range of interests and enjoyed being a weekly boarder. Todd listened to Vicky and was of the opinion that she should be the one to speak to him. Todd was busy seeking planning approval to build a poultry unit; he had studied the market and the cost of rearing the birds and was confident it would show a good return. The pig rearing unit was plodding along and making a small return. It had 42 farmers in the scheme and Drysdale Meats, although they had been sold to a West German company, were still trading under the same name. He was dealing with their agent, and it was all working smoothly. Vicky was still fretting over the pollution of the salmon stocks in the River Barle. Neil, the solicitor, had taken legal opinion from an eminent QC and the findings were in his favour, in short the insurance company was responsible for the claim, but again it was still not fully proven. As the initial policy was with the National Farmers' Association who had placed the cover with the Three Cities insurance company, Todd was taking action against the NFA, who were now sounding more positive, although the Three Cities insurance company were dragging their feet. Todd still remembered Neil's comments: "This will be a long, drawn-out case but I am pretty confident you will get 90% of your claim."

Vicky had a phone call from Renée who was staying with her niece. "Vicky, how are you and how is the business?"

"Well, as you know, I had this very friendly letter from Robert Stansbury stating the five-year lease on our part of the shop was up and they would like to take it back, but they were keen for us to continue with the wedding hire business and they would like to employ us. As you appreciated at the time, I was a bit shocked, but have been informed that they are within their rights to terminate the lease, I was not sure what to do, but as you suggested I got on to Chope's and they have come up trumps."

"Yes, Vicky, I could clearly see your dilemma. Robert is a nice chap, but I think money is tight and he assumes we are making large profits. I am so pleased that Chope's have stepped in with the same conditions. But look, if you get problems I do know the MD, Fred Bromley; his sister had a beautiful singing voice and..."

Suddenly Vicky cut in. "Sorry Renée, how are you and when can we expect you back? We are all missing you."

"Well Vicky, dear, I've never felt better, and I've got a lovely man in my life. It was through my niece; his daughter is one of her pals. I can't wait to introduce him to you. He's about my age and plays the trumpet in the local brass band. He worked for the council; I think he was in highways, but, look, I'll be back next week. I have finally decided to sell the house and move down here. In fact, I have already had an offer from a friend. I couldn't live there again, and I love Norwich and I'll be near my niece. Look, we can discuss all this next week, but it is time for me to retire and Ben and I have lots of plans." Vicky finally had a chat about her children, Charlotte, Heather, and Simon, and they arranged to meet up the following week. She felt so sad when she put the phone down. Renée had always been a tower of strength. The thought of her retiring made her feel very depressed.

Vicky brightened up when she took a call from Rod.

"Have you moved yet?"

"What do you mean?"

"Well, the farm, of course."

"No, we move next month. It's just outside Chard in Somerset. It's a county council farm but at the moment we are living with mum and she is not very well. Gloria, as you know, is pregnant and is blooming and just about to give up work. We would love to come up and see you all, but we are so busy. I was so sorry to hear of Edgar's death and, of course, our thoughts are with Simon." They had a long chat, catching up on mutual friends, and Rod promised to try and come up to see them after the big event.

o o o

Bob was so excited with the birth of his baby daughter; he received congratulations on all fronts. It was the big day of the Cup draw. He got over to a packed clubhouse; it seemed that half of Godstone was there. On their journey in the competition they had beaten Waterstone Wanderers, but only just; it was very close and was decided by a penalty shoot-out. Bob had never seen so many people in the clubhouse; it was bursting with supporters and there were crowds outside in the stands. The local TV shop Phillips had set up large screens inside and a larger one outside. Bob was virtually carried in and was standing on the bar next to Johnnie Mortimore, surrounded by pints of beer. Johnnie gave him a hug.

"I like these draws; it's good for the bar takings. I realise this success can't go on forever. Poor old Ted Drake is out of hospital, but he's gone off to Cyprus to his daughter. I also had a call from Don Rowbotham; he hoped to be with us for the big match. Well, at last things seem to be going our way. We are slowly turning the corner and we now have a manageable overdraft, although the bank wouldn't agree. Look, you haven't got a drink."

Bob smiled. "I'm okay." The noise was deafening, everyone talking at the top of their voice.

"I think I'd better quell this mob." Johnnie held up his arm and shouted into the megaphone for silence. He then looked across to the door and spoke to the groundsman on duty. "Pete, shut that door, and don't let anyone else in."

"Now, first I want you all to raise your glasses, and you lot outside, I know you can hear me: to Bob, our acting manager, to congratulate him on the arrival of his little baby daughter, Pat. Suddenly there was a thunderous shout of 'Pat' inside and outside the clubhouse.

"Now listen, the raffle will take place after the draw. We are nearly there but, briefly, I want to bring your attention to some of our sponsors who have given us so much help over the past years: Streets Coaches who make very little out of us, and then Williams the TV shop, Squires fish and chips who provide all our catering and, of course, Brand Hotels. Look, I could go on, but I must mention Lipton's, the food stores. I want you all to support our sponsors over Christmas. Remember, they have been good friends to the club over many years. Right, the draw is just coming up so let's have hush." Suddenly all went quiet and the camera went over to Lancaster House, the HQ of the Football Association. There were 64 teams left and they now would include the upper divisions. The coloured number balls were jumping around in a glass bowl and officials wearing gloves carefully removed them one at a time and passed them on to an associate who shouted out the number and the name of the team.

Most of the teams had been called, when they suddenly woke up to hear Torquay United versus Godstone United. There was a big cheer from around the ground and the noise in the clubhouse was deafening. Johnnie quickly picked up the megaphone to shout for silence. "Look, I've got Bob here, our Assistant Manager, who would like to say a few words."

Without warning, the megaphone was pushed into Bob's hands. There was warm applause and cheering from all quarters. "Friends, before I start I would like you to join me in giving a big vote of thanks to Johnnie Mortimer. He seems to have given all his time to helping the club. I just feel sorry for his family. So let's have a rousing three cheers for Johnnie." After the deafening din, Bob continued. "Friends, we are at last starting to see some success but, let's be honest, we've had a lot of luck. We had the rub of the green but we are now playing with the big boys and if it's done nothing else it will help the club's finances. Bear in mind we are still very close to the relegation zone and it's important we do not take our eye off our league position. We've got to strive and get back to where we were four years ago. It's sad to hear that Ted Drake is not well and is convalescing in Cyprus with his daughter but I was pleased to hear that Don Rowbotham is better and hopes to be at the next match. Finally, my friends, you must all pat yourselves on the back because we could not have achieved this success without your support. I'm now hoping that the season will end on a high, and that this is the start of good things to come."

They all started to cheer. Johnnie jumped off the bar and was soon in the thick of it, squeezing flesh. *So, there we are,* thought Bob; *certainly a tall order,* but he was aware they had had a large measure of good fortune to have got so far. In no time they started to disperse. As Bob looked around the crowd, who were all very excited, some over the top, he spotted some of his players, in particular Jimmy Greaves and Billy Steele, with two girls. He thought he recognised one who worked for Rosemary as a waitress; she had a familiar face and red hair.

Bob quickly slipped off home, trying to avoid the free drinks from well-wishers. Rosemary was in the kitchen preparing the supper. "Darling." She rushed over and gave him a big kiss. Freddie jumped off the kitchen stool and hugged his leg. "As you know, we've got Pat and Claude coming over for supper. She tells me Claude has made tremendous progress and is looking forward to getting back to work. Saying that, I don't know any of the details, but Pat mentioned on the QT that there had been a major problem at the bank, and they were missing him. Look, if she does mention it, pretend you don't know anything. Now, can you put Freddie to bed and read him a story. I must get on and peel these potatoes."

"Do I have to go to bed?" said Freddie with a long face.

"If you're good, then daddy will take you down to the football tomorrow. Now I really must get on and, oh yes, lay the table; I'm so behind."

They were pleased to see Claude looking much better, although he was very pale and had seemed to have lost a lot of weight. In no time, Pat and Rosemary tiptoed upstairs to see baby Pat; they seemed to be gone ages.

Claude was very interested in hearing Bob's news, in particular details of the club's finances. "Yes, as a general rule, we avoid football. In fact, we steer clear of leisure activities, and also the entertainment market. We burnt our fingers in the past and the public's taste in these matters can be so fickle."

"So, when are you going back?" asked Bob, picking up his glass of wine.

"Very soon. I do miss the cut and thrust of work and we've got some problem so I'm going back in next Monday."

"That's rather soon."

"Oh yes, but they requested me to look in. Well, you might as well know, it will soon be in the papers, but my temporary replacement Christopher Barrington, who I have always found to be very sound and reliable, is being investigated by the police. Again, I don't know all the details, but I gather he was involved in disposing of a body. Yes, it does make the mind boggle. Still, they want me back as soon as possible. No one could be more surprised. He really is a very quiet chap, softly spoken and respected by the staff, but no doubt the facts will unravel over the next week or so. Now, more important than anything else, I am so looking forward to meeting little Pat; we were all over the moon to hear of your wonderful news."

Little Pat was brought into the sitting room and passed around, she was finally put to bed and they sat around with their coffee. Claude looked at Bob. "Well, how is it going?"

Rosemary stood and immediately answered. "He is not just responsible for coaching the team; as far as I can see, he is Godstone United, like an uncle to them all. Most of them are quite young and seem to have problems; either it's girlfriends or money. Of course, they are all part-timers. Then he's very involved with the fundraising activities."

Bob looked up. "It's not as bad as that; they are all very inexperienced and need some help."

"Well," said Rosemary, picking up glasses, "remember your family should always come first. I hope we don't have to take second place to football. If so, I'd rather you go back to being an electrician when life was so much simpler." Pat noted the steely look in her eye.

"Still, let's change the subject."

Pat and Rosemary had a chat about baby Pat and then about the luncheon club. They were delighted that the new catering manageress was doing an excellent job. It was noted she had already sorted out some of the younger unreliable staff, but they were concerned about the lack of orders.

Finally, Pat and Claude left by taxi after a very enjoyable evening.

Chapter 15

Claude got back to the office weighed down with an armful of files. He could quickly see that all the staff was pleased to see him back; even the General was very amenable, but so far all the facts concerning Christopher Barrington were still vague. The police were tight-lipped. They had changed the indictment from first-degree murder to perverting the course of justice. They were also pursuing leads with their European colleagues and trying to track down two Polish villains.

Suddenly out of the blue, Claude and Pat received an invitation to attend a cocktail party at Kensington Palace. Pat was so excited and started to plan what to wear; she was also very nervous about the possibility of meeting the Queen.

She was now back to her old self but was not fully recovered from the devastation of Edgar's death. They had attended his funeral in Farnham. Poor Rita broke down; the blow had left her completely overwhelmed, but Doug and her boys had been a great strength. There were well over 200 mourners and Tom Owen assisted with the service. There were old friends from Wadham Developments who were saddened by the events, in particular Maggie and Philip. Bennington House school principals, Ian and Margaret Hogg, attended; also, directors from Irvin Insurance. The wake took place at the Castle Hill Hotel, which seemed to be packed. Simon had read a lesson. He seemed to have matured. He was now 17 and attended Downton College. Todd and Vicky came down with him and planned to go back on the same day. There were also a number of old friends: Rosa Dyer, who in the past helped with his planning applications; also June the ex-bar maid, who looked after Charlie, Edgar's father-in-law; and Lord Henry Marchant drove Tom Owen down. There were also a few old army friends.

There was great relief when it was clearly established that he died from natural causes. It would seem he experienced a 'petit mal', collapsing in the bathroom and hitting his head on the side of the sink.

The day finally came to an end and all the mourners left, feeling dejected and sad. It would seem a bright candle had been extinguished. Poor Rita found the occasion to be a strain. Doug was able to give the final blessing. It was such a sad occasion. Edgar had that rare quality which was admired by all those who knew him. Both Pat and Claude were devastated. Pat had a quiet word with Vicky. "Please don't take offence, but if there is any way I can help regarding Simon's education please let me know; it will be an honour to assist in any way." Vicky thanked her but stressed that Simon was now quite a wealthy young man.

Tom Owen sat in a corner drinking his tea and waved to Pat. She came over and sat next to him. "How are you Tom? I know that Edgar was so looking forward to your trip to the Isle of Mull."

"Yes, I enjoyed his company, but it was a long drive and I had to call on my daughter to collect me, and she lives in Truro. But Edgar was an exceptional man, often misunderstood; it would seem he lost his way after those two big disappointments. Sorry, I'm starting to sound like a 'shrink'. But we did have a long man-to-man talk on our way up to Scotland. Sorry, I'm getting old; I shall be 83 shortly. I've seen it all before. It is particularly sad when I could see Edgar was slowly putting his life back together. I knew all along his death was an accident."

"Yes, I'm sure you're right," said Pat, taking Tom's empty cup and placing it on the table. "But it's so nice to see you again, Tom. I hope we will meet up in the near future."

"Thank you for coming over. I can see Lord Marchant hovering around. I think he is ready to leave so I'd better make a move." Pat leaned over and kissed him on the cheek and then slipped away.

On the way home, Claude could see that Pat was upset and sat quietly looking into space with tears in her eyes. This brought back the memories of Hilary which he could not get out of his head. *No, no, I must not ring her*, but he kept wondering how she was. He eventually received news of her from a third party. It would seem after a lengthy period of rehabilitation and plastic surgery she had regained her health and was living in LA close to her daughter and grandchild.

Finally, Claude got back to work, he was faced as he predicted with a banking crisis. All aspects of the economy were going through difficult and demanding times. The government was under pressure and inflation was getting out of control. The Bank of England pushed base rates up to 15%, which had to be implemented by all the banks. These levels were unprecedented and causing much distress to many institutions. Established businesses were going to the wall and it would seem wherever Claude looked he was faced with serious problems. He thought back to the abortive attempts to make acquisitions in the USA, which he was pleased were unsuccessful. Three of the big five banks had to seek substantial loans from the government. Claude managed to stay out of their clutches, which he realised in the short term could be disastrous. He made the astute move to have on call £5 billion from a wide range of institutions at a low interest to prepare for the pressures that were predicted.

Claude was always in demand but quickly realised that he needed to nurse his health. Pat was supportive; he was now 64 and had gone through a very serious illness. Life became easier with General Harding on the board; he was now a director and he was very much of the view that, if you can't beat them, join them. He seemed to have watered down some of his most stringent demands, but the Chancellor was delighted with the far-reaching reforms being implemented by the London and Edinburgh. Claude was invited to sit on three government committees but reluctantly refused. He also refused an invitation to speak to the Institute of Bankers in Australia. Then suddenly he received an invitation to address an influential committee of the World Bank in San Francisco entitled Banking Practices in the European Market. He decided to accept this invitation, but to avoid any suspicions he asked Pat to accompany him. She readily agreed, knowing that Hilary lived close by on the West Coast.

Claude spent much time monitoring those companies who were experiencing difficulties. He also set up a small committee to study the implications of major economic cutbacks. He had to face the fact that the bank was losing serious money and would need an injection of new capital in the next six months. He examined a list of companies seeking substantial loans. The first on the list was Theatre World; this group had a gigantic empire of theatres in both the USA and the UK. Although they were seeking a substantial loan, Claude could see that in the long term they were a sound investment, but time was not on the bank's side. He also read a detailed analytical report from the risk management team and reluctantly decided to refuse the loan. He then turned his attention to Lucas Laboratories; they were a pharmaceutical company in Runcorn and had designed two important drugs dealing with arthritis and advanced dementia. They were shortly to receive licences to market these products. The company had changed hands twice in the past five years. An American company had taken over and then got into difficulties so there was a British management buyout. It would seem, according to the company's accountant that the sale was agreed at £220 million but they had difficulty in raising the final £40 million. However, the Americans generously agreed to leave the final payment on the table. Claude was impressed with their goodwill but again decided to refuse their request and suggested they approach the United Arab Bank.

He continued to study the accounts of a list of companies with a numerous number of reports appertaining to their health. Armed with a red pen, he refused the applications of Zola Fashions; their shares had dropped in value and their chairman, who lived in Monte Carlo, had a very dodgy reputation. He studied the accounts of a healthcare firm, a freight company, and finally Larson High Temp. He was familiar with this business and had dealt with them in the past; they specialised in heavy water chambers for nuclear power stations and also had a lucrative design for a medium-size drilling platform which could be used in fracking, but they had disposed of this to a Chinese company. Yet again he refused their request and suggested an alternative broker.

Claude then drafted a long, detailed report to the management committee highlighting his chief areas of concern. He stressed that at the end of the day there would be substantial shortfalls and did not want to be knocking on the Treasury door with his cap in his hand. He therefore suggested a two-pronged attack to overcome these difficulties. He would arrange a meeting with the United Arab Bank and other associate banks with a view to raising a substantial loan and he would instruct the committee to consider introducing a list of draconian measures to cut down the bank's overheads.

He decided before going any further to speak to Sir Peter Lipton, the Chairman. He realised these proposals would have to be pushed past the board before they could be implemented and was very conscious that three of the directors were Jewish and would be hostile to the thought of working too closely with the United Arab Bank.

Finally, Claude spoke to the Chairman. "Yes, I can appreciate the urgency and really we cannot procrastinate. I am due to have a meeting on Monday morning with the directors' executive subcommittee and it would be sensible for you to be present to outline these measures."

Claude agreed. "I should stress that we are very much on the back foot and these changes will set up tremors through the bank. I know we will get a lot of stick from the unions, in particular with reference to closures, and I appreciate a tie-up with the United Arab Bank will be frowned upon in some quarters."

"Yes, CD, you're quite right. I can think of two Jewish members on the executive committee but, more importantly, have you approached the Exchequer with your plans?"

"In principle, the Chancellor was quite supportive, but the Governor of the Bank of England was less enthusiastic. But look, I will get this draft report over to you before Monday. Please keep it under wraps; the media would have a field day if they got their hands on it.

"Just one final thing, Sir Peter; as you know, I recently had a spell in hospital and my doctor who I've known for over 20 years and can be rather formidable has lectured me. Well, to put it simply, if I don't cut back on my commitments then the consequences could be disastrous; he gave me 12 months, and of course this could not come at a more inconvenient time. We all know that very shortly the bank will be hit by a tidal wave; sorry to use such emotive language. I have therefore arranged talks with the personnel general manager regarding the restructuring of the management committee, which bluntly means I will be stepping down in, say, and the next six months. I do hope we do not have a debacle as took place with the temporary appointment of Christopher Barrington, which incidentally caused less of a stir than I anticipated; still, he is due to come to trial shortly and no doubt we will get the usual biased press coverage, but really this is one of our minor concerns."

"Thank you, Sir Claude, for putting me in the picture. But you're right, these are momentous times and I know the board will join me in thanking you for your commitment and endeavours. In fact, we look upon you as the London and Edinburgh. After your discussions with personnel, no doubt you will present me with your findings, which then will have to go up before the board but, the big decision is replacing your good self. Have we a man of your calibre or will it be necessary to parachute in an outsider? We can discuss this later when, I would also like to discuss with you my own future with the Bank. Look sorry, Sir Claude, to cut you off. I'm just about to go in and chair a meeting of Lombard Insurance. I will come back to you soon."

o o o

Pat could not get Edgar out of her system. At night when she was trying to sleep he would appear, with those large blue eyes, that friendly smile. She thought back about their relationship which she had curtailed and realised he had been faithful to her but was very ambitious for his property company. His sister Rita had always been so supportive and had hoped Pat would marry him. She deduced his wife Heather had not been easy, although very intelligent, Oxbridge educated and highly respected by those who worked with her. She heard Heather had black moods and, after the adoption of Simon, turned her back on him and finally drove Edgar out of the house. She thought about their lovemaking; it had been heavenly. He was always so gentle and so caring. She would have erotic dreams just thinking of him. Pat remembered vividly her last meeting with him when he had kissed her at the door and whispered, "I shall always love you." This caused her pain as she thought of darling Edgar. *Oh God I love that man.* She remembered him every night in her prayers.

Pat reflected about Claude. He had been a kind husband, but it was not the same. She regretted having played it safe. Her memories floated back to her mother Emily who had been a poor role model. Emily had run away with a flashy, unreliable Irishman, which had not lasted long, and was the beginning of a long list of most undesirable partners who abused her. After a cry for help, Pat found her living on her own in squalid accommodation in Brixton, not being able to cope, and she had a serious drink problem. Pat had finally taken her in and cared for her so that her last years were peaceful, although her mental capabilities started to deteriorate.

o o o

Pat was worried about Rosemary, but then she cast her mind back to her early years. *She's got it made, what with a part-time nanny for the children and a sensible manageress for the luncheon club.* She noted that the luncheon club was losing money. Rosemary's biggest problem was Bob. They seemed to be drifting apart. She complained they never seemed to be at home together enjoying a family life; he was always out fundraising and would come home smelling of beer, and one evening she noted he had lipstick on his shirt. *I must not get involved,* but she decided to have a quiet word with Rosemary when the opportunity arose, possibly asking her to try and be a little more supportive with Bob. She knew Rosemary could so quickly fly off the handle; she would have to pick the right moment.

As Pat was putting the dirty laundry into the washing machine, the phone rang; it was Rosemary, in a very agitated state, to say that Bob had not been home that night and she was worried sick because she did not know where he was. She had checked the joint bank account and he had withdrawn £1,200 but the cheque stub was blank. When there was no word by midday, Rosemary rang the police. They sent around an officer who took down all the details and left with a photo. They immediately put out a routine enquiry with the details of his car. Pat went over to Rosemary's who was now frantic with worry and she started to think the worst.

Then out of the blue in the late evening they got a call from the police informing them that Bob had been found and had been admitted to Farnham Hospital with a head injury. It seemed that his car had left the road and ploughed into a copse. Fortunately, it was spotted by a farmer who helped him out and rang the police. Pat stayed with the nanny and children and Rosemary rushed over to the hospital in a terrible state. She found Bob sitting up in bed with a bandage round his head and looking very sad. She rushed over and threw her arms around him and burst into tears. They finally sat back over a cup of cocoa.

"How are you feeling, darling?"

"Well, a bit groggy. I've got a terrible headache, as if I've cracked my skull. A good night's sleep might help."

They parted very affectionately with tears streaming down Rosemary's cheeks. "I'll be in first thing in the morning."

She was approached by an elderly doctor as she left. "Now, there is nothing to worry about; your husband is a healthy young man. We carried out all the necessary X-rays and he is suffering from mild concussion but he will soon be back on his feet."

"Thank God for that. He is the manager of a football team and I think he's been overdoing it."

"Well yes, it will take three or four days at the maximum and he should be back to normal, but he should try to slow down and get up to full speed next month."

She decided to ring Johnnie Mortimore.

"Yes, I heard about his driving accident. I'll look in and see him tomorrow." She explained that he was suffering from concussion and would need to take it easy.

"Don't worry. I will hold the fort until he gets back. He will be sadly missed by all of us, in particular the players, who hold him in great affection. We are due to play Torquay next month in the FA Cup but will have to face that when it happens. Rosemary, leave everything to me; the club is now in its healthiest state since Bob took over. Don't let him come back until he is fully fit."

o o o

Two weeks later, out of the blue, Claude received an invitation to a cocktail party at Kensington Palace. Pat now started to get worried. "Darling, I'd love to go, but really I won't know what to say. I'll be out of my depth and, meeting the Queen, what will I talk about?"

"You may not meet her, but just be yourself; she is very perceptive and will respect you for who you are."

"Now, come off it, Claude. Have I ever tried to put on airs and graces?"

"Darling, of course not, but don't become tongue-tied. Pick on your strong points such as your experience in the catering business."

"Yes, you're quite right. Then, of course, what do I wear? I have the most difficult figure to cover."

"Well, I don't know. I bet you get the glad eye from men on occasions."

"Yes, but certainly not the type I want to attract."

"Hello, what does that mean?"

Pat blushed. "Stop it; you know what I mean."

So they arrived at Kensington Palace at six and were quickly ushered into the large hall where the reception was being held. It was already full of groups chatting away and a posse of servants meandering with silver trays of drinks and nibbles. They were met at the door by a small entourage, including Princess Margaret and, after introductions, were escorted into the large hall and offered a cocktail and introduced to a small group. The noise was overpowering; everybody seemed to be talking at the same time.

Claude whispered, "Be careful what you drink; they have a reputation for being rather strong." Finally, they joined a group that Claude was familiar with and Pat was quickly introduced and understood the group were bankers.

Pat was chatting to one of the wives, who she felt was a real pain and never stopped showing off how clever her children were and then started dropping names and went on about her last holiday on the QE2. Claude was in detailed discussions with a short man with olive skin. Pat looked around but did not recognise anybody and then she spotted Lord Marchant with his wife Diana. *Anybody will be better than this ghastly woman.* "Sorry, please excuse me but I've just seen a dear old friend."

She slipped away from the group and was warmly welcomed by Lord Marchant who introduced his wife; she had a reputation of being a cold fish, but Pat was surprised; she obviously could not hold her drink and kept laughing at odd times. "I was so sorry Edgar had a breakdown but glad he managed to control his drinking." She smiled. *That was rich coming from her.* "Pat, you must come down and visit us. My hubby, he thinks the world of Sir Claude, thinks he should be running the country. Must keep my voice down; I can see the PM over there." From then on Pat was in her element. She had two drinks and felt quite relaxed. Suddenly Diana introduced her to a tall slim lady in her late forties, and then quickly the penny dropped. Lady Anne, the Queen's daughter. She seemed to be intelligent and well informed.

"Now, you must be Sir Claude's wife; my mother was looking forward to seeing him." Suddenly they seemed to be standing alone. Pat was now starting a third drink and starting to feel hot and a little wobbly.

"Sorry," said Pat, "but I feel a bit warm and unsteady."

"Come and sit down. I agree, this room is very warm and really these cocktails are too heavily laced with gin."

They broke away from the small group and sat on a sofa at the side of the hall. "Look, I'll get you a glass of water. I gave up drinking; it must be 18 months ago. It was not easy, but I feel so much better." A glass of iced water with lemon suddenly appeared. After drinking half a glass Pat felt better, but very embarrassed. "Sorry about that."

"Don't worry; we often have problems with some of the foreign diplomats. They overdo it then we have to help them to their cars. Do tell me, I recognise your West of England accent; where were you brought up?"

Pat smiled. "I cannot hide that."

"No, you certainly don't need to. So where do you hail from?"

"Well, Devon, a long way from here."

The Princess smiled. "I love Devon."

"Well, yes. I come from North Devon, a little bit off the beaten track."

"Really? I know it well. I have a great friend, Bertie Hillingdon; he has a large farm and in the past I've taken horses down there for training. It's just outside South Malton. But I have not been down recently. I have given up competitions. Really, I'm too old, but my daughter's very keen."

"Well," said Pat, feeling a little more confident. "My father was a farm manager and then we moved to Surrey to a large farm." They continued talking about farming.

"Yes, I would have loved to be a farmer but my ex was army; sadly, it didn't work. Still, that's all in the past. Well, Pat, it's been lovely talking to you but I can see my mother is looking for me. I do hope we meet up again. Please excuse me." She quickly slipped away. In no time Claude was at her side.

"Well, darling, I think it's time we left." The room was starting to become quieter as guests started to drift away; even the main lights were being dimmed. In the car, Pat seemed to be very animated.

"Did you speak to the Queen?"

"Yes, she was charming, but I could see she had another side. She asked some searching questions about where interest rates were going and asked for tips regarding stocks and shares. Yes, she was certainly switched on; it was like having an audience, and then she turned her attention to other guests."

"Well, that was rather rude, wasn't it?"

"No, not really; she seemed to be working all the time, but I have a feeling she had a prepared agenda; it was all well organised."

"Did you have a word with Princess Margaret?"

"Well, yes; it was very brief. She was very much in demand."

"Well, I must say, meeting Princess Anne made my day. She had a very caring nature, although she did have a rather austere temperament but a wonderful dry sense of humour. I was very pleasantly surprised."

"Well, darling, it's still quite early; shall we go out for dinner somewhere?"

"I'd rather not. I feel tired. Let's go home and play some games."

Claude smiled. "That sounds a much better idea," he said, squeezing her hand.

Chapter 16

Six years later...

So, my friends, sadly we are now approaching our destination. Many of the players from the past are still with us, but what has happened in the past six years? Equally important, what does the future hold for them?

o o o

We find Sir Claude and Lady Dibbs on a flight to New York for a short holiday to visit his great niece, Steph, and her small family. They are sitting in the first-class compartment of the Boeing 787. Pat felt quite excited. The plane took off two hours behind schedule due to a strike by the baggage handlers. They had carefully planned this holiday and wanted to avoid any publicity. He had been invited to give a presentation to a fringe meeting of the World Bank but decided to cancel that engagement. Claude was now highly respected on both sides of the Atlantic, but they wanted to get away for a quiet break.

The plane had been airborne for 40 minutes when suddenly there was an almighty explosion and an ear-piercing alarm screeching. The whole structure seemed to shudder, all the seats started to vibrate, conversation became inaudible. The lights went on and off and oxygen masks and their feeds were dangling in front of their heads. The air became polluted and hazy, locker doors were knocking and baggage was flying across the cabin. The speaker system went on, it was crackling, and then they heard the captain's voice above all the clamour. "Now, please, please, stay seated and don't panic. Make sure your seat belts are fastened. We are returning to Heathrow due to unforeseen complications."

o o o

Sir Claude Stocker Dibbs, now 73, had been Chairman of the London and Edinburgh for four years and had accepted a life peerage to sit in the House of Lords as a government adviser. The PM wanted him to be a deputy minister due to his intimate knowledge of banking legislation, which he and his team had framed in a White Paper. He refused but was frequently asked to make judgments on the interpretation of the Government's Banking Act. Pat was occupied with charitable work, mainly with the Catholic Church, and was always on hand to help her sister Rosemary with her growing family. Her husband Bob, after his success at Godstone United, was now the assistant manager at Southampton United, very much on the recommendation of Johnnie Mortimer, but he was finding life hard in the Premier League and was getting very disillusioned with all the shenanigans taking place in the transfer market. They moved to a house outside Bournemouth, but Bob found it difficult to settle. Rosemary had sold her shares in the luncheon club at a loss but could now sit back and enjoy bringing up her family.

o o o

Simon, Vicky's adopted stepson, studied law at Durham but was also a member of a pop group which was snowed under with engagements. He had a girlfriend, Amy, who Vicky was not impressed with. Vicky was worried that Simon was neglecting his studies and would fail his degree. He had a Trust Fund, for which Maggie, Vicky, and their solicitor, John Philips, were the trustees. It would not be released until he became of age. She finally cornered him and, red-faced, gave him a severe lecture. She did not hold back, and he stood head bowed with a tear in his eye, she five feet three and he six feet one; but it seemed to do the trick and in no time he left the pop group and finally got his head down and achieved an Honours degree in law. He was still pondering his future and decided with Raj and some pals to go on a gap year to Australia. He wanted to meet up with his Aunt Rita and her two sons, Freddie and Colin, in Sydney.

He decided to speak to Uncle Neil, a solicitor in Leeds, about becoming articled in his law firm when he got back. He was determined to train to be a solicitor and wanted to stay close by. He spoke to Neil over the phone, who was delighted, and they agreed to finalise the details when he got back.

"You must appreciate, Simon, I am a very small outfit, being the only qualified solicitor, so you will have to be versatile, dealing with a range of cases in the magistrates court, writing wills, dealing with house conveyancing to mention a few."

Vicky and Todd had made little progress. They had taken on an additional small farm on the Callington estate. The new agent was a pal of Rod's. They found him to be most helpful. Rod mentioned that the estate was experiencing cashflow problems and was open to offers from some of their tenants. He promised to keep them in the picture.

The pig co-op seemed to fluctuate, with numbers in the mid-30s, but it was holding its own, whereas the grain business had grown by leaps and bounds, and they were now marketing specialist pet foods. They were renting a redundant mill, which increased their overheads. The poultry business was now picking up after an outbreak of chicken flu, which had meant all the stock had to be slaughtered; Neil had taken out insurance to cover such disasters. Vicky's bridal business had gone from strength to strength and she now employed her eldest daughter Charlotte, who initially had been very unenthusiastic but was now on duty in the shop three days a week, liaising with the brides and their mothers, and seemed to enjoy the responsibilities.

Renée sadly was seriously ill and needed radium treatment but had refused all forms of help and wanted to die naturally. Vicky spoke to Susan, her niece, who reported her health was deteriorating, but she was in good spirits. Her friend Ben had been a tower of strength and took her out most days, but sadly she was failing; Susan reported that Renée was due to see her solicitors and wanted to leave the business to Vicky.

"Would you like me to come down and see her? She's been like a second mother to me."

"Well, it's up you, but she is a very private person, and I suggest it probably better to give her a ring."

"Well, if that's what she wants I quite understand, but do give her my love."

Vicky felt very sad; her youngest daughter, Heather, was in her last year at school and seemed to lack any ambition and spent most of her time helping her mother in the kitchen.

Poor Todd had put on a lot of weight and Vicky continued to nag him regarding his drinking. He had no hobbies and tried taking up golf but just could not afford the time. His biggest regret was not having a son. Vicky was worried about his health; he was in constant pain due to gout and also needed a hip replacement and seemed to have lost his sparkle. She could see that he was wracked with pain, added to which Todd's sister Norma was being difficult. Her husband left her. He confided to Todd that she was impossible to live with, and their two sons had left home too. Todd's health suddenly went into sharp decline. He was starting to find it difficult to walk and suffered from shortness of breath and was finally found in the piggeries collapsed, lying motionless. He was quickly rushed to hospital. After exhaustive tests, they found his heart was malfunctioning. Diagnostic tests showed he had a hypertrophic obstruction and needed immediate surgery. It was finally decided to perform open-heart surgery. It was a complex procedure which entailed the use of an artificial heart, but the operation was a success. Vicky was now twice as busy seeing to the farm and she called Rod for some advice.

He could quickly see the problems. Together they appointed a farm manager on a short-term contract. He was a retired farmer, very sound on all the practical duties, but was hopeless with the paperwork. He'd lost his wife but Vicky found him to be very reliable and he had now been with them for two years. Rod negotiated, subject to planning, the sale of 30 acres to a very upmarket leisure campsite company. They had plans to build 42 log cabins, but the planning authorities were not very positive. The planning application was refused so they went to appeal and Rod, who had specialised in planning, finally had the refusal overturned, which included costs.

Todd was back at home after a long period of rehabilitation and was now working half time but was suffering from depression. He would sit for long periods with no conversation. Vicky was worried and thought he would need some professional help.

Simon had come down from Durham, finally getting an upper second in law. He was now planning to take a gap year in Australia with his pal Raj, who was an art student and had Indian parents. His father was a master tailor and had three gentlemen's outfitters. Simon was so looking forward to meeting up with Auntie Rita's son Freddie, who was now in the New South Wales police force. They heard that Doug, the vicar, and the boys were getting on well, but Rita found it difficult to settle and wanted to come home. Vicky was secretly amused when Raj the art student, short in stature with large brown eyes and black curly hair, always with a ready smile, said he would like to paint her because she was a very interesting subject.

"Well, yes," she answered when he came forward, looking very earnest.

"But would you mind if I painted you in the nude?"

Vicky blushed. "Certainly not; whatever would my husband say. I think we better forget this conversation." But she suddenly felt he had other thoughts on his mind. As she turned to the sink to wash up the tea things she felt her hormones take off; since Todd had been ill she was missing their intimate and sensual relationship and she could see Raj was well endowed and made no secret of it.

She rinsed her face with cold water just as Simon came through the back door with his golf bags. "I must give that game up; the more I play the worse I seem to be. Mum, do you mind? I am meeting up with some chaps at the pub tonight."

"Well, what about Raj?"

"Oh, he wants to catch up with some letters. I think he is planning an exhibition when he gets back after our holiday. Incidentally, where are the girls? One of my mates suggested I brought them along."

"Certainly not; a pub is not the place for my daughters. Even so, Charlotte is spending the weekend with a school friend and Heather is staying with Auntie Caroline. Why can't you take Raj? I don't want him under my feet; it would do him the power of good."

"Okay, I'll try, but how's dad? He certainly seems to have gone off his food."

"Yes, poor darling; he's not himself and seems to spend a lot of time daydreaming or sleeping. He has an appointment at the hospital the end of next week."

o o o

Rod and Gloria could not be happier. They had a darling little daughter, Gaynor, but Marilyn, Rod's mother, was starting to suffer from mild dementia. She so missed her husband and was now living in a small cottage nearby. He had recovered enough to return to work after that tragic accident years ago when he was trapped under a tractor and lost a leg. He was playing quite a lot of golf and had got his handicap into single figures. He was very busy working for a firm of land agents in Dorchester. He had set up the office and was now a partner. He had qualified as a chartered surveyor, which opened the door to a wide range of opportunities. The firm's HQ was in Taunton where the competition was cut-throat, but he had connections and quickly established a close relationship with two banks and was spending an increasing amount of time setting up commercial loans. He specialised in carrying out valuations on large country estates and still carried out assignments for the London and Edinburgh. But the highlight of their lives had been the birth of little Gaynor. They had been married five years and had nearly given up on a family when suddenly Gloria knew. She could feel the changes and then early morning sickness and after a visit to the doctor she started to laugh and cry as she told Rod. Only a woman can fully understand the emotions experienced at this momentous time. Needless to say, his mother Marilyn was so excited. They had grown over the years to respect each other but, of course, Rob was the centre of their lives.

o o o

Wadham Developments' architect Philip's life had now settled down. He had fallen in love with Barbara and finally went to live with her and thought had at long last found a partner. She had two lively boys, who were wild, but Philip avoided any confrontation and let their mother lay down the law, although he would at times try to lend support; they were 10 and 12 and needed constant attention. They seemed to resent his presence and missed their dad, who had taken them to the park to play and also to the swimming baths. Suddenly one evening, with no warning, after they had been together for 18 months, they were sitting by the fire in the lounge when Barbara suddenly put down the novel she was reading and spoke. Philip lowered his paper.

"I had a call from Pete last week, my ex."

"That must have been a big surprise."

"Yes, he's left that girl. I think he caught her with another man."

"So what?"

"He wants us to get together again."

"I hope you told him where to go."

"Oh no, I'm worried about the boys and I think they need their dad. Let's be honest, you're not much help."

"What does that mean?"

"Sorry, Philip, but I think we will try and get back together again."

"But what about me?"

"Philip, I'm very fond of you, but I still love Pete, and I think this time we can make it work."

Philip stood. "I think I'd better move out."

"No, Philip, don't go yet; we can still be friends." A tear came into his eyes. He stood with his head bowed and within the hour left the house with two large cases.

Then suddenly out of the blue and just two weeks later, Philip had the biggest surprise: a phone call from Claire. He had not seen her for years.

"Is that you, Philip? This is Claire." She spoke with that warm Geordie accent.

"Where are you? I read you had been sent to prison."

"Yes, yes, but my sentence was reduced. I am now working and hope to get married next year. Philip, I've been meaning to ring for ages. I'm just so sorry for what I put you through. I know I made a lot of mistakes in the past. I could go on, but I've changed."

"Tell me, Claire, what do you do?"

"Well, when I was inside, I studied and became an accountant technician. But look, I've changed my name to Christine Grey, which was suggested by a friend, and so far it's worked. I'm responsible for the wages, the accounts, well really the books, of two hotels. I then liaise with the accountants with reference to taxes and allowances, et cetera. I love it. I did try and carry on my studies to become chartered but really I just do not have the time or the discipline. Sadly, I gave up Winston to an adoption society. It was the biggest sacrifice of my life; it's left a deep scar that will never heal. But look, Philip, sorry for everything, but I must go; I can hear my partner's car. I'm sorry for what I put you through. Take care."

Suddenly the line went dead. Philip sat back and lifted his glass. *Well,* he thought, *am I ever going to find a partner?* He put down his glass of whiskey and thought, *I am getting into some bad habits.*

o o o

Vicky was lying in bed thinking about her daughters, and she was also worrying about Todd, when she heard a car drive up. She looked out to see it was Raj. Vicky slipped back into bed and could hear Todd snoring quietly; they now slept in separate beds. She listened but all went quiet, so she slipped down the back stairs with just a flimsy dressing gown on to look in the kitchen. There was Raj lying back in the old armchair, with blood across his face; his clothing was torn and dirty and he was whimpering and gulping in breaths.

"Raj, dear, are you alright? Whatever happened?"

He looked up with tears in his eyes. "They hurt me. They beat me up because I was talking to some girls."

Vicky put her arm around him. "Now slowly tell me what exactly happened."

He took a deep breath and rubbed his eyes. "I went down to the pub for a drink and it was full, and there was a singsong, a talent competition or something, and I was talking to two girls. I bought them a shandy. I saw a bloke giving me a dirty look. One of the girls said she had chucked in her boyfriend because he was too bossy. They then left and I went out to the car and they were waiting for me. I never really saw them properly. I got hit on the back of the head. They knocked me to the ground and spat on me and one of them peed over me, laughing all the time.

"You poor boy. Look, go up and have a wash and get to bed. I'll bring up a hot drink and a sandwich."

She finally came up and found him lying on top of the bed dozing. He opened his eyes and smiled.

"I brought some ointment as well, and some gauze to clean up those cuts on your forehead." She leaned over and gently cleaned the grazes on his forehead and his face when, without warning, he put his arms around her body, drawing her in and kissing her gently on the lips. Suddenly, her hormones seemed to be on fire. *No, no,* she thought. *I must be mad.* She tried to pull away but could feel his large hands pressing her bottom, pulling her onto the bed, and then felt his manly weapon pressing into her groin. She only had a light dressing gown on that fell apart and she could feel the warmth of his naked body. Any resistance seemed to dissipate and she could feel his urgency. He certainly was well endowed. She thought it was remarkable that such a small man had such large hands and an enormous weapon. Her frustration and worries seemed to be all forgotten and in no time she was in bed and he was astride her. It was such a wonderful experience. It was heavenly. She could feel his large tool, which was smooth and slippery, and felt her vagina starting to be stretched. Conflicting messages were shouting at her: *God, it was never like this with Todd; whatever am I doing; this is the most wonderful experience I've ever had,* and then suddenly she could feel him explode and felt his warm juices flooding everywhere, and then she experienced a heavenly orgasm and then felt so tranquil and relaxed. They lay in each other's arms drifting off to sleep when suddenly Vicky awoke to that little voice in her head screaming. She quickly managed to slide out of the bed and slipped into the bathroom, experiencing a whole range of conflicting emotions.

Finally, at the end of the week, Raj packed up his car and they departed for their gap year. Vicky secured a cheque for Simon and then gave him a lecture on being frugal; he was very appreciative. She was glad to see the back of Raj. His presence was difficult but thank goodness he avoided her. Charlotte, her eldest daughter, seemed to be very restless.

"What's the problem, darling?"

"Well, I've chucked in Bill. I know you didn't like him. I found out he went out with one of my best friends. She's welcome to him; I was finding him to be a real pain."

Vicky looked puzzled. "Did you sleep with him?"

"Mum, what a question to ask!"

"Well, pet, my family are my life and I think of you all the time."

"Don't worry, Mum; he did try but it won't happen until I find the real one. Glad that Raj is gone; he kept trying it on, touching me. Simon did warn me he's got a bad name with the girls, and I must be three inches taller than him. I did notice you seemed to give him the cold shoulder."

"Really? It was not intentional, but I have been worried about dad."

"Mum, I've been meaning to have a chat. I like the job in the shop, but I seem to be in a bit of a rut. It's just that, I don't know, I just feel like a change. Now, don't have a fit, but I have been thinking of joining the police force." The conversation was cut short when the phone rang; it was Gloria, who wanted a chat with Vicky.

It was a week later that Vicky experienced discomfiture in the area of her vagina, with a burning sensation when she peed. She thought it was cystitis; she'd had that problem in the past and had some medicine, but it was now becoming very intense. So, reluctantly, she paid a visit to the doctor. He was quite young and was a keep-fit fanatic and always wore shorts. He examined her carefully for 10 minutes. "Look, Mrs Hosegood..."

"Please call me Vicky."

"Well, Vicky, I need to take more tests, but it would seem to me that you have picked up a mild strain of chlamydia. It is not uncommon today and can be treated, but I can assure you that it is not cystitis. It's not the sort of infection that can be picked up from a lavatory seat or off a towel. It is caused in the main by sexual intercourse. Now, I know you might find this embarrassing, but my next question is obvious. But please remember I have signed the Hippocratic Oath so anything you say to me will go no further."

Vicky blushed. "Well, yes, my husband is a semi-invalid and I feel ashamed but, yes, I had a one-night-stand with a student. I think he was the culprit."

"Right, Vicky, thank you for being so frank. We have caught the infection in time and, as I said, this is not uncommon today. I'll give you an intensive course of antibiotics which should eradicate the problem. I feel it would be prudent for you to speak to the student and ask him to seek medical help; he can be carrying this infection without knowing it and, Vicky, please, if it happens again, make sure you have safe sex."

"Don't worry, doctor, it will certainly not happen again. To think I have been lecturing my daughters about these dangers."

After a month, Vicky's problems seemed to disappear, and she was pleased to see some improvement in Todd's health. He had given up the drink and he'd lost some weight and was now more mobile and taking an interest in his daughters and the farm. Todd seemed to snap out of it after a flaming row with Vicky. The pressure was getting to her and she never did things in half measures. It seemed to do the trick. Vicky felt guilty and wanted to apologise, but she was like her mother, who always found it difficult to say sorry.

She had a chat with Rod who said, "I've had it on good authority that the Callington estates are having major cash flow problems."

"Yes, there has been a rumour floating around up here that Callington Estates are in trouble."

"Well, yes. I gather that Lord Henry who took over the estate decided to pass the management over to an investment company in the City and, from what I have been told, it's been a disaster and they have got to raise substantial capital. To put it briefly, and from what I can glean from the new agent – incidentally, I was at crammers with his brother; they have got to sell some of their smallholdings. In fact, he wants to get out and tells me Henry can be impossible. Vicky, look, I must rush, but I suggest you have a chat with Todd. Here is an opportunity for you to buy your farm. It would not command a particularly high valuation on the open market due to your lease so you could probably look to a 40% discount. Sorry Vicky, I've got an important customer waiting. Have a talk with Todd. I can handle the application and sort out the loan; you won't have this opportunity again."

"Oh, how exciting. Thank you, Rod; we will be in touch and I hope the holiday park is still interested. It would certainly help us in raising the necessary deposit."

The good news helped their strained relationship as this was the only topic they could think about and discuss. But Vicky as ever was very cautious. "Look, darling, we are not there yet so let's slow down. You get on to Rod and give him the okay."

o o o

Claude stepped down as chairman of the London and Edinburgh. Many of the directors had changed, but he had taken pleasure in appointing Veronica Arlott-Trefuss, who was a past vice chairman of the Association of Chartered Accountants, and Professor Amos Gold, a director of the LSE. Both had served on the committee when drawing up the report for the Royal commission on banking reform. There was some opposition to Professor Gold, who was an ardent socialist, but Dibbs was very impressed with his sincerity and felt it was good to have on board a paid-up member of the Labour Party; he would be useful in dealing with the unions. Sadly, General Waldron Harding had died. He had been chairman of the Shareholders Association and could be tiring and rude, but he had at heart the interests of the shareholders, in particular the military pension funds and their beneficiaries.

Finally, after numerous requests from Pat to move out of London, they had a house in Lymington in their sights, but first they needed to sell their house in Holland Park. Unfortunately, house prices were dropping. Pat tried to keep in contact with all her old friends. Steph, Claude's niece, the granddaughter of his older sister, was due to come over to see them with her young son and her husband, who was now a lieutenant in the New York Police Department. Steph had not changed: tall, slim, hyperactive and very noisy but with a generous disposition. Pat had at last made contact with Joy Bulley in Australia, who had had a fling with Shane, the famous Australian cricketer, but was now married to a retired farmer and happy, except he did have two daughters and they were both hostile. Pat invited her to come over and stay. "Thank you, Pat. I would love to come. I am now financially more secure than when you first knew me, and I shall always remember your kindness. Eric is 78 next month and really not well enough to travel. I could maybe come over alone. I promise we'll meet up in the near future."

Finally, Claude moved towards retirement. He vacated his seat in the House of Lords where he had never settled. He found it to be riddled with insincerity and intrigue. He also resigned from the Government as an adviser on financial affairs and from the boards of a dozen companies. Initially, it was a matter of attending the odd meeting, but he was now being pressed to give judgments. On some occasions he would be at odds with the legal opinion of a team of QCs.

So it was they finally left London and moved into a large four-bedroom house in the attractive town of Lymington. He then joined a club for retired businessmen, Probus, and in no time was appointed to be the treasurer. He also joined a Bridge club but had given up trying to teach Pat; she was far too erratic and made some outrageous calls.

He was also busy writing a book on banking espionage, which he enjoyed but realised it had a very limited market.

Then suddenly he had an urgent call from his physician, John Ritchie, to attend Saint Mary's Hospital. He was met by John and a lady surgeon, Kathleen Darnley. She pointed out that he had an aortic aneurysm which had been monitored over the past five years and was now approaching a dangerous level. If action wasn't immediately taken, it would burst. They went into details, stressing the importance of the various procedures. There were two main types of surgery: endovascular, a graft inserted into a blood vessel in the groin, with a 98 per cent success rate; or open surgery, possibly making a cut in the tummy and repairing the aorta valve. There were greater risks with the latter; bleeding, blood clots and erectile dysfunction were common.

Kathleen, a short attractive lady in her early forties, with blonde hair and a ready smile, then took the lead. "Now Sir Claude, we have had a multi-disciplinary appraisal and agreed to go ahead with the procedure immediately, so please make an appointment to see the registrar.

Before leaving, Claude had a quiet word with John Ritchie. "That lady surgeon, Kathleen Darnley, please don't take offence, but she seems to be very young; how much experience has she had?"

"Now, Sir Claude, I do appreciate your concern. We have known each other a long time; it must be nigh on 30 years, so please rest assured I have made a detailed examination of her history and you have nothing to worry about. So please excuse the pun, but you are in safe hands."

Pat was naturally very concerned but in no time Claude was admitted to St Mary's and Kathleen the surgeon immediately performed the clinical procedure, which went very smoothly. After four days, Claude was sitting up. He had left intensive care and was now eating a little food and taking a few strides. All seemed to be going well when, the day before his release, he had a relapse. He was rushed back into the operating theatre where they performed an operation to repair the leaky blood vessel. Suddenly his life took a nosedive; his survival was in the balance. He was placed back in the intensive care ward on life-support. Pat received an urgent call from the hospital and dropped everything. She met Dr John Ritchie, a big fat man, waddling across the car park. In no time, they were with a locum surgeon who explained the problem and the action he had taken. Kathleen Darnley was not available. She had taken some leave and turned off her mobile. The locum was an elderly retired grey-haired surgeon with a very placid manner.

"Look, I've come up against a similar problem 20 years ago. I think we know what happened, but we must carry out further tests. We do not want to jump the gun, but it would appear there has been some partial blockage. I have replaced the stent and the blood flow is now back to normal, but this arrest can cause long-term problems. As we speak, he is under a general anaesthetic to help his body to cope. I cannot at this stage evaluate any damage. Fortunately, it was only a partial cutting off of the blood so we must pray there has been no long-term damage."

Pat looked very concerned. "Well, whose fault was it?"

"Now, Lady Dibbs, I am not here to make judgments; my main concern is to get your husband back to full health. You must make an appointment to see the chief executive officer but it is far too early to jump to any conclusions."

Pat rubbed her forehead. "Sorry, you're quite right. I do fully appreciate all you have done. No doubt we can sort this out later, but when can I see him?"

It was three months later that they had a call from John Ritchie. "I just recently got back from New Zealand. My wife would like to have stayed but it was a joy to see my grandchildren. Now briefly, Sir Claude, I've studied all the relevant reports and I am of the opinion that the hospital took all the necessary precautions. I've seen the minutes of the multidisciplinary meeting and also read the hospital's report on the cause of the relapse, but there is no clear answer to the cause of this rupture. I will get my secretary to ring you about an appointment. You can, of course, take a legal opinion, but when you get involved with QCs they can sit on the fence, and their fees are exorbitant. Quite frankly, if it was me, I would put all this behind you, but if you wish to take a civil action it will be long and messy."

"John, you're quite right. I had made up my mind. I am now feeling fine and I was more than pleased with the hospital. Yes, you're right. I will let the whole matter drop."

Claude was surprised when he discussed this with Pat. She was in full agreement; he expected her to be more aggressive.

They had decided to take a holiday in New York. Pat was excited and so looking forward to seeing Steph and her little son.

o o o

After 40 minutes out, everything seemed to go wrong. The plane started to pitch, roll and shudder. It seemed to be out of control; then the lights had ceased, all the seats were vibrating, locker doors were slamming and items of clothing were flying across the gangway, The emergency light stayed on to give them faint illumination. There was a loud screeching of metal and the smell of burning rubber. The air was becoming polluted with a fog of gases.

Pat held Claude's hand and leaned over. "Darling, I love you. If we are to go, let's go together. I have no regrets. I've had a wonderful life."

Claude bent over and kissed her. "We will pull through."

They pulled on the flimsy oxygen masks and attached the air feeds.

The plane continued to pitch and bump as if the pilot had difficulty in holding it on course. The noise was deafening. They heard the faint static noise of the loudspeaker. "We are now approaching Heathrow. Now please," Then suddenly it ceased to function. The emergency light went off and the engines could not be heard. There was an eerie silence.

Then, without warning, there was a tremendous flare up, with flashing lights and the acrid smell of burning latex. The plane pitched onto its side and seemed to be completely out of control. There was one almighty explosion as the plane hit the ground. And finally a deadly silence.

...to be continued?

Printed in Poland
by Amazon Fulfillment
Poland Sp. z o.o., Wrocław

64796622R00134